BLOOD LEGACY

THE V V INN BOOK FIVE

C.J. ELLISSON

First eBook Edition 2015

Revised Second Edition April 2017

Copyright © 2015 by C.J. Ellisson

eBook ISBN: 978-1-938601439

Print ISBN: 978-1938601347

For Peter.
My best friend, staunchest supporter, and greatest
inspiration.

CHAPTER ONE

VIVIAN

After almost being killed by silver poisoning, I'm recovering nicely. Most people think vampires are immortal, and I can understand why with how long our kind can normally exist. But if you can be killed by *any* means, then you aren't technically immortal, right? I prefer the term semi-mortal. Lord knows I've certainly killed more than my fair share of vampires, and I can attest that we are not immune to death.

I stretch on the chaise lounge, gazing up at the late afternoon cloud coverage revealed by the clear atrium panels above me. It's a nice winter day in late June, three weeks after I escaped from capture, off the southeastern coast of Argentina, and a semblance of peace finally fills me.

Drew, one of the vampires in my seethe, or vampire family, strides into the inner garden of our large Spanish-style hacienda and clears his throat. "Vivian," he says, calling me by the nickname most everyone uses instead of my real name,

Dria, short for Alexandria. "Do you really think shipping us home to Alaska is the best idea? We all want to stay and help."

I glance up at the tall, slender man, noting his healthy hue and the sexually satisfied air about him. Judging by the noises drifting from his suite every night since our return to the island, he and Chelly have been exploring their new relationship status, vampire and servant, every chance they've had.

"You're not strong enough for this fight, Drew, and neither are the others. I appreciate your loyalty and decision to stay to see things through, but I won't risk your safety for my own."

Frustration appears to simmer beneath his smooth facade. "I take it there's nothing I can say or do to prove we'd be an asset?"

I rise from my comfortable spot on the lounge chair. "Think about it—*you* might be a help, but what about the others? Can you say the same for any of them?" I angle my head and go for a low blow. "Could you live with yourself if your desire to protect your master led to *their* deaths? Would you sleep well during the day knowing Chelly died before she had to?"

Drew's handsome face crumples, his noble intent twisting within. "Not fair, Viv. Not fair. Dammit!" He paces away before whipping around to face me again. "Deep down, I know you're right, but that doesn't mean I have to accept it without complaint."

I walk toward him, reaching out a hand in comfort. My grip rests lightly on his forearm as I push my will into him, not quite using my full manipulator traits that can sway any vampire to my way of thinking, but I give him a mental shove past his immediate anger to offer clear thinking. "I know where

2

your heart lies, and I don't mean regarding Chelly. I know you would fight to the death beside me, without hesitation. But I have need of you elsewhere." His brow quirks up in question. "*You* will be the one to protect all I hold dear. *You* will be the strongest left in Alaska should trouble befall them while I'm gone."

Irritation at my words spills into his tone. "What good will I be in Alaska during the summer? I'd be living indoors and traveling via the tunnels the entire time."

"Do you really think a vampire weakened by the sun is still not strong enough or clever enough to protect those who matter to him? Do you think a man, or group of men, could outwit you at your lowest? You are over a century and a half old, Drew. By no means are you on the same level—in any sense—as Paul or the werewolves."

He smiles. "I see exactly what you're doing, you conniving woman. Building me up to make me feel important with what you want me to do. All right, I'll go quietly—whether I agree with you or not about how much good I'll be while cooped up inside."

"Good. Now, onto the more important question: Do you trust Paul to share the flying duties home with you?"

"Uh... no, not yet. But either way, we can't fly during the day."

I smile, glad the issue of them leaving will be dropped. "Not to worry. I've arranged for several top-notch pilots you can pick up in Buenos Aires."

Once Drew departs, I return to the personal suite I usually share with my human husband, intending to do some yoga. The stretching and muscle work has helped realign my spiritual balance with the physical healing. Thanks to Rafe,

I've fully regained my strength from the silver trauma a few weeks ago.

The ones responsible for my imprisonment and torture, Coraline and her cohorts, were killed by my husband in a brutal display of his defensive nature. Only one man—Rolando —remains for us to track down in Buenos Aires. Hopefully, finding him will put an end to the hunt for other manipulator vampires like me. As far as I know, I'm still the only one who has escaped extermination over the last few centuries.

While I rested and recovered, Rafe explored the underbelly of the Argentine city extensively, making sure his casual occupation stayed unnoticed by the ruling Tribunal of Ancients. His protective instincts toward me have barreled to the surface, and I've found I rather like this side of him.

After the worst of my damage was healed through copious amounts of blood and lots of deep restorative sleep, the dead-to-the-world type only the undead can take, we split up—him staying in the city to investigate, and me journeying back to our island off the coast of southeastern Argentina to tend to the family of caretakers. Their minds needed delicate fixing from the damage done by the same people who tried to kill me.

The island caretakers were not harmed permanently, and I have to admit, what was done to their minds was so subtle it didn't require much effort on my part to repair. The island hideaway they help keep in tip-top shape is where we spend most of the Argentine winter, only venturing to Buenos Aires when there's a big Tribunal shin-dig.

But this year was different.

Not only did we initially arrive weeks earlier than normal, with most of our new seethe traveling with us, but now we're sending Drew, Chelly, and the others home to

Alaska during the region's summer months—which is typically singe and die season for vampires above the Arctic Circle. The extensive tunnels and safeguards built into the resort will keep the returning vampires alive, so I'm not worried on that end. They'll be safe and—by the end of the long stretches of seemingly never-ending daylight—bored with cabin fever.

I'm sure Asa, the ex-military vampire responsible for the resort's security, will be happy to have them back. Recently, he's had his hands full with helping to exorcise ghosts at the inn. The apparitions were of the humans and supernaturals who'd died during the past year's adventures. By the lighter lilt in his voice during our last conversation, it sounded like Asa may have found a female diversion this summer, too. Good, the man needs to let someone in.

Sending them home while Rafe and I get to the bottom of things here is the smartest solution. I will not let guilt sway me.

I n the end, it was the others and not Drew who protested nonstop about returning home last night, tempting me beyond belief to force them to my will, but I managed to resist and smile benignly during their blathering.

Above all, Rafe and I need to focus on finding Rolando and putting an end to this drama. Having the others here, even if they stayed on the island and not in the direct path of my enemies, could be dangerous—not to mention a distraction I don't want to take on. I'd worry about their safety.

Someone could succeed in finding them again, even on our tiny middle-of-nowhere island, to use against me. In comparison, the inn is more of a secure, secluded fortress than many of them realize. It's the perfect place to await an enemy, especially when you know the property as well as we do.

Doubt creeps into me and I squash it, determined not to second guess my resolve regarding Jon and our plans to fly him down. As an alpha werewolf, he would be the best choice to stay and safeguard the seethe at the inn. But, whether I like it or not, I need him here by my side, to hunt down Rolando.

What prompted a hidden sect within the Tribunal—one hell bent on tracking and killing manipulators, a rare breed of vampire thought long exterminated—to hunt me down?

Has the story of Coraline's tampered memories, which I was responsible for on her last visit to Alaska, spread among their supporters? Did I reveal myself unknowingly through another channel? Has my arrogance in always assuming I could handle anything thrown my way with a simple bending of my will finally backfired on me?

How did they know to look for me? Who pointed them in my direction? Have others, vampires older than me, suspected my secret for centuries and yet never acted to eliminate me? And if yes, why? Was it out of fear, or with the hope to someday use me and my skills to their advantage?

I shake my head, eager to dispel the uncharacteristic self-doubt. The wondering of why and how my hidden traits have been discovered is not important. Tracking down those who wish me harm and killing them *is*.

Resolve swells within me, strengthening with the deep breath I draw into my lungs. I will find those responsible. I will secure the safety of those pledged to me. I will—

My cell rings, cutting off my internal diatribe.

The screen reveals it's Rafe. I grab the device and answer it. "Yes? Why are you calling me on the phone?" Referring to his choice to use technology rather than connect with me telepathically, as he usually does.

"Your thoughts were all over the place. And growing rather dark, truth be told. I thought calling you might snap you out of it better than rudely barging into your private musings."

"Fine. I was also thinking of Jon—did you catch those thoughts, too?"

"Yes, and you're right. We do need him here. He'll be an asset more than a hindrance, I think. When can he get here? And will you have him fly to the city or the island?"

I bite my lip, ruminating on his questions. "He's scheduled to leave in a few hours, and will arrive late tomorrow. I think having him journey directly to Buenos Aires would be the smartest use of time. I've chartered a plane and will fly in tonight."

"Good. Did the others leave already?"

"Yes, last night, right as the sun went down. They had a brief stop in the city to pick up more pilots."

"Time to do what we mentioned months ago—'beard the lion in his den.'"

I snort, unable to contain the sarcasm waiting to escape. "Oh yes, that worked so beautifully for us last time, didn't it?"

"Hey, things didn't go as planned, I'll grant you that, but any battle you can walk away from with your life is considered a win, trust me." A teasing note enters his voice. "Are you sure you're not more annoyed that I did most of the killing and maiming this time?"

Flashes of blood and dismembered bodies skitter across my mind, small glimpses of what I recall from when I awoke in the underground rooms beneath the Tribunal headquarters, also known as the Seat of Darkness and the base of all vampire kind.

Rafe's actions may have surprised our new seethemates who were with him, Drew and Paul, but I've known what my husband is capable of for a very long time. "I don't think that's it. Or more accurately, I don't think that's the only thing." A sigh escapes me. "I think we walked into a bigger mess than we bargained for, and I'd rather make sure it doesn't happen again."

"We can't begin to formulate a plan of attack until we're well aware of who our enemy is and where they're located. The basic knowledge of where the Tribunal lies is not enough. Who else is visiting this season? Are all the ancients in attendance or are some traveling? Where do they stay during their restorative sleep—meaning a private residence or in the extensive underground holdings of the Tribunal?"

He's not saying anything we haven't discussed before, so I redirect and ask about recent developments. "Have you had any luck in tracking down Rolando?"

"No, none. And it's damn frustrating, I can tell you that. The big bastard didn't up and disappear, that's for sure."

"What about Justin? Have you discovered where he lives yet?"

"I've narrowed the wizard's location down to a diverse *barrio* on the outskirts of San Telmo, one of the city's older neighborhoods. But no set address. The area has lots of herbal shops with hard to find magical ingredients."

"That sounds more like an ideal location for a coven of witches than a wizard."

"Well, where would you have me start looking? Should I

knock on the Tribunal's door and ask where they hide their pet wizardling?"

A grunt of frustration seeps past my lips. "No. You're fine. I almost hate to admit it, but tracking is better suited to Jon's natural abilities than yours."

"Oh yes, the furball. Do you plan to have him take his wolf form and sniff like a dog to track?"

"Come now, dear, don't make this harder than it needs to be. He is a strength. He is a valuable asset to us."

His voice tightens, showing his inner turmoil and anguish. "Who are you trying to convince—me or you?"

"You, you dork. I know I need him. Now more than ever. Suck it up, buttercup." My voice deepens, taking on a husky tone. "It's not like I *want* him the way I want you. He's not the one I dream of every time I close my eyes. It's not his love, his very essence of life, that brought me back from the edge of insanity and darkness," I say, referring to the moment I nearly died and Rafe's devotion and love saved me.

"Okay, you've made your point. I'll play nice with the werewolf. Any hint or rumor he may have found a mate during last month's big game hunting fiasco with all the werewolves?"

I shrug, realize he can't see my movement, and say, "I'm not sure."

"What? How can that be? How could you not be sure of what your vampire servant is doing at any given time?"

"You know I gave him distance when we left—and I don't mean physically, I mean with our mental connection. He's still there, in the back of my mind. But I've given him privacy, not wanting to intrude when he has the chance to be free of my influence for once."

"Is that the best course of action when you claim to 'need him' now?"

"I'll allow the connection to strengthen when he journeys here, but I want to keep some mental distance in place for him. He needs it. His uncontrollable obsessive desires were overcoming his waking thoughts, he needed the break to heal and find himself again."

"All right, enough about the poor lost puppy. When did you say he'll arrive?"

"Tuesday night. We'll meet him at the airport in the city. How is the house hunting coming along?"

I hear the happiness in his voice. "I've found several suitable accommodations," he says. "You'll like them, I'm sure."

A rush of images floods my mind. Stately residences in the posh neighborhoods near the heart of the city, rooms with high ceilings and ornate moldings, and hearths with big roaring fires.

"Good. I miss you, my darling. It's only been two weeks and I still think it's too long."

"You're just hungry for my blood, aren't you?"

"Among other things..."

A gentle tingle of sensation indicates my husband's mind reaching out to mine. *And I miss you too,* liebling. *We'll be together soon. Not to worry.*

CHAPTER TWO

RAFE

We hang up and I check the time on my phone. The real estate agent should arrive in a few minutes. I purposefully projected images of grand homes to Dria when there was mention of the house shopping. In reality, I've picked three older places, all in different sections of the city—and none of them grand. I smile, anticipating her reaction.

I like to think of it as a private joke between us.

My wife happily resided—for years—in a drafty cabin on our island, *instead* of the existing farmhouse already on the property. It was purely out of personal preference due to past horrors she endured in an old English farmhouse. In the end, I know she'll be fine in any home we consider safe, no matter the trappings.

But still, I can't wait to see her face when she sees the places I picked. The one we close on this afternoon is a row house that's seen better days, another is a basement apartment under an old, closed bank, and the third is a ramshackle structure with sewer access—perhaps it was an old worker's dwelling.

We will never be caught like rats in a hole. We will change locations daily, if needed, ensuring trackers can't find us while we plot and plan how to ferret out the dissension in the Tribunal's ranks.

A car pulls alongside mine, maneuvering to park in front. The door opens and a tall, attractive woman in her forties, dressed in a royal blue business suit, exits from the vehicle, her long dark hair secured in a ponytail at the nape of her neck. She smiles as she approaches my car, watching me as I climb out. "Hi, Mr. McAndrews. Ready for the walk through?"

I return her smile and extend my hand. "Yes. Mrs. Rameriz, thanks for meeting me before closing."

She shakes my hand, her smile firmly in place. "You and your wife certainly know how to close a house sale quickly." The lovely woman is referring to my wife's favorite "cash is king" mentality.

Well, when you've got the money available, why not? No need to delay matters with bank applications and loans. I return her smile, offering no further explanation. After all, she doesn't need to know too much of our business. "You still agree it's a good location for my wife's preferences?" I explained that we travel extensively for business, and Dria wants a private residence she can enjoy instead of a crowded hotel. The other locations were acquired through different agents and purchased under different company names, so no one from the Tribunal would be the wiser.

"Oh, yes. Quiet, all residential, mostly families and retired couples. Grocery shopping is close by, only a couple of blocks south." She indicates the direction with a sweep of her arm.

"Restaurants and small businesses are three blocks to the north. Crime rate is low. I think she'll be happy with your choice." A wisp of panic crosses her face. "You did send her the listings to review, right? I'd hate for her to be unhappy with the house."

"Yes, of course." I've done no such thing, wanting to surprise Dria, but I keep that to myself.

Once more, I glance at the brightly painted homes—pink, salmon, robin's egg blue, yellow, green—you name it and it's here. Wherever your eye lands, you're sure to be assaulted by color. I inhale deeply, enjoying the smells of cooking food drifting on the air. The inner-city neighborhood is exactly what we want—discreet and unobtrusive. No one would expect a wealthy master vampire, her husband, and a werewolf to reside here.

"Shall we go in?"

At my nod, the agent produces a key and leads the way to the entrance, a solid door a few feet from the sidewalk. We enter the small furnished home, my eyes taking in the stucco walls, pristine tile, and compact floor plan: kitchen in the rear, living space and dining room laid out at the front.

The decorating style is simple and clean. No fussy fabrics or chintz, more of a minimalist decor in an urban setting. "Nice," I say. "It appears all the furniture we asked them to include is here. Do you have a list?"

She produces a file from her large bag. "I'll double check while you look around."

We wander through the first and then second floor, with her checking off items as we go.

And now, onto what really drew me to the listing. "How

about one last look at the basement and root cellar? Just to make sure they were cleaned thoroughly."

"Oh yes, right this way." She leads me to a small bathroom on the first floor. "I know it seems odd, but I kind of like that the entrance is through a hidden door in here. Very different."

I try and hide my smile. This dark hideaway is exactly why I bought the place. It's probably a remnant from a paranoid German who moved to Argentina after the Holocaust. Lots of German nationalists who supported Hitler fled to Argentina to avoid persecution after the war ended. They may have easily adapted to creating their own hidey-holes, like the ones used to hide Jews when the Nazis had a stranglehold on Germany.

The doorway is tight, I literally have to turn sideways to enter, but after that, the stairwell opens up and I'm able to descend normally. The stairs are illuminated by a single bare bulb, indicating the lower floor has electricity. There's no trace of the damp, musty smell we noticed last week. It's been replaced by the scent of astringent cleaners. A low hum from a dehumidifier and air purifier sound below us.

We reach the bottom of the stairs, revealing the room's about half the size of the main floor. Empty shelves line the walls, devoid of the household detritus stored there previously.

Exposed beams in the ceiling and the underside of floorboards from the rooms above loom over us, leaving maybe seven feet of headroom. I plan on installing insulation and dry wall this afternoon after the closing. Tomorrow I'll be painting and building pre-made furniture down here. The floor isn't dirt, like I'd initially feared, but a serviceable ceramic tile— newer by the looks of it. Nothing a nice area rug won't warm up. This is where I plan to make us a hidden bedroom. It won't be glamorous, but it will be safe.

A small wooden door, slightly bigger than a large kitchen cabinet, sits in the center of the far wall, leading toward the back of the house.

"Do you mind if I check the root cellar, too?" I ask.

"Not at all, allow me." She moves to the door and lifts the latch, then swings it inward and retreats to grant me a better view.

I step forward and stick my head inside. It's very dark, only the light from the basement slipping past to illuminate a few rickety, empty shelves made of rough wood. But it smells like they cleaned in here, too.

"Here," she says, clicking on a flashlight and handing it to me. "I always have one in my purse just in case an attic or basement is unlit."

I scan the interior once more, noting the very low ceiling and an old ladder about eight feet away. "Where does this lead?"

"Before the basement was hand-dug to allow more space, the area was used for food storage. Outside access to the garden, via that ladder, was the only way in, until the tiny staircase was built in the bathroom closet. If I'm recalling right, the ladder leads to a ground-level storm door behind the garden."

Perfect. "Looks good. I'm ready to finalize the sale."

"Great. Let's go sign the paperwork. You'll have the keys before you know it."

We spend the next hour in a nearby attorney's office, hashing out the details and then I ask to see another property I've singled out as a possibility. It lies on the other end of town, bordering a more isolated section of woods. Just in case Jon needs space to run as a wolf, I thought it prudent to acquire a spot with land.

"Oh, you're interested in more than one location?"

I smile, knowing we'll probably make her month with two sales in one week. "Yes, we are. The next one doesn't need to be habitable right away. We'd like it for the property."

She returns my smile, "Well, let's get started." She packs her portable document scanner into her briefcase, finished with emailing the signed documents to the seller's agent. "We can swing by their office on the way to get both sets of keys. The house is yours." She thrusts out her hand to shake mine. "Congratulations."

The next hour flies by. We draw up a contract for the place I earmarked for Jon. It's further out than I thought, but heavily wooded and backs a park. Once again, I'm grateful for my wife's preplanning that has allowed for bank accounts filled with millions in various countries around the world—with even more in Argentina since we have the island off the southeastern coast.

With the later part of the afternoon still ahead of me, I hustle and get the supplies needed to insulate and drywall the basement. The simple, but tedious, task of shoving the insulation in and slapping up dry wall and the first layer of mud takes me a few hours. I won't be able to apply the next coat over the seams until this one is dried, so I climb back into the shiny, new, dark blue Audi I purchased last week, and drive to the Tribunal's neighborhood. I say neighborhood because they literally own the whole block, plus adjacent homes to ensure their safety and privacy.

I park a few doors down from the main townhouse, the one we entered last month for the autumn ball, and the one the other houses on the street connect to underground—vampires really do love their secret tunnels and hidden exits.

The trees lining the darkening street are bare of leaves, casting eerie shadows as the sun slips below the horizon. A harsh wind kicks up the few dead leaves from under a hedge, whirling the mass into the air before moving on.

The flip of seasons below the equator is a welcome change of pace, especially for a species that thrives in the dark, but occasionally I do miss having a chance to enjoy the warm days of summer. I sip coffee while watching the doorways. Nothing much reveals itself, just the average comings and goings of employees needed to keep a large residence running smoothly.

What I haven't seen in a week is hide nor hair of their pet wizardling, Justin. If he stays on schedule, he's due back today to renew his magical wards. I'm hoping to get another glimpse of him before Dria and Jon arrive.

How do I feel about Jon coming to help? To be honest, I'm relieved. I may tease the arrogant bastard who watches my wife a little too closely, but I'm used to having him by our side, protecting both of us, even if he swears he's only watching Dria's back. This was our first extended trip out of the country in years without Jon, and with all the danger flying around my wife, I hope it's our last trip without him.

No matter what I say to Dria, inside I'm racked with guilt. If I had insisted he come, could things have ended differently in late May? Would he have been able to stop Dria from being taken and tortured? Would his presence have kept her safe? Seeing the ravaged body of my wife again in my mind's eye makes one thing very clear: I will accept anyone in our lives to keep her safe. Jealousy and self-doubt have no room among the fear of an absolute there's no return from: the final death of an undead.

I check the messages on my phone and see Dria is already in the air. She'll be here in a few hours and we'll be able to have an intimate reunion before Jon arrives tomorrow night. Good. I need it.

Movement on the townhouse's grand steps draws my eye. My luck has finally changed. The familiar lanky form dressed all in black descends, taking the stairs carefully, with his attention turned inward. By the subtle movement of his lips, I'm guessing Justin's either talking through a Bluetooth earpiece I can't see, or perhaps checking the strength of a safety ward.

Luckily, a lone human parked on the street during the day when the vampires are asleep, hasn't triggered an alarm. Maybe the ancients' arrogance doesn't normally allow for fear of one lowly human. Local residents carrying pitchforks and torches? Probably, yes.

Justin reaches the sidewalk and strides toward a small black SUV, the kind that looks like a hybrid of a car and a four-wheel-drive vehicle. Excited by my stroke of good fortune, I start my car moments after his and follow.

This will be the second time I've been able to tail Justin, and hopefully this time I'll find out exactly where he lives. I've also scouted the local residents of a dozen vampires who've left the Tribunal grounds, none of who have led me any closer to finding Rolando.

Could the slick crafty bastard still be residing in the Tribunal or could he have left via a hidden route? I'm only one set of eyes, and staking out various entrances day in and day out can only be so accurate.

The wizard leads me on a merry chase, stopping at a restaurant before finally pulling into a small residence not far from the dwelling we closed on earlier today. I wait ten minutes to ensure he's not dropping off something for someone else, then leave my car to approach the house. Like most of the homes in this section, the front door is right off the sidewalk, no front yard or driveway to give it distance.

I stand outside a window off to the side and quiet my breathing. I take out my phone, glance at the screen, and lean against the wall. With luck, I'll appear to be stopping to check something and not draw attention from neighbors.

In a moment, I hear a TV on inside the small house and a scrape of a chair against the floor. Sounds like he lives here. And possibly alone, as I don't hear or sense anyone else inside.

Perfect. When the others arrive, we'll start with questioning him. Time to go wait for my wife's flight. I can't wait to see her.

CHAPTER THREE

JON

I settle in Dria and Rafe's apartment, way more comfortable in their home, surrounded by their scents, then I'd care to admit. Meeting Candy has transformed how I think about my relationship with the owners of the inn. She gives me the intimacy and sense of belonging that comes in a new relationship, and being with her has also helped me achieve a personal balance I was lacking earlier.

Sure, since the rogue vampire Emiko ran loose across the resort, things have been tighter between Dria, Rafe, and me than ever. But now, it feels more like a partnership than a longing to be part of what I can never have. Is that what Dria hoped when she allowed a summer season at the inn to become a haven for werewolf packs? I'd never have expected her to play matchmaker, but I think maybe that's exactly what she's done.

I grab a beer out of the fridge and wait for Diane. I invited her here to ask about topics she's more capable of answering than anyone I know. In a few minutes there's a light knock at the couple's front door and I answer it.

"Thanks for meeting with me, Diane," I say to the inn's resident witch and my former lover. Much to my relief, she came dressed normally. No low-cut blouses meant to draw my eye, or skin tight jeans begging me to grab her ass. I like it. Her appearance bodes well for a successful conversation with no sexual undercurrent.

"Of course, Jon." She tosses her long strawberry-blond spiral curls over one shoulder, follows me through the suite, and takes a seat across from me at the round kitchen table.

I thought meeting here, rather than my secluded cabin, might be smarter—and perhaps it wouldn't send a vibe like I was trying to jump her bones, as I've done repeatedly in the past. The seethe's conference room in the basement would have been the most neutral and professional location, but only a handful of us are aware of its existence, and she isn't among those in the know.

Perhaps sensing my discomfort, she smiles, and it almost reaches her eyes. "No worries, Jon. We can still be friends. I know you've hooked up with Candy, and I'm happy for you."

I clear my throat, hoping for a way past this awkwardness. "Gee, news travels fast. Didn't you just get back yesterday from visiting friends in the lower forty-eight?"

"Yeah," she answers while nodding. "It was a great trip. But hey, you aren't doing yourself justice. News of your 'unique' uh... girlfriend... reached me from friends here even while I was away."

Refusing to be drawn into conversation about my girlfriend who can shift to any form, including that of a man, I grab my note pad and read over the bullet points.

"Did you also hear about what happened in Argentina to the rest of the seethe?" She nods again, encouraging me to keep talking. "Okay then, that saves some time."

"I only heard the basics—Vivian was captured, along with Paul and Drew. And it was Rafe who saved them all." Vivian is the name the employees and guests call Dria. It's an old play on words from when she first opened the V V Inn years ago. People shortened the name and called her Vivian—it stuck.

"That's enough. It's not my story to tell, so I can't reveal too much detail." I lower my eyes again, unwilling to be grilled for gossipy tidbits that will be spread among the employees before the bosses return. "I asked you here for information on a topic you are much more suited to than I."

"Ahh... I get it." Her eyes light up and tension eases from her slim shoulders. "You want to talk about magic, right?"

"Yes. Can I trust you not to say anything to the rest of the employees?"

The phrasing was just what she needed to hear, as Candy suggested it might be. It puts her in a position of power, knowing more than her fellow employees, and might garner her trust in sharing witch knowledge with an outsider.

"After everything we've been through, you should know I can be discreet, Jon." Her sexy smile is back, like the old Diane I know so well. "Besides, most of them would prefer to forget that I'm a card-carrying witch."

"Fantastic, thanks. Vivian prompted me to ask you first, and then do more research on my own before I join them. I'm tempted to call Cy, too, but don't know that he'll be able to dig up anything you don't already know firsthand."

I glance down at my notes again, even though there's not much listed there. The diversion helps to keep me from looking into her pain-filled green eyes. She might deny it, but I can tell she still has feelings for me. Dammit. I never wanted to hurt her.

I start with the first item on my list. "Can you tell me the difference between a witch and a wizard?" My pen is poised to begin taking notes as soon as she starts speaking.

"I can tell you what my aunt explained to me when I first came into my powers, although I'm sure there is a more definitive answer in an ancient book somewhere. A witch is born with magic, whereas a wizard is not. A wizard, be it a man or woman, takes magic from the world around them via spells, powders, magical objects, and a wide assortment of ingredients. Often leaving an imbalance in their wake if they aren't careful in their magic usage.

"Compared to us, wizards are considered abnormal. A witch or warlock, a male witch, is born with an affinity for magic. They are gifted in different traits found in nature, and all inherit a tendency to excel with one type of elemental magic over another. But with proper training and lots of practice, a witch can learn to use all the elements in their magic."

"What do you mean by elemental magic?"

"An element found in nature—fire, water, air, earth —get it?"

I nod and look back over the notes I'd just written. "How does one become a wizard if they are not born with inherent magical ability like a witch is?"

"They need someone to teach them. Many cultures have a form of elemental magic, and the practitioners aren't always called witches. Some are shaman, druids, wise women... you get the idea. But others not born with the innate ability still seek out the mysteries of controlling and using magic. I'm sure at one point the two types of practitioners were more closely knit, like say perhaps a sibling or child of a witch who had an interest in magic, who wasn't born with the trait, but still wanted to learn.

"Something must have happened at one point, because even if my theory is right, the division between the two magical practices is permanent now. I don't know how wizards developed their spells, how they draw magic out of the things around them without a born affinity, or how they expand their knowledge base. I do know that in certain instances, they can conjure spells that are more powerful than a single witch can do on her own—we use a coven for complicated magic.

"Mainly, I'd say wizards are more focused on amassing knowledge for self-preservation and material gain than witchcraft users. We're much more about balancing the whole and doing no permanent harm."

"Does that mean a wizard's spells are not balanced?"

"I don't know."

"And what happens with an imbalance caused by wizard magic?"

She shrugs. "Beats me. I'm not a wizard. Sorry."

"You're aunt never went into detail on it?"

Diane looks toward the bright window over the sink, gnawing on her lower lip. "Hmm... I was really young when we first talked about it. I think she mentioned 'bad things' would happen if the balance wasn't restored while casting, but she never went into what the bad things were."

"Okay, fair enough. I'll have to dig up more on my own." I check my list again. "What can you tell me about the vampire saying, 'never turn a witch'?"

"Huh, that's a new one. I've never heard it before. Could be because I'm not a vampire." She winks. "But hey, you've got one who's *real* close to you. I'm sure she wouldn't mind you asking."

"If you didn't have an answer that was going to be my next step." I look up from my notes, apprehension bubbling in my middle before I ask about the next thing on my mind. "You know the amulets you used to make for me?" She nods, a spark lighting in her eyes in remembrance of the sex charms I needed to enjoy the act and block images of Dria from overriding all else. "Is it possible to make something similar, but to help strengthen my mental shields?"

Understanding dawns in her intelligent gaze almost instantly. She's way more perceptive than I'd like. "You haven't told Vivian about Candy yet and you need to make sure the vamp can't easily pry into your thoughts?" She snorts. "Good luck with that. There's no spell I know of that can dull the bond between a master vampire and her servant if she *really* wants to get into your head."

I rise from the table, awkward now that I asked. "Thanks."

"Wait a second," she reaches toward me, dropping her hand when she realizes she's about to touch me. "What about meditating on your own and learning to build a wall to protect your innermost thoughts? It might help."

"Okay, thanks. I'll try that." Realizing I've never been particularly good at meditating I ask, "Do you have any suggestions on how?"

Diane smiles, the look in her eyes filled with more of a fondness now than anything else. "You betcha." She glances at the table and hard chairs. "We'll need to get comfortable. Follow me."

She rises and moves to the living room, no hint of guile in her movements. Apprehension seeps into me at the thought of sitting next to her on the couch. After all, this is the same woman who tried to tear down my pants and suck me off outside the gentleman's lounge a few months ago. We never did get together after that. I was too uncomfortable with her affection and determination to win my desire.

"Relax, Jon." She points to the oversized chair while she takes a seat on the couch. "If we can't get the tension out of you, you'll never be any good at this."

I take the offered seat, feeling stupid. "I'm not tense."

"Uh-huh, sure. You look like a nervous virgin on prom night. Chill." She winks. "I've had you, and not that I'd kick you out of my bed for eating crackers, but I can understand you're not on the market anymore."

I settle back in the soft cushion, a deep sigh easing out of me. "Thanks, Diane. We never had a chance to really become friends and I'd like it if we could."

Sadness flits across her face, quickly replaced by determination. "Okay now, close your eyes, be quiet, and listen to my voice. I'm going to start with a simple guided meditation. If you like it you can download others off the Internet—I'll give you some site recommendations."

Her voice slows as she begins to walk me through basic relaxation techniques. Very soon, I'm floating in a peaceful cloud of contentment, happy to picture the serene images she's painting with her mellow voice.

We spend the next hour going through several techniques and mantras to build inner walls within my mind. Kind of funny that a guy has to ask how to deliberately hide his feelings and thoughts when most of us have been doing it unconsciously our whole lives.

When she leaves, I feel good. Good that I may be able to have a friendship with a former lover, good that I've begun to build a sense of self away from the dynamic couple, and even better that I have Candy waiting for me in my cabin.

Speaking of which, I've got a surprise planned for her. And I better get going.

CHAPTER FOUR

VIVIAN

I settle back into the seat, grateful the flight is almost over. I prefer flying in my own jet, rather than renting a private plane, but there was no choice since Drew and the others flew back to Alaska in ours.

Apprehension tightens my gut. I know, somehow sense, Jon has been physically intimate with someone from the big game hunting trip last month, but I don't want to ask who she is. Prying is not my style. I want him to find happiness more than anything, and I think having to discuss his recent relationship status with Rafe and me will add unwanted stress to a budding attraction.

He's young, almost twenty-nine, and could easily grow his small pack. The real problem is making sure said pack remains happy right where Jon is, by my side, which won't be changing any time soon.

The smartest move would be to enlist his whole pack as my vampire servants, but I don't want the responsibility of so many souls bound to mine. Especially if something were to happen, like if Coraline succeeded in killing me. Rafe and Jon are strong enough to stand on their own if I died a true death, never to return from the dark abyss. But what about a weaker person, or a newer bond—how would they fare?

Yes, this is definitely *not* the time to experiment and try to find out. Eric and Pat, the new werewolves in Jon's pack, are both capable young men, but in the coming years they could decide to break from this pack to start their own—which would be impossible if they were bound to me as well. A vampire servant is usually bound for life.

I know I could break such a union if I had to. In dire circumstances, I've been able to destroy other people's mate bonds, which is the the binding between a vampire and a servant that makes them virtually equal in power. Doing so comes with inherent risks, like death, so it's not something I want to do on a regular basis.

I've often thought that only a strong mate for Jon could be a viable second vampire servant for me, but finding a woman who fits that role is not up to me, it's up to Jon. I could essentially make a bond work with anyone, of that I have no doubt.

Will he think about what it means to the three of us when he allows someone close to him, or will his passion rule his heart and head?

Either way, I have to keep my mouth shut. If he hasn't been paying attention the past seven years, then I've really failed as a master. I may never have set out to have a seethe of my own, but I've always known how to treat people with decency and have never forgotten how the struggles in my early years as a vampire shaped me.

The solitude of the private plane's cabin is disturbed only by the deep breathing of one of the snoozing, off-duty pilots. I decide to indulge in quiet meditation for the rest of the flight, all too aware that I need to be sharp for the next stages of our investigating.

Before I know it, the plane touches down smoothly on the runway. I stand when the pilot says it's safe, smoothing my long sweater over my leggings. Within minutes, I'm descending from the plane in a private hangar.

"Madame," an attendant calls to me. "There's a room ready for your arrival, if you'll follow me." A private suite sits in the back of the small hangar, obviously set up for elite passengers while a plane becomes ready. It will be a perfect place to relax and wait for Rafe to arrive.

"Do you have a status on the flight to Alaska?"

"Yes, ma'am. It's received great tail winds and is expected to land ahead of schedule. Should arrive very late tonight and be ready to fly back within a few hours."

I nod, smiling my thanks, and follow the trim young woman to the far end. She opens a steel door and steps back, ushering me in before her. The moment the door opens, I smell him. Rafe is already here.

"*Liebling*," he says in a quiet exhalation of breath, calling me the German endearment for darling. The lines in his rugged face smooth out at my arrival, making him look younger than his normal appearance of a man in his mid-thirties. He towers over me by at least five inches, even in my heels, his heavily-muscled body dwarfing mine by over a hundred pounds. He's wearing dark casual pants and a thin navy sweater. Both drape over his frame like they were made for him.

I step into the room and my husband's thick arms wrap around me. "I've missed you, my dear."

I mimic his actions, draping my arms over his shoulders, nuzzling his neck, and take a deep breath, drawing in the familiar male-muskiness that's unique to him. "Me, too, you big lug."

His large hands roam down my spine, settling at the small of my back. "I don't sleep as well if you're not near me."

"Really?" I say, a slight teasing note in my voice. "That says a lot, considering I rarely *sleep* in bed with you."

He pulls back, far enough to place his lips on mine. It's a tender touching of mouths, not a hungry devouring like I'm aching to do.

He ends the kiss, his warm breath tickling my cheek. "Maybe that's because what we do in bed when you're *not* sleeping tires me."

"Oh?" I kiss his cheek tenderly. "So what you're saying is you miss me as a work-out partner?"

He chuckles, the sound rumbling through his chest into mine where we touch. "You do help keep me in shape." He circles his hips, teasing me with his blatant arousal. "Can you feel how much I've missed you, love? Haven't you missed what only I can give you?"

I smile. A wicked grin, I'm sure. "Did you come here hoping to 'mark' me before Jon arrives? Really, darling, we have all night and all day tomorrow, and besides, he knows I'm yours. He's known it for years. You don't need to beat your chest every time he's near."

Rafe fists a hand in my hair, tugging hard, tilting my head back. "This has nothing to do with Jon. I swear. Perhaps it's something in the air..." He trails kisses over my face, leading to my mouth. "Perhaps it's the constant danger of trailing vampires and staking out the Tribunal..." His mouth locks onto mine for a sweet kiss that quickly deepens to passionate. "But I need you—for me. Not to prove anything to anyone."

One hand shifts to my front, sliding between us to grasp my right breast. He squeezes hard, displaying his urgency better than any words. "Will you deny your husband?"

I stare into his bright blue eyes, overcome by the love and desire I see shining back at me. "Never."

My hands slide down to his pants, urging him to take them off. The two-week separation from him has me creaming in my panties, eager to satisfy a craving only he can fulfill. He complies with my subtle request in lightning fast movements, divesting us both of our confining clothes in record time. Once we stand nude, staring at one another, the heat of lust coloring our skin, I lurch forward, clasping him to me in desperation. My mouth locks onto his and I'm lost to the passion that rolls over us.

F ull darkness has descended as we leave the hangar in search of transportation. Rafe grabbed my bag, left by the attendant near the door. I scan up and down the narrow drive, looking for the lights of our hired car.

"Over here, my love." Rafe palms a shiny key fob, depressing one of the buttons. A tiny chirp sounds from a sleek sedan parked nearby. Glossy, dark blue paint reflects the distant street light.

I change direction toward the expensive car. "Bought yourself a new toy, did you?"

"Can you blame me?" He runs a hand lovingly over the

hood in passing, making his way to the trunk to deposit my luggage. "I'd never get to drive something like this on our snow-packed roads on the resort."

I glance at the front emblem of four interlocking circles. "I agree. No need for an Audi above the Arctic Circle."

He opens my door before proceeding around the car to the driver's side. "I knew you'd understand."

I withhold the snarky snort itching to escape and settle into the buttery soft seats. "I'm glad it makes you happy. It's only money."

"Spoken like only someone with a whole lot of it would proclaim."

Rafe starts the car and steers us to the main road, proudly showing off the posh interior features in case I might care. Which I don't. And he knows. But he's so excited and I'm currently content, so I see no need to burst his bubble of joy.

Once we approach the older section of the city, I break into his ongoing sales pitch for the Audi. "I want to go to the Tribunal. Tonight."

Concern furrows his brow as he pays attention to the busy streets. "Are you sure that's a good idea?"

"I know you've got your doubts, and I can understand your side of things. But I don't think the entire Tribunal was in on what Coraline and the others were doing. They may be perfectly willing to serve Rolando up on a platter to keep the peace. I won't know until I ask."

"You plan on barging in and demanding they tell you where he is?"

"Yes, because that worked so well for Drew and Paul a few weeks ago, right? Their time in the Tribunal's underground holding cells was not pleasant, I'm sure." I stare out the window and consider my choices. Rafe hasn't been able to track Rolando from the Seat of Darkness, nor has he questioned anyone with any success. I'm a long time member of this stupid governing body. I have rights to stop by and ask to see someone if I want to.

Rafe must have been listening in on my thoughts, because he says, "Oh yes, and of course it's no big deal to waltz right in after you were held hostage there, possibly unawares by the eleven ruling ancients, we're not sure, to *demand* to see one of the inner circle who was known to betray you recently. Yeah, sure. That'll happen."

A tiny bubble of annoyance blooms within me. I'm unsure if it's directed at him or me.

"We can make it casual."

"Uh-huh. Yeah. And they'll know that. That's why someone from the Tribunal asked about you after I broke you out, sent flowers while you were healing... oh, wait. That never happened. These people don't care about you, liebling. And I will not have you walking into danger—again. I don't want you to go tonight. It's risky, there's no plan of attack, or one for escape, for that matter. I don't agree with this course of action."

I smile in the dark. My husband's frustration fills the car between us like a buzz of angry bees. "You almost sound like you're ready to proclaim 'I forbid you from going.'"

He snorts, the tension easing out of him. "I know you. That would go over like a fart in church."

I glance at his strong profile, love warming my chest. "How about we compromise?"

"Just like that? You're going to roll over and listen to my

advice without a knock-down-drag-out fight, or me having to talk you into it until I'm blue in the face?"

"See? An old dog can learn new tricks."

"All right. What's this compromise?"

"We enter the first floor, limit how far we're willing to be drawn in, and ask to speak to someone. I still have friends there. I know it."

"Hmph. And where were they that night?"

"That *night* you're referring to actually started right before dawn, remember? I was taken, as were you, while most everyone else was sleeping away the day. I refuse to believe everyone who attended the fall party that night is a suspect."

"Fine." Silence fills the car as we finish the journey.

Rafe drives to the Tribunal's stately townhouse, done in the old English style, smack dab in the middle of the two residential blocks the Tribunal owns.

He pulls the powerful car to a silent stop across the street from the elegant townhouse steps. Every light on the block is ablaze, indicating the residents within are up and about, even past midnight—which is certainly normal for a group of undead.

"Just the foyer?" Rafe questions. "No farther? We leave the door open and whoever we talk to must come to us?"

"Yes, dear." I have no intention of asking whoever is at the door to leave it open, like I'm a child afraid of the dark, but I agree to placate my husband. Which he should recognize by now, right?

We alight from the vehicle and make our way across the darkened road. Before we've gone ten feet, a familiar voice booms across the quiet street. "Vivian? Is that you?"

The vampire I nicknamed a wall of meat, George, calls from the top of the porch steps. He's one of the few vampires I've ever met who makes Rafe look small.

"Yes. It is." I try for a casual tone. "How's it going, George?"

The large man rushes down the stairs to greet us, sweeping me into a big bear hug before I know what hit me. "I was so worried about you! Why haven't you come by sooner?" He looks at Rafe and raises an eyebrow. "And hello, Mr. Vampire Slayer. The internal video feed caught *all* your adventures that night. It's a good thing you know your way around a fire poker, eh?"

Rafe doesn't respond, a small upward turn of the corner of his lips the only indication he heard the man.

"Funny how you were worried about me, George," I say. "After the shit we faced that night... let's just say it's amazing your superiors aren't gunning for us."

He lets me go and ushers us toward the stairs. "Not at all, Vivian. You had to know what Coraline did was not sanctioned by the Tribunal. We have no idea why she behaved the way she did, or tortured you, but obviously you aren't to blame. You're the victim, the video clearly shows that."

Not expecting such a warm welcome, frankly any welcome at all, I'm at a loss for words. Rafe trails behind us as we ascend the stone staircase to the front door. There's no apprehension or warning bells in my head, like I felt a few weeks ago when we arrived at the fall party... but I still feel uneasy. Is there a surprise awaiting us inside?

"Did you really worry after all your years of service that you'd be in danger? You've got a lot of friends in high places."

"And enemies, too," I whisper.

George looks back at Rafe, his expression growing covetous. "Not anymore, thanks to your husband. If he wasn't spoken for, you can bet there'd be a bidding war for the right to claim him."

"Ha!" The short bark of laughter rips out of me before I can stop it. "That wouldn't stop most of these bloodsuckers, as you well know, George."

He winks at me as we step into the brightly lit foyer, high ceilings vaulting away above our heads. "You speak the truth. Best to watch your back where he's concerned. Even the men showed more interest than I'd consider healthy."

I nod my understanding. "Duly noted. Thanks."

George takes our coats and asks who we'd like to see.

"Are any of the inner circle in to receive callers? I'd like to ask one of them a few questions."

"I'll see who's in and willing to see you." He looks at Rafe again, not hiding his own spark of interest in the quiet man. "You two know your way to the parlor. Please, go on ahead."

Uncertainty tightens Rafe's shoulders for a second, and then he relents, striding toward the parlor. Our heels ring out over the polished marble floor as we pass several sets of closed doors. I rest my hand on one of the door knobs and open the mental connection between myself and Rafe.

That was weird, no?

Damn skippy it was.

Did you get any vibes we might be walking into a trap?

No, he responds, resting a hand in the small of my back to lead me in toward a grouping of couches and chairs. *But I'm not comfortable venturing to the lower levels or any of the back rooms.*

Me, either.

Not sure I'm ready to sit, I stand near the roaring fireplace, its heat a welcome after the chilly autumn night.

We're only alone a few minutes before the doors open again and the tall form of Persephone glides in.

CHAPTER FIVE

RAFE

"It's good to see you again, Dria. You're looking well... considering."

"Oh, you mean considering one of your *treasured* inner circle members tortured me for information I don't have?"

Dria's surprise at seeing one of the ancients instead of someone lower in the hierarchy seems pretty clear by her response.

Persephone hides a grimace. "We don't keep them on leashes, my dear. You know that." She shrugs one elegant shoulder. "Vampires are a pretty ruthless, back-stabbing bunch on the whole. Why are you surprised?"

I rest my hand on Dria's shoulder, sensing in her thoughts the desire to blurt out exactly what's on her mind. And that wouldn't be good for anyone. Persephone's next question confirms it was a good thing to make my wife hesitate.

"What were they questioning you about?"

Tension spills through our connection, even though my wife's face remains neutral. The false concern I hear in the ancient's inquiry makes it apparent that even though they may have had a video feed, there was no sound on the video to reveal why Coraline and Rolando abducted her.

"Does it matter? You saw what they did. Could anything matter that much?"

The ancient vampire tilts her head to the side while watching us carefully. "That would depend on the situation, I'm sure."

Dria waves a hand dismissively, seemingly unwilling to answer the question. "What I really want to know is where Rolando is."

The other woman straightens up at that. "Really? And what does he have to do with what happened to you?"

Confusion knits Dria's brow. "I thought you saw the video? He was there. He got away."

"I think you're mistaken." Sympathy crosses Persephone's face. "He wasn't in the room where you were held. It was all Coraline and Lucas who administered the silver and... the rest." Distaste crosses her face, as if she can't bring herself to talk about the numerous cuts and deep wounds inflicted on my wife hour after hour while she was questioned.

Anger begins to burn slowly in my stomach. I know what my wife saw because she's had nightmares about it since that night, and I've seen it in her mind while I soothed her back to sleep. Rolando was there. But I can't reveal how I know without making my wife appear weak.

Dria composes herself, smoothing her face of any trace of emotion. "Is that the story you're going to stick with? Are you sure?"

Persephone looks away, toward the fire, her silence her answer.

My wife stalks forward, pushing into the other woman's personal space. "He was there. I know it. I heard his voice and I saw him myself. Maybe he altered the recording."

"There's nothing I can do, *dear*." She smiles, the look calculated and bordering on mean. "But you can rest assured, your husband's life has been spared."

Shock and anger radiate from Dria. In a heartbeat, she locks the emotions down, refusing to glance my way in reassurance of my continued safety.

Persephone steps deeper into the room, careful not to appear to be yielding to Dria's advance, but removing herself from a possible confrontation. She glances my way, a blank expression on her face. "We've never had a human wreak so much destruction in the Seat of Darkness. There was a call from many for his head."

Power pushes out from my wife's carefully concealed aura, engulfing the three of us, expanding to fill the room. Tingles run over my skin, like a buzzing of insects waiting to swarm a farmer's crops. "Anyone who thinks to harm my mate will have to go through me first."

"Relax, Dria. Control yourself. Quite unseemly. Like I said," she looks straight into my eyes, a hint of approval and interest in their depths, "he's safe from retribution. It was—how do you say? Extenuating circumstances."

"Your disbelief in my account of that night doesn't change the fact I want Rolando—on a platter. I will find him, with or without your help."

"Good luck with that. He's been strangely absent since you were here last." She nods toward me. "Your husband scared off a lot of our permanent residents that night. Many are seeking shelter off Tribunal grounds now."

"Rolando has been gone since the night I was tortured here, where I should have been safe—and you don't think that's revealing of his guilt?"

Persephone stares down Dria. "No, I do not. Are you sure you don't remember anything about what your captors wanted to know? Why they took you in the first place?"

"I never said I didn't remember."

"You didn't? Then why didn't you answer me?"

Dria moves to my side, returning the older vampire's stare. "Isn't it obvious? I don't trust you."

Quiet descends, blanketing the two angry vampires. After a moment, I clear my throat, not sure where we can go after a remark like that.

Persephone says, "Well then, it's good to know where we stand with each other. Is there anything else I can help you with?"

"Not for now. I'll be back when I get to the bottom of what the hell is going on."

Dria stalks toward the parlor door, her body stiff with anger. Persephone calls after her, "Are you sure you don't want to tell me what you know? I can help."

"Yeah, sure. 'Cause you've been great so far. No thanks."

My hot-headed wife storms out of the elegant townhouse, her furious steps echoing on the polished floor. I watch her, trailing behind at a slower pace.

"Keep an eye on her, Rafe. She's liable to do something rash in her rage."

I glance back at the ancient vampire and nod, not willing to trust myself to respond politely. Once she leaves, I track down George to retrieve our coats and ask after the bags we'd brought that fateful night three weeks ago.

Turns out, someone repacked our things and put them in storage. He retrieves them and I hustle out to join my wife.

When I return to the car with our luggage, Dria has cooled off a bit, pacing back and forth on the chilly sidewalk. I unlock the doors so she can enter, and place our things in the trunk, next to her bag from the airport. I slide into the driver's seat and start the car. Tension seems to vibrate in the compact space.

"Want to talk about it?" I ask.

"Not really."

The car pulls away from the curb and I direct us toward the hotel. "I closed on the house earlier this morning."

Dria doesn't respond.

"It's not ready yet for us, but will be by the time Jon arrives tomorrow."

This time she grunts once, indicating she heard me.

Determined not to let our strike-out at the Tribunal ruin our reunion, I tell her the rest of what I accomplished today. "I found out where Justin lives."

She whips around in the car, giving me her full attention. "You did? And why didn't you tell me earlier? We could have been at his place questioning him instead of wasting time with that woman."

A grin tilts up one side of my mouth. "You didn't exactly give me any time to tell you. Demanded what you wanted the second we left the hangar."

"Dammit! You could have said something on the way over."

"You were determined and didn't seem open to listening to alternatives."

"We'll never know now, will we?" She fumes in the seat next to me. "Are we close? Can you swing by his house?"

"I think we should wait for Jon." I check the time on the car's clock. "It's after two a.m. We can't barge in on the wizard now."

"He's used to working with vampires. I bet he's awake."

"No. We're not going. It's late. We're going to the hotel."

"Just tell me the address and I'll go while you're sleeping."

I squeeze my wife's thigh. "Not a chance, liebling."

The rest of our trip to the hotel is silent. Within twenty minutes, we're in our room. I turn on the TV while Dria pouts silently. She doesn't stay mad long, but I know enough to let her work through her issues on her own. She'll talk when she's ready.

While she's in the bathroom, I lay back in the bed, hopeful I can entice her out of her funk with another round of lovemaking. Best to give her a few minutes before attempting, as she doesn't seem receptive to my fabulous idea just yet. I flick through the channels via the remote until I find the news. Expecting a repeat of an earlier broadcast, I'm surprised by a late-breaking story in a nearby barrio.

Images of an attractive young woman in her thirties appear in the foreground of the screen, overlaying the live broadcast with ambulance lights and crime scene tape. In Spanish, the local newscaster informs us Sophia Delgado, a store clerk, was found dead in the alley behind an herbal shop. No leads have been discovered, and if anyone was in the area between ten and midnight and saw anything, they are asked to call.

Dria enters from the bathroom midway through the reporter's plea for information. She listens until the segment is over and then turns to me. "I'm heading out. Going for a run."

She's dressed in gym clothes, indicating she feels the need to burn off anger and tension.

"Be safe," I call out as she leaves.

As the door closes, an irritated snort reaches me. *As if I'm ever not careful?*

I refuse to rise to her baiting. She's fuming and looking for a fight. And I won't be the one to give it to her.

Waiting for a pissed off vampire to cool down is never a good way to spend your time. Instead, I opt for sleep, drifting off while thinking of all the small tasks I need to complete tomorrow to make the new house ready for our stay. She'll either be open to make love again when she returns, her anger run out of her, or she'll be tired and randy after she sleeps.

I know my wife well, and her desire to feed sexually is stronger than her need for blood. She had plenty of the latter while we were apart, but none of the former. She'll come around soon. I don't doubt it.

When I arise late the next morning, Dria is nowhere to be found. She's old enough that a little winter sun exposure won't harm her, so I'm not overly concerned. But it has been a rough month. I reach out to touch her mind, hoping to discern where she is and what she's doing.

In a tingle of sensation, I sense her and what she's feeling. The cool splash of water runs over her limbs in a steady motion. She's making use of the hotel's indoor pool to burn off even more nervous energy. She'll only be able to rest when she's tired herself out completely. I've seen the same behavioral pattern year after year. Too keyed up to sleep, she has to be doing something.

I back out of her mind, giving her peace and space— exactly what she needs.

She'll be back to rest soon. I shower and eat from room service, then leave her a note. Which will give me plenty of time to finish the hidden basement room in our new house. I head out, my list of to-do items in my pocket. If she doesn't get more loving soon, she's liable to start climbing the walls. Smiling in anticipation over our upcoming sex antics, I hum a mellow tune.

CHAPTER SIX

JON

After Diane leaves, I check in with Asa one last time and then make the sunny trek to my cabin, eager to spend my last few hours with Candy before embarking on the long trip south. She's agreed to take care of my wolf-dogs while I'm gone, and thankfully the animals have accepted her. We've only been together a few weeks, but I trust her, even if Eric and Pat still seem undecided.

She's opened my heart to feeling again—true feelings embedded in real emotions, and not the unhealthy obsessive, possessive ones I've had for Vivian the past seven years. Candy makes me smile, makes me laugh out loud, even at myself, and she turns me on like no other woman before.

We've talked about her taking on any form in the past, even a man's, which she secretly lived as while staying with my old pack in Manitoba. I really don't care. I accept her and everything she had to do to survive, with no qualms.

It seems rational that if you were scared and alone you'd hide as something, or someone, else. She's a shifter, it's what they do. Having no one left of her family, she lived as a male werewolf to protect herself among strangers. Truth be told, I'm not as unsettled by the idea of her growing extra parts as I thought I would be. It's still her underneath any skin she might take on.

And more importantly, she's been able to be herself with me this past month. No hiding behind another form.

And the sex has been incredible. Sure, the obvious thought has occurred to me: to have her transform into the image of Vivian. But strangely, when I'm with Candy, I don't feel the compelling need to possess the despotic redhead anymore. To Candy, such a request might mean nothing, and she would probably readily agree, like we were role playing. But for me, it would be a slip in the wrong direction.

I'm feeling free for the first time in years, and I rather like it. A part of me is worried about seeing Viv and Rafe again. Will I begin once more, against my will, to have haunting dreams about the three of us sharing a bed? Or will my new relationship with Candy help to stave off the old, not-so-hidden desires?

Above all, I need to focus on my duty to the couple. If Candy journeyed with me, I might be distracted. Or she might be the strength that helps me resist the seductive pull of the passionate couple. Either way, I do know introducing the subject of Candy to Vivian will be a delicate matter. Will she freak out or allow me to choose my own mate? Is it too soon to name Candy as my mate?

I shake my head, eager to dispel the conflicting thoughts for a few more hours. I'll have plenty of time to be paranoid and stew on the plane. As I approach my cabin, with the special dinner the chef prepared for us, desire begins to flow through my veins. I know what awaits me beyond the heavy wooden door. A woman who wants me for me—not a partner who wants what I could become for her, like Diane did—but someone who desires me as I am: a man self-bound to a ruthless and very strong master.

I grab the knob and turn, pushing the door into the warm interior. "Hey," I call out. "I'm back."

Candy steps out from the bedroom, her long dark hair shining in good health, lying over one sexy bare shoulder. She's clad in a skimpy pink nightie I've never seen before. "How did it go with Diane? I hope it wasn't too awkward for you."

My mouth dries up at the sight of her pert, firm breasts thrust against the thin silky material. "Uhh...."

She smiles, her pleasure over my dumbfounded reaction spreading across her face. "Cat got your tongue?"

I say the first thing that pops into my head. "I dunno—do you plan to change into a cat next?" Yup, I'm a born romantic.

"Only if you want me to," she says while strolling languidly toward me. "But I hope you like me just as I am, I'd rather focus on something else than changing shape."

"Really? And what would that be?"

She stops in front of me, nimble fingers from one hand skating up my jacket-covered chest, while the other hand grabs the bag of food and sets it on the floor. "Let's get you out of this coat and I'll fill you in."

Faster than she can blink, I've unzipped my coat and unceremoniously thrown it to the floor near the door. "You were saying?"

Her surprised laughter spills into the room. "Talk about motivation. Maybe I should always dress in baby-doll nighties."

"If that's what that pink frothy concoction is called, then yes, I second that opinion."

She turns around and shows me her full, rounded ass through the sheer fabric. Candy reaches out a hand and grabs the back of a wooden chair, leaning forward slightly and pushing her bottom out farther on display. "I might get cold, wearing nighties all the time. Or attract the wrong kind of attention."

What the hell are we talking about again? All I can feel is the weight of my hard cock in my pants, weeping to be set free to play. "Uhh..." Without further thought, I step closer and run a hand lovingly over the plump curve of one cheek. "Yeah, that sounds good."

"Are you sure, Jon?" A teasing note enters her voice as her hips circle, pushing her bottom more firmly onto my hand. "I'm not so sure I'd want everyone to see *your* ass on display."

"What? I think I may have lost what we're talking about." I gesture toward the current physical predicament in my pants. "It's hard to think straight with your pretty little bum begging to be touched."

"See, that's the problem, Jon."

Warning bells go off in my head at the word "problem." "Did I miss something, are you angry?"

She straightens and turns toward me, stepping close enough to run the tips of her breasts against my shirtfront. "Does it look like I'm angry?"

"No... but I'm not the brightest bulb when it comes to women."

"Well, there is something I want to talk to you about." And with that, she leans in and captures my mouth, tracing her tongue over my closed lips, tempting them to open.

I dive in, all thoughts of talk completely out of my head. One hand rises to caress the back of her head, tilting her slightly for better access as I plunge my tongue deep inside, claiming her mouth as my own. Her response is immediate and red hot. She slides one hand over my hip and to the front, clasping my hardness through my jeans.

A small mew of pleasure escapes her as she thrusts her hips forward to grind against my thigh. "I need..."

"Yes?" I ask, leaning down to nibble along her neck. "Tell me and it's yours."

She stiffens in my grasp. Somehow, what I said was not the right thing. I pull away and look into her face to see what the problem is. "Hey, are you okay?"

She nods, lowering her eyes to the ground. "I want to ask you for something, something I want sexually, but I'm worried how you'll take it."

The beautiful, vulnerable creature in front of me has my full attention now, and I cup her face in two hands. "You don't need to worry about me. We're good. Tell me what you want." I skim a hand down her front to tease one erect nipple. "I'm sure I'd be open to anything you want to try." I think back to the wild stuff we've done already and wonder what has her so hesitant.

Candy takes a deep breath, and blurts out, "I want you to spank me." She looks up at me through the fringe of her lashes, like she's trying to read my reaction.

"Excuse me?" I say. "You mean like BDSM kind of stuff?" I smile, confident I can try to please her even if my experience with the lifestyle is none existent.

"Yes, and no."

"Okay. That's not too clear. Care to elaborate?"

"I... uh... I don't need punishment games, like I'm a bad girl and you have to discipline me. I..."

I grin, unable to help myself at the prospect of slapping her ass. "Just want a little slap and tickle?"

She frowns at me, but nods. "I like it. The arousal when the blood rushes to my cheeks is intense... and overwhelming. Is that weird?"

"Darling, I've lived for seven years on a supernatural resort that caters to the sexual tastes of a myriad of creatures from around the world. Did you really think you'd shock me and I'd refuse you? Or make you feel embarrassed by your desires?"

She shrugs and turns away, moving to lean a hip against the square wooden table in the center of the room. "I dunno. I just... haven't really brought it up with other boyfriends before. Once I did and he refused, saying he wouldn't hit a woman."

"It's not hitting you—"

"Exactly what I said!" Her face lights up. "So you do understand? It's just something fun I like once in a while. You don't think I'm weird or sick?"

Eager to show her I'm game to try whatever this fantastic woman desires, I pull out a solid wooden chair and take a seat. Patting my thighs, I indicate she should lean over and assume the position.

With a wide grin splitting her face, she complies, spreading herself over my lap. The thin material rises up due to her position, revealing the bottom half of two firm globes I can't wait to smack.

"Someone else is liking this already and we haven't even started," she squirms on my erection, my eagerness prodding her middle, while she faces the floor.

"Once I walked in and saw you wearing this..." I skim the

sheer fabric even higher, uncovering all of her butt. "I was lost."

I reach one hand out and slowly caress her flesh. She wiggles a little, pushing herself toward my palm, eager to encourage me.

I deliver one resounding smack to her right cheek, causing her to squeak and squirm more. "Not so fast, missy. I'm the one handling the butt-smacking. You lie still." Holding her down, I land three more quick slaps to the same cheek, then switch to the left one and rain more blows down on her tender skin.

Pausing, I smooth a hand over the heated flesh, admiring the faint pink tinge rising to the surface. "Like that, Candy?"

"Yes!" she pants, eagerness in her tone. "God, it felt good."

"Not too hard?"

"You can go harder if you want. I'll tell you if it's too much."

I nod and run a hand between her thighs, pressing lightly to spread her legs. Going on a hunch, I send two questing fingers inward, testing her arousal. Moisture coats her swollen outer lips. "You do like this, don't you, you naughty girl?"

"Shut up and give me what I want," she replies, a hint of backbone in her tone. This one won't be cowed by her desires, and I like it.

"Yes, ma'am," I say, raising my arm.

Images of Candy and our recent sexual escapades seep through my conscious, teasing me and making sleep on the plane impossible. A sigh of contentment escapes as a grin curls the corner of my mouth. Damn, that woman is fine. So passionate in her desires, and unselfconscious in getting *exactly* what she wants. If I close my eyes, I can still see her wiggling in discomfort with every smack of my palm.

I've had women who liked to play a little rough, but never a woman who knew what she needed and had no qualms about taking it. It's sexy, and freeing.

All I know for sure is I want more of her. I want her every day of the week, every morning when I rise, and the seconds before I close my eyes to sleep. And all the time in between.

Holy shit. Could this be love?

One part of my mind immediately scoffs at the idea. Another deeper part of me realizes she's exactly what I need and want in life. I just have to be man enough to realize it and act on it.

What about Vivian? What will she say?

Now there's a question I can't seem to escape. What will she say, how will she react? I have a feeling the feisty redhead is prepared for anything in life. If I'm able to remain loyal to her and still fall in love, she'll know it from reading my mind. If I'm not...

What then? Would she kill Candy? Would her possession and jealousy push her to drastic measures?

Come on, it's not like Vivian is a stalker with an unnatural attraction. She owns a part of you. She will always see the truth.

And what exactly is that truth?

Ahh... now that's the sixty-four thousand dollar question.

Unwilling to examine my inner thoughts, especially when I have no idea where I stand, I decide to focus on meditating to strengthen my mental shields. I relax into the chair, reclining the seat to a sleeping position. The mental walls I've pictured —tall, thick, made of stone and reinforced with steel—rise around the "inner" me. Shielding my closest dreams, fears, and desires, shutting away my intimate moments with Candy... everything I value that I can't share with the woman who is my master.

The only way I can be certain my waking thoughts don't betray me is to control the barrier between them and the outside world. Slowly, I draw the recent memories inside the wall with me. My hope is with practice I will be able to block a casual reading of my random thoughts.

Fear of messing it up and unleashing a whole world of hurt on myself and Candy doesn't act as the incentive you might think it would, so much as it acts as a painful reminder of what I have to lose if I don't perfect this skill quickly.

After an hour I take a break, pulling out the folder with all the research I've done on witches and warlocks, wizards, and the "never turn a witch" vampire saying I discovered earlier. I didn't find out anything new on the phrase, but I did learn more about South American magic. What the locals practice is called *Brujería*, the Spanish name for witchcraft or witch healers, but from what I read, it seems similar to what Diane practices.

None of what I found could explain how Justin became such an accomplished wizard so far from where the majority of them live, which is in North America and Europe.

Who could have taught him? Wizards normally learn from someone else, especially as the knowledge is written and passed down. It's not a practice one could easily pick up on their own.

Okay, maybe I'm missing something. What do I know about him so far? We've got a youngish guy who knows enough magic and packs enough mojo to get hired by the Tribunal.

How did such a man make the initial connection? Who did he know who helped land him the job? Did he do similar work for someone else, possibly a human, and the word spread to the supernatural community?

I.shake my head at the unlikelihood of such a scenario. It would make more sense that he was referred by another supernatural. What mystical creatures are native to the area? Werewolves wouldn't have evolved there, but a pack resides there nonetheless.

Which reminds me, I have to stop by and pay my respects to the local pack to keep the peace. If they discover I'm there first, things could get nasty. I met the alpha, Hector, years ago on one of my visits with Vivian and Rafe to the city. He's an amiable sort and didn't give me too much trouble once he realized I was passing through.

I grab my tablet and open the browser, wanting to pull up a map of the city and try to recall the exact location I previously met the Buenos Aires alpha. I think it was a bar on the edge of Centro. As I scroll through the windows I opened earlier, searching for the map image, a news alert from the Argentine city pops up. Once again, I'm grateful for the convenience of traveling in a luxury jet—unlimited Internet connectivity on the long journey.

A murder was discovered late last night in a small barrio, or neighborhood, in the city. The young woman was beaten to death behind an herbal shop, no leads yet on her killer.

I read over the minimal details and then skim the rest of what's happening in the city. It's winter now in the southern hemisphere, but thankfully the weather never gets too cold in the subtropical climate. I never would have expected such a moderate fluctuation of temperatures in South America.

The average for the entire year is low fifties to the mid-eighties.

Vivian and Rafe sure can pick locations for second homes. Supposedly, the couple owns residences in over a dozen countries around the world, but this is the only one I've visited with them since joining their two-person seethe almost eight years ago.

Closing the news site, I get back on track, examining the map carefully. I believe I first ran into the scent of the local pack in Monserrat, near the San Telmo barrio. They never took me to their "den," for lack of a better term, or pack home, but met me in a neighborhood bar the pack frequents.

From what I recall, the city has around three dozen werewolves registered in their group, with maybe a few rogues who live further out, but they'd be loner wolves, rarely causing trouble with an established pack. As long as they kept to themselves and maintained a low profile, the established pack should leave them alone.

I blow up the image of the city until I find the neighborhood I'm looking for. There. Lupine Luna. That's the place the pack hung out. I'll have to stop by within twenty-four hours of my arrival. It's never good to make a pack of Weres wait if you don't have to.

Comfortable with where I need to go and what needs to be done after arrival, I turn off the device and sink into the comfortable recliner. I practice making my mental walls stronger for a few more minutes then allow my mind to drift and relax, hoping sleep will overcome me soon. I know when I arrive, Viv and Rafe will be adjusted to night hours, and I'll need to keep up.

It'll be good to see them both again. I stifle the old urges threatening to burst through my carefully constructed mental walls, content for once with the platonic, but loving relationship, the three of us now have. And then there's Candy. My pants get tight as my mind drifts to smacking the shifter's tight butt.

My hands itch to yank my zipper down and pleasure myself on our memories. What the hell? Why not? The sound of the zipper rasping down in the dark cabin forces more blood to my heated flesh. Might as well enjoy the rest of the flight.

CHAPTER SEVEN

VIVIAN

Even though I missed my husband while I was on the island and he was here in the city, today proved that some days we need a mental break from each other. He knew I was annoyed and frustrated last night, and he gave me the space I needed. Today he worked on the new house while I slept, not revealing any details to me when he returned. The sneaky bugger.

He woke me before sunset and we made love again. The tension between us earlier has vanished. I'm not sure if its removal was due to pent up testosterone, but it could be. Rafe is smiling like a Cheshire cat. Could be the small sips of blood he took from me at the end, but I rather think he's just in a more mellow mood after an explosive orgasm.

After a short drive, we're lounging in the hangar, waiting for Jon's plane to arrive.

"I miss him," Rafe says, a tinge of shock in his voice.

"And why is that surprising? He's been with us a long time

and before this trip, we'd rarely go two days without seeing him. This month-long separation has been hard for all of us."

"I bet he won't feel the same. I think he's been having his own private 'Vivian-free Vacation' without you."

The grin on my lover's face doesn't amuse me. "And what the hell is that supposed to mean? I *wanted* him to have time without me. He deserved it. He needed time that was his own. To find someone he can share his heart with."

"Ahh... but will you let him find love?"

"I wish both of you would give me more credit. I'm not some sniveling teenager filled with angst, living in some misdirected love triangle." The immature tone in my voice sounds like I should be stomping my foot in emphasis. Yeah, that's sad. "I want him happy."

"Yeah, just not as happy as he is with you, right?"

"I resent that. He's with me because he has to be. Because he pledged himself to me. He's happy because I work hard to *make* him happy. That's not the same as being happy on your own." I slump in my chair, annoyed Rafe is badgering me about this right now. "Do you doubt my sincerity? Do you think I want him pining after me forever?"

"No," he says softly, drawing me into his arms. "That's not what I'm saying at all. And I'm sorry I've brought this topic up so poorly. I'm concerned with how you will react when he chooses a mate."

"Hmph." I glare at him, the desired effect lost because I can't stay mad at him when I've missed him and every other thought in my head turns to tearing his clothes off for more sex. "I think I'll surprise you both when he finds a mate."

"We'll see."

The topic is thankfully dropped and I quiz him about the

properties he's purchased. They all sound like suitable choices and I'm excited to finally see one tonight.

"I spent all day preparing the first place. It's the one nearest to Justin's house, too."

I nod to indicate I'm listening, but I'm more interested in the arrival of Jon's plane. The attendant knocks on the door, alerting us the time is now.

I bounce out of my seat and stride toward the door, glancing back over my shoulder at my husband. He shakes his head at my exuberance and joins me. The hangar is windy, the engines stirring up the air, sending my long hair flying around me.

In a few minutes, Jon leaves the sleek jet. His shorter, stockier body a sight for sore eyes.

"Jon!" I quickly close the distance between us, and wrap my arms around him in a big hug. His arms come around my waist and a deep sigh releases from his chest. "I've missed you."

"Same here," he mumbles. He pulls back from my embrace, a crooked grin on his face. "'Bout time you two came to your senses and sent for me." He winks at Rafe rather than his regular glare, which is what I thought he was going to do after the mild rebuke.

Rafe pats him on the back. "Yeah, well, we can't get what we want all the time. How is everyone back home?"

Jon looks away and then back to my husband. "Good, good. You know what's going on from talking to Asa and me earlier."

I sense there's much he's not telling us, right below his surface thoughts, and do my best to not rifle through his private musings to find out what he's not sharing. I set up the big game hunt with available women last month for a reason. I'll be damned if I muck it up by pumping him for details when he obviously wants to keep what occurred private.

"Nothing new to share?" Rafe presses, much to my dismay. If he was standing closer I'd kick him. Guys are shitty with subtlety.

"If there was, wouldn't I tell you?" There's a glint of challenge in Jon's eye. Not of one man challenging another for top-dog spot, like these two normally do, but more of a goad to see if Rafe or I can discover news on our own.

"Enough, you two." I let go of my right hand man with reluctance, wanting nothing more than to snuggle up to his neck and take a deep breath. His scent and Rafe's have a calming effect on me, rooting me to the here and now despite whatever worry may be weighing on me. "You must be hungry after the long flight. I know Rafe is. How about we get a meal and catch up on what's going on?"

"Sounds fine with me." Jon grabs his large duffle from the attendant and follows Rafe to the rear door leading outside.

We climb into Rafe's new car, a low whistle from Jon indicating his approval. "Sweet. This is one ride you could never have back home."

Rafe grins, pure male satisfaction showing on his face. "Don't I know it. I'm sure it will stay here when we leave. The house I'll take us to later has a small garage in the back."

We cruise through the dark streets of the city, making our way to a favorite tapas house. Before long, we're seated at a secluded table, placing our orders for mountains of tiny plates of food.

Rafe orders an expensive red wine, an air of celebration wafting from the larger man. When we all hold a filled glass and the waiter has left, he lifts his in a toast. "To Jon. I know I don't always act the best, and often goad you on purpose, but there's no man I'd rather have by our side than you."

Jon blushes, unused to praise from my husband. "Thanks, man." A touch of the mischievous Were leaks through. "Too bad you had to fight to the death—not once, but several times— to realize it."

Rafe doesn't rise to the jab, but nods solemnly. "I'm no stranger to killing when I have to, but you're exactly right. I swear to refrain from wanting to beat you to a pulp if you can refrain from lusting after my wife."

Jon looks him dead in the eye and returns his nod. "I don't think that will be a problem."

"Good!" I break in cheerily, eager to get off this subject. "Let's get down to business. Rafe has purchased several private residences for us, and assured me they're all secure." I look toward him for confirmation.

"Like I said, I'll take you to the first one after we eat. The others can wait 'til we need them. I even bought one with property backing to a park, in case you needed to run." Rafe looks to Jon on the last comment, seeing the surprise on the younger man's face. "The house we're staying at tonight is nice. It's small, centrally located, and not far from Justin's place."

"Furniture?" Jon asks, avoiding commenting on Rafe's thoughtfulness with the property near the park. Typical guy. I run my hand over my husband's thigh, pleased he made an effort.

"It came fully furnished, but I did purchase and build new items for the basement."

Jon raises one eyebrow. "Build? *You* bought furniture you had to build? Like *Ikea?*"

Rafe smiles and nods. "You'll understand when you see the place."

Our food arrives and the men dig in. I sip my wine, peace settling over me. It feels good to have the three of us together once more. My gaze settles on my husband. I can't wait to get him home and naked again. The hunger within me hasn't been satiated yet. Which of course, was delayed by my anger and frustration last night.

I hate this feeling of no control, reacting to stress and problems instead of being the one pulling all the strings. It's unsettling. And no amount of exercise or avoidance will make the feeling go away.

A television over the nearby bar draws my attention. The news is on and a gruesome report of another murder flashes across the large flat screen. Makes me glad we don't have such depressing local news in Alaska. The only people dying near us are usually on our property.

The announcer is speaking Spanish, and thankfully, all of us are fluent. Jon learned the first season we journeyed here with him over seven years ago.

The men continue eating, but I can tell by the shift in energy that they're listening to the news as well.

Jon speaks as the cameras cut to another view, "I read about another murder last night on the plane. A young woman beaten to death. Sounds like an intimate crime, you know, like the killer knew her."

Rafe nods. "We saw that on the hotel television last night, too."

The female announcer's dulcet tones carry clearly from

the bar, and thanks to our supernatural hearing, we don't miss a word. "This recent killing appears to be an animal attack, although the medical examiner has not determined the type of animal, or if there may have been more than one animal. The identity of the victim has not been revealed at this time. We should have more details later, after the family has been notified."

"Should we be worried?" Jon asks. "A vicious animal attack? The details sound sketchy at best. What type of animal in a city could do the type of damage needed to kill? A big, rabid dog?" He shoves more food in, chewing with a contemplative look on his face. "There aren't any shifters in Argentina except werewolves, are there?"

Rafe shakes his head. "Not that I know of—and we've been traveling here for over fifty years. I think we'd have heard chatter of another species moving in, wouldn't you?" He directs the last question toward me.

My brow wrinkles, uncomfortable with the implications of a savage animal attack in a large cosmopolitan city. "At the very least, you'd think the masters of the city would know. Maybe it will turn out to be an escaped animal from the zoo."

The news segment cuts to the weather and our attention returns to the table. Rafe reaches for another small plate of food. "I'm sure the Tribunal will have their thumb on the pulse of the matter shortly. You know how they are regarding supernatural activity in 'their' city." He uncharacteristically uses air quotes when speaking to show his emphasis. "Or you could go back and question Persephone again. It worked so well the first time."

I stiffen my spine at his dig, pulling my hand from his

thigh. And this is the man I want to have sex with later? "Hey. I did learn something. It wasn't a total waste of time."

Jon finishes his next small plate and says, "Hold up, now. Am I hearing this right—you went straight to the Tribunal already, without me? What the hell?"

Rafe nods. "And now you see what I'm dealing with. Very little regard for planning or safety. Just jumps right in whenever she sees fit. Drives me crazy."

I scowl at my husband, noticing the commiserating look of understanding on Jon's face at the same time. Bastards. If they weren't on the same side and being agreeable with each other, I'd blast them into eternity with a scathing reply. "I learned that Persephone is lying to me. She does know where Rolando is, and she does know what they asked me during the interrogation."

"How?" Rafe asks. "She never revealed the info directly."

"Because she harped on the question too much—and if the video was of decent enough quality, she'd have been able to read their lips."

Jon responds before Rafe can, picking up his beer before speaking. "That's a big assumption you're making—like if the camera had the right angle, if the lighting was good enough, if they were facing the camera when they grilled you. I dunno. Lots of 'ifs' in there."

"And how did you logically draw the conclusion that she knew where Rolando was, too?" asks Rafe.

I shrug one shoulder and take a sip from my wine, wishing it had blood mixed in. "They're close, and have been for years. Call it a hunch."

The two exchange a glance and don't say anything else. I

have a feeling they think my hunch is a bunch of crap. Fine. Nothing new with the two of them doubting my instincts.

Jon sets down his now empty beer glass and turns to Rafe. "What did you learn while staking out the Tribunal?"

A grimace appears and disappears quickly across my husband's full lips. "Not as much as I'd hoped. I've got locations for the residences of a dozen lesser vamps in the employ of the Tribunal, but no one from the inner circle or the Ancients themselves.

"For all I know, they could all live underground in the Seat of Darkness." He dabs his mouth with a cloth napkin and sets it aside, clearly done with eating. "The greatest breakthrough occurred right before Dria arrived last night. I finally nailed down Justin's location. I think we should question him tonight."

Unwilling to have us go off on a tangent, I say, "I still think finding Rolando should be our main focus, not dwelling on what Justin does or doesn't know."

"I'd have agreed with you before talking to Diane," Jon says. "But now I'm not so sure. What exactly does Justin do for the Tribunal? Who hired him? How does he pay for his spells?"

Rafe answers him. "We know he does protection and detection spells for them at the very least. I've witnessed him doing last minute fine tunings as he leaves. I'm sure he's compensated well enough to be able to pay for his spells and still have money left over."

Jon shakes his head. "That's not what I meant. Diane explained that wizards work differently than witches when it comes to using magic. Whereas a witch can naturally work magic, a wizard forces it, conjuring the magic himself with ingredients, chants, and whatnot, but doesn't have the ability to call magic up spontaneously like a witch can."

"Don't witches use focuses and ingredients too? I know I've heard spells being spoken—so what's the real difference?"

I speak up on this one. "It's more like the witch has the magic in her blood, it's a part of her. Whereas the wizard is a normal human who learns, through years of study and practice, how to master magic. But forcing the use of magic instead of channeling it naturally means there can be an imbalance in the world left behind from wizard magic."

"Do you know how they stabilize or fix the imbalance?" Jon asks. "Diane was unsure."

"No, I don't. I've never heard of a witch—and they're the only ones I have experience with—casting a spell that resulted in an imbalance. Or the need to fix it."

"What about the phrase 'never turn a witch'?"

Rafe jumps in, his mind filling with apprehension and pushing it toward me through our bond. "Where did you hear that? It applies to a vampire code, one not spoken of often."

Jon looks to me, not bothering to answer Rafe, as if he's waiting for me to expand on the phrase. "I know it's hard to believe, but the rule came into effect way before I became a vampire. I was told to never turn a witch, with no real details given. I assumed it was because the witch wouldn't survive the transition."

"Okay, it might turn out to be a dead end anyway," he says.

"What made you ask about it?" I ask.

Jon shrugs. "I'm not sure really. Just a feeling I had. It triggered something inside me when I read it."

"Where did you read it?" Rafe inquires.

"Uhh... I... umm..." He looks to me and quickly away.

I raise an eyebrow at his odd behavior. "Now you've made me curious. Spit it out, Jon."

A harsh breath wheezes out of his chest and he slumps. "I know I should have asked..."

"Yes?" Apprehension coils in my middle. Has he violated my privacy more than I bargained for?

"I read the term in one of your journals."

Shock hits me in the gut. "What? Why would you read those?"

Rafe breaks in, sensing my rising tension. "Liebling, the leather-bound books are stored on the shelves in our office. And he has been staying off and on in our apartment while we're gone. If you really didn't want anyone to see them you should have locked them up."

I wave off his response, knowing full well where the books are kept. "That's not the issue. I'm just surprised he didn't ask —and why he'd want to read them anyway."

Jon finally looks up, meeting my unflinching gaze. "It was too much of a temptation. I know I should have asked. And honestly, I only read the first one."

"Okay, but again—why?"

"I wanted to get to know you better, Vivian. What experiences made you who you are today. How you became a vampire."

I'm not sure how to respond. Why didn't he just ask me? Am I that unapproachable?

"Are you angry?" he asks, his face a mix of emotion, guilt being the most prominent.

"No, I'm not. I'm more curious—why didn't you ask me if you wanted to know?"

Rafe chuckles and pats Jon on the back. "It's okay, man. I

get it. You didn't think she'd tell you the truth, right?"

"Honestly, he's right. I wasn't sure how you'd react. Especially after I read all you went through."

I raise one shoulder, refusing to dwell on my past. "Whatever. It was a long time ago."

"*Whatever*? You were raped weekly for years. You were forced into blood servitude. And after six years, a shell of yourself, you were changed into a vampire against your will and used as a pawn in vampire politics."

His words don't affect me as they probably should. When I think back upon those dark years, it seems like what I'm remembering happened to another person. "Should I quote a popular song and remind you that what doesn't kill you makes you stronger?"

"Or crazy," Rafe says with a wicked smile. "Or maybe a little of both."

"Seriously, though," Jon says, "it was dark and depressing. After the first journal, I couldn't read anymore. I don't know how you survived to become the person you are."

I look away, unwilling to allow any of my past to crowd my mind and drag me back to the edge of darkness again. "I did survive. So let's move on."

"Well, that's where I read the phrase 'never turn a witch.' It was in a section where Mikov explained some rules of existence you'd needed to know as a newly changed vampire."

I nod to indicate I understand, but I'm glad I can't recall the original conversation any longer. I wrote those entries almost twenty years after the events occurred, which was still over five hundred years ago, and I'd rather not revisit them for anything in the world. I look to Rafe, hoping he can change the topic and save me from further discussion of my early years.

CHAPTER EIGHT

RAFE

I see the expression in Dria's eyes and on her delicate face. She's struggling to maintain a hold on the present. Having her slip back into those dark memories would not be good for any of us while we're in a public place. Not that I think she'd hurt anyone, but if I can spare her pain of any kind I will.

"Okay," I say, "now we know where you read it—let's move on to what we're going to do next and how we can find more information."

Jon looks like he'd like to discuss the journals more, but after a glance at me and Dria he nods once and settles back in his chair, content to let the topic drop for now.

"Rolando, when we finally find him, might have the answers we need regarding the phrase," Dria says, her voice steady with no trace of the distress I read in her eyes a moment ago. "Or maybe I can contact someone at the Tribunal and ask."

I reach for my wine glass. "Have they been forthcoming

with this type information in the past?" I take a sip, examining the small plates stacked on the table, debating to search for more food.

Dria raises a hand, signaling the waiter for additional plates to be brought. "You know how they are. Some days they will talk to you... other days they shut you out completely."

"During my stakeouts, I witnessed the protocols we've dealt with for years at the Tribunal abandoned. No one is manning the phones—I called a half a dozen times. Non-vampires are not permitted in the house at night, with the exception of bonded mates. I didn't seen any blood donors like we saw at the party, either. It's like the whole place is in lock-down mode, functioning on a skeleton crew under strict orders."

The waiter brings six more plates filled with delectable food. Jon reaches for two, saying, "What about Justin? You said you'd tracked where he lives. I think we should start with him."

I nod, grabbing two plates for myself, he's echoing what I've been saying all night.

"I still feel Rolando should be our main target, not the wizard," Dria says, squirming in her seat. I bet her hunger is rising again, and not the one for blood. I stifle a smile at what that means for me.

"I agree, darling. Eventually he will be the one we need the most, yes, but maybe Justin can lead us to him."

"Why would that bastard care?" my volatile wife hisses. "He was the one who helped them catch me in the first place."

I settle a hand over hers, attempting to send calming energy to her. "He did what he was paid to do, having no idea what they planned when taking you. I've told you, he was the one who helped me locate you in the underground warren of rooms. I could have searched for hours and never found you before the sun set. And by then I would have been dead.

"I trust him. Not with my life or yours, but I do trust he won't deliberately try and sell us out or hurt you again."

"Hmph," Dria mumbles, turning her hand over to clasp mine, her thumb teasing a circle in my palm.

Jon finishes scarfing down the rest of his food and cleans his mouth with a napkin. "I don't have much input on what happened before I got here—and based on past experience, I'm inclined to let Vivian trust her gut—but I do agree he sounds like a good person to question."

"Well, that's settled then," Dria says when I indicate to the waiter we'd like a check. "We'll visit him first and then see the new digs." She glances at her watch, horniness making her movements jerky. "Let's go."

I smile, glad she's able to push past her doubts and go with the majority.

T he quiet hum of the expensive motor idles at the curb before I shut it off. "We're here."

Dria shifts in her seat, her rampant arousal slowly leaking through our connection. She had an extensive internal debate going on while I drove, where she was seriously considering asking Jon to get out and walk so she could ravage me in the new car. The feel of the leather under her hand almost did her in. Damn, it feels good to have her back.

I smile to myself, glad to have the shoe on the other foot. A little pent up lust will be good for her. I got the distinct feeling before that I missed her more than she missed me. Childish, I know, to be pleased she wants me, but we're both feeling vulnerable after her close call.

"Which house is his?" Jon asks, popping his head between the front seats from the back.

I point to the right, ahead of us. "His house is the blue one with the lime green shutters." Thanks to the streetlight on the corner, and our excellent night vision, we can make out the colors of the small abode.

Jon asks, "Are we knocking like civilized visitors, or breaking in and surprising him?"

Dria arches one dainty brow. "Really? Break into a wizard's house when he could have the place wired with magical traps and wards? That doesn't seem like the smartest choice."

Before we can decide, his front door opens and Justin's tall form fills the doorway. He looks our way, unsurprised to see us there. He's once again dressed all in black, his shoulder length hair looking cleaner than when I last saw him. If I had to cast him in a role, I'd say he looks like a younger, handsomer version of Professor Snape from the Harry Potter movies. But I keep the observation to myself, knowing I'll get an eye roll from the two I'm with for a movie reference.

Jon climbs from the car first, ready for action should the wizard cast a spell, and I follow, opening my car door. "Looks like the bugger had detection wards farther out than we bargained for and he knows we're here."

Dria huffs out an impatient breath while exiting the car. "Well, can't change that now. Let's go say hello."

The three of us walk toward Justin, trying our best to look

casual—our hands are empty and none of us are projecting anger or displeasure. Thankfully, he's able to read our body language and doesn't bolt for an exit. Then again, who knows whether he would run or not when he's got the benefit of protective wards at his back.

"Hi, Justin," Dria calls once we're closer. "Do you remember me?"

He nods, his stoic expression revealing nothing. "Not every day you get tricked into helping abduct a master vampire, so yeah, of course I remember you."

"We offer no retaliation, I promise." Her hands are open, arms spread at her side in a non-threatening gesture. "We came to talk."

Justin's eyes flick to Jon. "He's new. Don't recall him from the Tribunal that night."

Jonathan tilts his head in acknowledgement, but remains a step or two behind Dria and me to ensure our safety and keep a look out for associates of the wizard we may not know exist.

"Yes, he is," Dria admits, but doesn't expand further. "Would you like to go inside to chat or would you feel safer here on the street?"

Justin smiles, a lazy over-confident grin if I ever saw one. "Please, join me inside. I have your word you intend no harm?"

Dria's answering smile is brittle, allowing no room for humor. "If I did, you'd be dead already."

The wizard's aplomb looks shaken for a second, but he quickly hides it behind a mask of indifference. "Please, come in." He sweeps open the door behind him and ushers us in with one arm.

We file in, one at a time, with Dria in the lead. I know she'd prefer to meet any threats head on, protecting us from the worst of whatever might await us. As much as it triggers my own fears, I don't even bother arguing about her safety or any possible dangers we might be walking into. She'd do whatever the hell she wants anyway.

Her blasé attitude makes her hard to protect, but I've adjusted over the years to recognize I have to let her have her way in matters such as these. Arguing with her in front of someone would undermine not only her authority, it would make me look stupid as she is clearly the strongest of the three of us.

I pass over the threshold, feeling a tingle run over my skin. Another protection ward perhaps, I'm not sure. The living room beyond appears normal enough, a couch, two chairs, small TV, everything in drab, dark colors. The man obviously likes black. No sign of the magic the wizard wields or items he might use in spell preparation. Then again, what the hell did I expect? A staff of magic or a pointy hat? Maybe a black cat lingering on a cushion? Wait, that's a witch, right? I shake my head at my fanciful rumination. Need to focus.

Justin shuts the door behind Jon and proceeds to the center of the room. He motions toward the small grouping of furniture. "Please, take a seat."

Jon stays near the entrance, his stance revealing he's too keyed up to sit, while Dria and I sit on the couch, and the wizard selects a chair facing the door.

"What brings you to my home? And should I even ask how you found it?"

Dria nods toward me. "Rafe has been keeping tabs on the comings and goings of anyone associated with the Tribunal. As I'm sure you can imagine, we're looking for Rolando."

Justin tenses in his seat, perhaps drawing the correct

conclusion that he led us back to his home, an unwanted occurrence for anyone who wants to maintain privacy from vampires or anyone else in the supernatural community. "I'm sorry, I can't help you."

My deadly wife cocks her head to the side and stares deeply into the wizard's eyes, "Can't help us, or won't?"

"I assure you, madam vampire, I have no idea where he is. I would help if I could."

"And *why* would you help us?" I ask. "You were helpful weeks ago when you didn't have to be, and yet you still work for those in charge at the Tribunal."

"As far as working for them, I didn't have a choice in the matter. We've got a signed contract. And if I break it, my name in magical security will go down the tubes." His open expression bespeaks of truth, but only Dria will know for sure if he's lying. I may be experimenting with learning mind control on the inn's employees, but I would never attempt to enter a wizard's head without more practice. If I messed it up, he'd go on the defensive and Dria would be even more annoyed than she already is with what I've been attempting on the side.

Jon speaks up near the door. "So you were hired to set up the wards and protect the vampire's territory in the city?"

Justin nods, angling his body to partially face Jon and us at the same time. "I installed wards for danger, magical use, unannounced supernaturals—that one was tricky, had to meet all the vampires in the immediate area and make sure the spell included them. But the wards don't really cover a 'territory,' just the property surrounding the Seat of Darkness. They control the whole city, but that's too big for me to cast around."

"What does that phrase even mean, 'the Seat of

Darkness'?" Jon asks. "I've heard it used several times, but no one has clarified."

Vivian answers, "It refers to where vampires originated from. No one kept written records thousands of years ago, but when we first organized to form a governing body it was here. There was the highest concentration of vampires living here—long before the city was called Buenos Aires."

Jon nods, scoping out the rest of what he can see in the small house, appearing to pay more attention to our surroundings than the three of us.

"What made you take on the task of helping to catch Vivian?" I revert back to using my wife's nickname as that is what most everyone has called her for the past century.

"Same as I told you that night—money. If I had any idea what they were really planning I never would have agreed to the job. Which is exactly why I led you to her when I found you in the underground halls.

"Coraline was always rather intense. I hadn't realized her obsession with your wife was borderline crazy until it was too late."

"Fair enough," Dria says. "How deep does your involvement go with the Ancients? Or do you mainly work with underlings?"

"Coraline was the highest ranking person I worked with, and she was part of the inner circle, as I'm sure you already know." He lifts his shoulders in a show of nonchalance. "What can I say? I never even saw Rolando involved. I'm just the hired help."

"Do you know what he looks like?"

"Nope. Never met the guy."

Dria's eyes glint. "So he could have been involved in the abduction and you wouldn't have known?"

"I guess that's possible. Coraline handled my security contract. I also met a dude named Lucas and was always supervised by different sentries when I came back to renew the wards."

Jon begins an entirely different track of questioning. "What do you know of the recent murder on the news? The one involving an animal attack."

Dria glances at the Were, but remains quiet. A tingle of sensation indicates my wife is about to communicate with me telepathically. *Let's see where he's going with this, love. Maybe he senses something.*

Whatever you say, liebling. I'd just assume any line of questioning could help.

"Nothing, man." Justin sits up straighter. "I know the same as you do from the news. Happened a couple of blocks from here, in *El Centro* I believe. No one I know, I don't think."

He's lying, she says. *He knows something, but I can't tell what without going deep into his mind.*

Save that for later, I reply. *I don't trust he doesn't have security measures in place that could reveal your attempts.*

Oh, he does. On that, I'm very sure.

Jon doesn't always possess the same degree of subtly that Dria does, and calls Justin on what he sensed. "Your scent changed, Justin. Like you might not be telling us everything you know."

Justin clams up, his entire posture indicating he's said all he's going to say tonight. "Think what you want. I don't know of anyone who has the capability to kill so ruthlessly." Sweat breaks out on his forehead. He looks to my wife. "Except for the city's deadliest predators. Any chance one of you could be behind it?"

Dria tilts her heard while answering. "Until I learn more about the attack and the victim, there's no way I could answer that. But if you're asking could a vampire kill someone and make it look like an animal attack, then the answer is yes."

"I thought so," the wizard says. "It could easily have been a four-legged supe, too." He pointedly looks at Jon, making us aware that he does indeed know our companion is a werewolf. Could be the odor. Jon is a musky son of a bitch.

"Do you know of other large Weres, besides werewolves, in the community?" Dria asks, no longer pretending Jon is human.

"I've heard of a tribe of snake shifters in Brazil, ones that can become as large as anacondas. But the wounds inflicted on that poor guy could never have been made by a snake."

Jon pipes in with, "Assuming the perpetrator was in animal form when the killing took place."

We're all quiet for a moment, letting his words sink in. A supernatural shifter is naturally stronger than an average human. Strong enough to have inflicted deadly, animal-like claw gouges and knife wounds without ever having to change shape.

Dria smiles, looking like she's hoping to diffuse the tension in the room. "Good thing we're not here to solve a crime. What I really need help with is finding Rolando. Think you might be interested?"

"Me?" Justin's eyebrows shoot up his forehead. "You barely know me, and I helped them catch you a few weeks ago. Why would you want to hire me?"

Dria looks deep into his eyes, by my guess she's attempting to slip into his mind. "Because you're wearing an amulet more powerful than I've ever seen a witch make—and it's keeping me from controlling your mind."

A slow arrogant smirk turns up one corner of the wizard's mouth. "It's the only thing keeping you bloodsucking bastards honest. If not, I'd probably never get paid."

Jon takes a step closer, one hand raised in a stop motion. "Wait a second. You *can't* read his mind, therefore you trust him? Seems counter intuitive."

Dria nods. "You bet. If I can't get into his head, then that means neither can the others. And his motivations for striking a deal are more clear cut... more pure."

"I bet I can guess what his motivations would be," I say, running a hand over Dria's knee. "Money—and lots of it."

Justin's look, if possible, becomes more smug. "Maybe. Maybe not."

"Oh, please," Jon grouses. "You're like a prom date up for bid, willing to put out when the magic number is reached."

"Jon! A little decorum, please." Dria returns her attention to the wizard. "Can you help me find where his non-Tribunal home is?"

"You're asking me to find and reveal a vampire's daytime resting location, and one of the inner circle at that?" Justin shakes his head. "I'm not so sure that's a smart job to take on— for any price."

"All right, how about you try to set up a meeting with him for yourself? No need to feel like a sellout."

I glance to my wife, suppressing my smile. That was her objective all along. She asked about finding his home, knowing he'd decline, and countered with a more *palatable* idea. She's a clever bitch, that one.

"Hmm..." Justin's gaze shifts to the floor. "Let me think about it. I'd have to see if it could be arranged. He might not be willing to meet with me."

Dria smiles and rises, extending her hand. "Thank you for your consideration, Justin. And when you're ready to get away from this city and seek out a more peaceful existence, maybe we can talk."

Whoa—what the heck did that mean? Does she intend to invite him to Alaska? We're going to have to talk about that when we're alone. He seems like an okay guy, but that doesn't mean I want him to join our seethe. And judging by the annoyance in Jon's eyes, he probably feels the same.

We wrap up the conversation, promising to return if we think of anything else. A part of me is annoyed Jon spoke out about the animal attack when he did, but consequently, we'd already learned everything we were going to at that point and Justin's reactions were revealing all on their own.

The three of us make our way to the house I purchased yesterday, which lies several blocks to the north. Farther from the crime scene, too. I open the door with a flourish, presenting our new local residence.

Dria laughs when she enters, the sound full of good humor. "Not anything like what you hinted at."

I smother a grin. I knew she'd be fine with whatever I picked, as long as it was safe and there was a bed. When it comes right down to it, she demands very little in physical comfort.

"Not bad," Jon says while sauntering through the small living room. "Is it big enough for your highness?"

Dria shoots him a nasty look. "I will adapt. Not to worry. If it feels too cramped for space, you're welcome to sleep in the backyard."

Jon snorts. "Glad to see you haven't lost your bitchy edge while were we separated."

"Never," she replies with a deadly grin, striding to the small kitchen in the back. That's a look I've seen many times before, and one Jon should know by now means to shut the fuck up. She's ready to blow, and I don't mean in anger. She wants what only I can give her, and it warms my soul just knowing it.

Hoping to break the tension, I motion to the staircase. "How about I show you to your room, Jon?" Without waiting for an answer, I ascend to the second floor. In a moment, I hear him on the steps behind me. "You'll have this whole floor to yourself."

"Really? Where will you guys be? Doesn't look like there's space on the main floor for a bedroom. Is it off the back or something?"

"I've got a safe place for us in the basement. I'll show you next."

Dria trails behind us, content to check out the area at her own pace.

I open the door to the largest bedroom with the adjoining bath. It's serviceable, containing a queen bed, nightstand, and tall dresser. The accommodations aren't the Ritz, by any means, but comfortable and clean.

"Not bad," the wolf says. "I've stayed in worse."

Dria mumbles from the doorway, "You've lived in worse, but who's counting?"

Jon doesn't respond, tossing his large duffle onto the bed. "Let's see the rest and then I have to take off for a little while."

"Where do you need to go?" I ask, unsure how I feel about leaving the doors unlocked while he's gone.

"I have to check in with the local pack. Don't want to piss off any big dicks while we're here."

I toss him the set of keys. "Take these. Lock up behind you. We need to get another set made tomorrow."

CHAPTER NINE

JON

I catch the keys, and follow Rafe down the stairs. He shows us the rest of the small main floor and then leads us into the tiny half bath off the dining room.

"Not much room in here," I say. "Did you really need us all to cram in?"

Rafe ignores me and uses the toe of his shoe to kick the molding along the floor, triggering a section that pushes in. It's a spring latch. Depressing it opens a hidden wall section, swinging it inward a couple of inches.

"That's some cool shit. How do you guys always have secret passage ways in your houses? Homes don't normally come equipped with these."

"That depends on *where* you've lived, and *when*," Vivian answers, pushing the door further and peering down into the darkened opening. "Argentina has a lot of German immigrants from World War II. Think of all those secret hidey-holes the Germans used to safeguard Jews from the SS. The same mentality came here when people fled the country to avoid persecution after the war ended." She approaches the top step of the hidden staircase, looking eager to explore. "Although I doubt doing the same thing here was with the original intent— to protect their friends and neighbors who were unjustly hunted. I think whoever built this did it purely for self-preservation."

I stifle a snort at her description. "Sounds similar to *you* when you phrase it like that."

Rafe grabs a flashlight off the vanity, one he must have left earlier, and clicks it on to illuminate the way down. "There's a bare bulb with a pull chain a little further down. I plan on adding a stick-on light near the top tomorrow."

Vivian descends, and Rafe, then I, maneuver through the tight doorway to follow. "Now I see what you meant by having to 'build' the furniture for down here. You couldn't get much down these stairs." There's a soft whir of a motor below, and a light antiseptic scents the air, reminiscent of cleaners.

We reach the bottom and Rafe pulls the chain, lighting the basement. The space is bigger than I expected, with shelves lining the two long walls, a large bed dominating the middle of the room, and a small seating area with comfortable chairs at the far end. Floor lamps stand near the bed and chairs. Very soon, all the lights are turned on, casting a warm glow in the windowless space. There's a tiny refrigerator, sized for a dorm, in the far corner, with a microwave on top, and glasses and mugs sitting on the shelf behind both.

Shiny new books and magazines line another shelf, and new clothes hang on a pole strung in place of shelves in the next area down.

"How'd you get a king-sized mattress down here?" I ask.

"It's two twins, side to side, with a mattress pad over the top."

I nod, glancing up at the door, and the straight shot down to the tile floor. I bet he slid the smaller mattresses down easily. "Smart."

"It's perfect, my dear," Vivian says, throwing her arms around her husband's neck, lust clear in her eyes. "You thought of everything."

I'm surprised Vivian is okay with such a dark and dreary location, but hey, the things I don't know about that woman could fill a book. Wait, when I think back to all those journals, I'd say what I don't know about her actually fills dozens of books.

Rafe lowers his head to kiss her and I take that as my cue to leave. "Okay, guys, I'm out of here. I'll make sure the back door is locked as well as the front when I leave. Anything else I need to worry about?"

Rafe breaks their kiss for a moment to answer. "Nope, you're good. Just make sure the basement door latch fully engages when you close it." He resumes his kissing, hands roaming down to cup his wife's ass.

In the past, I'd be consumed with jealousy and longing at an awkward moment like this. But not now. I take the stairs two at a time, then turn sideways to exit through the narrow entrance. Now, I can handle their non-stop sexy times. I have Candy in my life and someone to return my affection. Life is looking up.

I close the hidden panel right as a low chuckle from Rafe reaches my ears. I'm sure the two of them will be busy for the next few hours and not even notice I'm gone.

Before I leave, I decide to touch base at home. I dig out

my cell and move to the couch in the living room, then realize very quickly my sensitive hearing can easily hear the couple downstairs going at it, and make the short trek up to my new room, hoping the extra distance will drown out the randy pair.

Candy answers on the second ring, sounding breathless. "Hey, how was the trip?"

"Long and uneventful. Except for the parts where I was thinking about our last night together. Those moments were more fun."

"You sound like me. I haven't been able to get you out of my head."

I picture her masturbating on the bed we shared, the sheets twining around her long, toned legs. Soft moans sounding in the strong light of an Alaskan summer evening. "Is that what has you out of breath?"

"I heard the phone ring and had to shift back to answer it."

"Oh? And why were you shifted?" I smile, still picturing her naked, but this time due to her fast change back. "And what—or who—were you?"

"Not anyone, I'm happy with the shape of me at the moment, thanks in large part to you. I was trying on different dog breeds, seeing if I like anything more than a wolf."

"And do you?"

"Not yet, but it's a nice challenge to try. Changing into an animal I've never seen outside of a picture or *YouTube* video is... interesting, to say the least."

"Having no idea how, I'll have to agree with you." A thought occurs to me. "Could you essentially change into any animal you only have a vague idea of, like something you saw in an old drawing?"

"I haven't tried it. But if I could identify the combined body parts and scale, I probably could. Why?"

"No reason, just curious." I hate not telling her the truth, but the idea that whoever killed the man I saw on the news could be a shifter, and not a species like a werewolf, is something no one has mentioned yet. Could also be because Dria and Rafe have no idea we have a shifter living at the resort.

It makes me wonder how many shifters are in the world. I know Candy has no idea, as she's mentioned before that she worries she might be the only one left.

"How are the dogs and pups?" I ask, referring to Eric and Pat with the puppy reference.

"I saw them shifted as wolves and out running the property early with the dogs. We haven't talked today, but they seem fine. Are you worried about them? Should I be checking in on them?"

I think back to Pat's awkwardness in the control room a few weeks ago. They probably need time to warm up to Candy on their own. Having her check on them might make them uncomfortable with her, like she was higher than them in the pack. And that's not the case, yet. "Nah, don't worry about it. If you feel like chatting with them, go ahead, but I'll check in with them tomorrow. I don't want to put you in that position. They're good kids."

The word "kids" sounds funny when they're only six or so years younger than me, but they haven't been Weres long and the term fits how I feel.

We talk for a few more minutes and then I hang up, the task of reporting in to the local pack weighing on me. I meditate for a few minutes, careful to lock all my feelings regarding Candy behind my mental shields. There's no way I want to be near the horny couple and have a random image of me and Candy pop up for Viv to catch.

Confident I've done all I can to keep my new relationship private, I return downstairs to check the map and locations I researched earlier on my tablet. The Were bar I want to visit is only a few blocks from here. It's half past midnight, I should find some Weres hanging out, still enjoying the evening.

As promised, I check the back entrance and exit via the front, testing the knob and door before leaving. We're in a safe part of town, but it wouldn't look good if I messed up something as simple as locking a door to keep the couple safe.

The cooler evening air feels refreshing after the summer in Alaska. At least here there's a noticeable, if slight, change in seasons. Back home everything seems to be in extremes. Even on the southern island, we get more seasonal enjoyment than Alaska.

The nights are longer this far south of the equator during the winter season, but it's still nothing like the enveloping blackness and gut wrenching cold of the deep winter above the Arctic Circle. I stride down the sidewalk, taking a left turn after a few blocks. Very soon, I'm near a more commercial and less residential section of the barrio. Restaurants, shops, and groceries line the streets, most closed at this hour.

Bars seem to be the only exception, with their warm lighting and appetizing aromas beckoning one to enter. A few more blocks and I'm near the less populated commercial section, where some of the businesses look like they've seen better days and a few lone warehouses can be found. A loud howl rips the air, the sound made by human vocal cords. I glance up at the sign. Lupine Luna. Yup, I've found the local

Were bar. And by the sounds of it, someone is having a great time inside.

I push open the wooden door and enter. The smells of cooked and well-seasoned meat waft around me, tempting me to sit and order a second large meal of the night. I walk toward the bar, conversation dimming a little with my presence. I've been seen. And more importantly, they don't know who I am or why I'm in their territory. Two men slip out the front door and I can't help but feel like I've driven them away with my presence.

I nod to the barkeep, addressing him in Spanish. "I'm looking for Hector. I'm visiting the city on business and need to let him know I'm here."

The short, dark-haired man locks his steely-eyed gaze on me, his full lips thinning before he opens his mouth to respond. "There is no Hector here anymore." The muscles in his biceps tighten, looking like he's holding himself back. But from what? And why?

Apprehension slivers up my spine. I wonder who took over the pack. I feel for Hector's wife, even though I never met her. He wouldn't have stepped down without a fight, and depending on how hostile his challenger was, Hector is most likely dead. I doubt he'd be absent for any other reason. The victor could have claimed his wife, but in most cases a new alpha would choose his own mate. "Can you direct me to the current head of the pack?"

All conversation stops as people turn to openly stare at me. The bartender tenses. "And where did you say you're from, mister?"

I smile and rest my palms on the bar, relaxing my limbs and trying my damnedest to look like I'm not a threat. For some reason, my asking about their leader has made the energy in the bar fly off the charts with agitation. "I didn't." I extend my hand in greeting. "I'm Jon Winchester, visiting from Alaska."

My casual approach and openness has done the trick. The Were behind the counter grasps my hand, giving it a solid pump up and down, and with his acceptance the tension around us lowers. "I'm Emmanuel. Manny for short. Welcome to San Telmo." He waves to the rest of the patrons with a slow smile. "I promise they won't bite—for now." He drops my hand and reaches for a pint glass. "Can I get you a beer?"

I look over the draft pulls on tap. "I'll take a *Dos Equis*. So, Manny, are you the guy in charge? I stopped by as a courtesy, to let the local pack know I was here on an extended business trip and not a loner you need to worry about."

"I'm not the alpha," his gaze drifts behind me, over my right shoulder. "But I—"

A sultry female voice rumbles behind me. "Thanks, Manny."

I turn, coming face to face with the sexiest female werewolf I've ever laid eyes on. She's tight and toned, close to my height, but still carrying an impressive set of womanly curves. Short black hair done in a messy, carefree style, frames a pair of sexy, dark-as-sin eyes, set in a face with full lips. "I'm Magdelena. Hector's former wife and the new reigning alpha."

Sexual pheromones fill the air between us, and I can't tell if it's from her or me. My breath freezes in my chest, ensuring I don't fall prey to my baser instincts and mount her like a horny dog. It's got to be her. Sure, she's hot, but what the hell? I do have a girlfriend I like a lot. It isn't like me to feel this way about someone I just met.

How is she their leader? Did she defeat the former alpha with her pussy?

My thoughts must be broadcast on my face because her expression turns surly when I don't immediately respond.

"Uh... hi. I'm Jon," I say, rushing in to erase the damage. She still doesn't look very happy with me as I stumble on. "I apologize for my reaction. You're the first female leader I've met who rules on her own—without a mate."

She shrugs one shoulder and cocks a hip against the chair next to me. "Not all of us are created equal."

My gaze travels up and down her body, noting the truth in her statement in a way she more than likely didn't intend. "So... er, uh... Hector? What happened to him?"

The sexy werewolf turns away, facing the rest of the Weres in the bar. "He didn't agree with me, so he had to go." She takes a moment to watch the reactions of the people around her, nodding once or twice at something she sees in the others. "And yes, I killed him—by myself." She returns her attention to me and holds up a delicate hand. Before my eyes it shifts and sprouts claws, the fingers lengthening and growing into a strong, weapon-like hand and paw mixture.

My cock lurches in my pants, surprising me with the immediate stimulus response that triggered arousal and not fear. She's the first female Were I've seen who can change into a combination of a wolf and a human, at will. I've only witnessed one guy who could do it—and that was at a yearly regional pack rally with other Weres up in Canada. He was a bit of a dick, too. Flaunting his skill to intimidate us. Romeo, my former pack leader, ignored him and the rest of us followed suit.

A full-body transformation would leave a human/wolf

hybrid creature—a true "wolfman." One that could kick serious ass over a Were in human form or one in full werewolf form. It's a powerful skill I've heard is usually confined to only a handful of male alphas.

Her nostrils flare, picking up my interest. I try and lock down the unwanted reaction, unwilling to send her the wrong message. I'm taken. No matter how fucking hot she is. I'm starting to fall in love with Candy, right? The attraction to another person—even if it is to a magnificent female alpha any werewolf would give his left nut to possess—feels disloyal.

Quick as a wink, she senses my emotional reaction, shutting down her onslaught of sexual hormones.

Her head tilts to the side as she examines me with curiosity. "Tell me what you didn't tell Manny."

"And what would that be?"

"Why are you here?"

The hand in my pocket closes over the house keys Rafe gave me, a very solid reminder of why I'm here and what I can't reveal. "Work, mostly."

She smiles. "Your words sound true, for the most part. I get the feeling there's more you aren't telling me. Care to expand?"

"I really can't, sorry. But you can rest assured I'm not a lone wolf looking to hone in on your territory. I don't know how long I'll be here, but I don't think I'll be here by the end of the season."

Her changed hand comes to rest on the bar next to one of mine, tapping out a deadly staccato, making dents in the wood surface with her long sturdy claws. "That's good, because we don't deal well with loners. Especially after what hit the news earlier tonight."

"Hold on a sec. You thought I might have been the animal

in the attack that killed someone?" I sink onto the high stool by the bar. "Of all the strangest things I've been accused of, that has to take the cake. But seriously, you think it might be a werewolf?"

She looks around the room once more, then settles her smoldering gaze back on me. "More importantly, the medical examiner thinks it's a wild animal who's bigger than any domestic dog or native predator."

"How did you hear that? I haven't seen it in the news."

"Friends in high places. Let's go to my office in the rear and we'll talk." Without a backward glance, she walks away through the throng of Weres, weaving a path toward a hallway in the back.

I follow, passing close through the tables, sensing every eye on me. I can't tell yet if these wolves are happy with their new leader, or plotting her demise. It's the oddest feeling.

We stride into a small office and she closes the door behind us. The thick wood mutes the noise from the bar, cocooning us in a pocket of relative quiet. "I miss Hector," she says in a soft voice, regret tingeing her tone.

"Then why did you kill him?" I ask, leaning against the wall, admiring her tight curves.

"I didn't have a choice."

"We all have a choice when it comes to killing, honey."

She lunges forward, her clawed hand digging into the wood paneling beside my head. "Don't 'honey' me, you cocky son of a bitch. You weren't here. You don't know the choices I had to make or why." Bitterness creeps across her face, dimming her beauty. "All you should concern yourself with is the fact I dealt with the issue on my own, when no other man in the pack was strong enough to do so."

I raise my hands to reinforce I'm harmless. "Take it easy, lady. I'm sure you had your reasons." I motion my head toward the door. "How did the rest of them take it?"

"At first, there was a lot dissension among the men. But once I kicked a few asses they settled into line." She retracts her claws, transforming back to fully human, her slim hand looking perfectly normal again, and wanders to her desk to take a seat. "But then the first murder happened two days ago and all eyes turned to me."

"You mean the woman beaten to death? I read about that on my flight over. Why would they think you were responsible?"

"I knew her. She was a member of a small coven of witches in the barrio." She gazes toward a high window in the stucco wall, set near the ceiling. A sliver of moonlight leaks in, illuminating the delicate lines of her face and shining on her short hair. "She was quiet, nice, stuck to herself—not a flashy witch—yet."

"Okay, well, that doesn't sound like a reason you'd kill her."

"I didn't. But the pack knew I didn't like her."

"Why?"

"Because she'd had an affair with Hector two years ago." A phone vibrates on the desk in front of her. She picks it up and reads an incoming text, not sharing the message or elaborating further. Not that I expected her to either.

"No offense, but that's a long time to hold a grudge, especially if you already killed the man."

She looks to me and nods. "Yes, I think most of them felt that way. Knew I wouldn't take action so long after the incident."

"Meaning if you were going to kill her, you would have done it two years ago when you found out?"

"Yes. But this second death—that's the real problem."

"Well spill it lady because I'm jet-lagged and the obvious isn't really happening for me right now."

"Whatever animal killed the second victim is bigger than a werewolf."

"Okay, so? Doesn't that mean you guys are off the hook?"

"Not when your whole pack knows you can transform into something much bigger than an average werewolf—and inflict damage none of them could emulate."

"You're saying your whole pack thinks *you're* the killer?"

She nods, pain filling her eyes. "Not the whole pack, I don't think, but definitely the majority. And most of them are avoiding the bar altogether." She straightens in her chair, smoothing her hands over the pristine desk blotter. "That's why I called you back here."

"Uh... need a little help? Still don't get it."

"You're an outsider. Not connected to me or my pack. I need you to help prove my innocence and catch the real killer."

My jaw drops open. You could have knocked me over with a feather, I'm so shocked. That sure as hell wasn't what I expected. "How? I'm here for my own... work. I don't have time to spare for your issues."

She stands and comes around the desk, leaning her bottom on the front edge. "Sure you do, Jon. Because if you don't, I'm going to tell them *you're* the one who did the killing. And I'll spread it to all the supes in town."

"Ha! Like anyone would believe you. Good luck with that. I was still in the air when the animal attack occurred." I reach for the knob, ready to let myself out and get away from this crazy she-wolf with the Napoleon complex.

"Maybe you'll change your tune when I tell you I've already had someone follow your scent trail back to the home you're staying in. How would your vampire master feel if she knew you gave away her location within hours of her arrival?"

Anger boils under my skin as I turn back and face Magdelena. That must have been the info she received via text. Could it have been the two Weres who left the bar right after I arrived? "You send anyone after her and you'll be signing their death warrants. She doesn't take kindly to unwanted visitors."

The woman chuckles. "She's only one vampire, and there are many supernaturals in the city. I doubt very highly she could stop them all. And my trackers reported she smelled very, very old. I bet she has a lot of enemies." She trails a finger across the smooth surface of her desk, seemingly calm and collected while she issues Vivian's death threat. She's one scary lady. "You have a decision to make, don't you?"

I storm out, the sound of her laughter burning a fiery pathway to my groin. Dammit, I'm aroused even when I'm so pissed I want to throttle the woman.

She shouts behind me as I leave, "You have twenty-four hours to give me your answer."

If I'd known tonight was going to turn out like this, I'd have stayed home and listened to the two love birds go at it all damn night. Even that would have been preferable to fucking up with the safe house location less than four hours after I arrive.

I resist the temptation to immediately rush home to check on the pair. My head is filled with self-recriminations at my own stupidity in not taking safety precautions with our new home. What the hell was I thinking?

Was I not thinking because checking in with the local pack was a routine task? Was it because my mind has been filled with Candy lately? Jesus, if I'm not careful, I'll prove to be more of a danger to Viv and Rafe than anyone else in the damn city.

I wander around the quiet streets for hours, watching the city slowly wake up. It's past dawn when I return to the small house, but with the time change from Alaska, it feels like midnight to me. I crawl upstairs and into the bed that doesn't smell like pack or home. A few hours of sleep is just what I need before I tell Viv and Rafe about what happened. Considering the guilt weighing on me, I'm sure I'll be up before the two of them.

When I next open my eyes, it's past two in the afternoon. I scramble out from under the covers and stagger to the bathroom for a shower. I wonder if there's food downstairs. Ten minutes later, when I stroll into the kitchen, I hear the unmistakable sounds of love-making through the floor.

All night long and those two still can't keep their hands off each other? Geez. I block the images from my mind and think of Candy. Maybe I should call her to see what she's doing today. I bet she's up by now. Pulling ingredients from the cabinet and fridge, I begin brewing coffee and prepping a meal. No doubt the two of them will be hungry when they finally make it upstairs.

I am not looking forward to reporting we have to leave this place as soon as possible.

CHAPTER TEN

VIVIAN

Sweat rolls down my back, gathering in the dip of my spine. The sexual energy released during our all-night love session has finally filled me to the point of satiation. I feel more like my old self than I have in weeks. The shadows of doubt and worry no longer grip so tightly to my soul. All thanks to my husband's tireless stamina.

"Holy hell, that was incredible," I mumble into the pillow.

Rafe collapses on the bed beside me, a thick arm latching onto my waist to drag me closer. His still-rigid cock presses against my backside as he tucks me tightly to his front. "Incredible? A more inaccurate proclamation has never been uttered. Woman, I just rocked your world. Own it. The experience was way better than a simple 'incredible.'"

A chuckle spills from me. "Someone has a highly inflated opinion of himself."

He presses his hips toward my bottom. "Hush now, or I'll rally for another round and prove my opinion is spot on." A warm hand caresses my hip with affection and then draws back to deliver a resounding smack. The small zing of sensation jolts me from falling asleep. "And with two weeks away from you, I'm more than able to go for round four. Say the word, liebling."

"Is this where I cry 'uncle' and admit you're the studliest man on the planet?"

He grunts and digs his fingers into my hip. "You aren't saying it like you mean it, darling. I think I will have to do you again, you insatiable wench."

I smile, content to lie here the whole day. I love goading him. "Oh yes, that's it. Do me. Then I'll proudly proclaim you king of all fuckery."

Before he has a chance to respond, there's a solid knock on the hidden basement door. A sigh escapes us both.

"What the hell could that furry bastard want?" Rafe glances at his watch. "Crap. It's after three. We really should get up."

I push back with my hips, grinding into his, unable to resist teasing him after he was so cocky a moment ago. "I thought you were 'up' already?"

He leaves the bed, taking his welcoming warmth and growing hard-on with him. "Rise and shine, liebling. Don't make me drag you out."

We dress quickly in the cold basement. As I watch my husband, a shiver steals over me that has nothing to do with the cold. He's heavily muscled all over and it takes a considerable amount of will power not to jump on him and feast from his throat while I ride him to another hard and fast orgasm.

"Dria!" he calls loudly, breaking into my naughty daydreams. His voice softens as concern lights in his eyes. "Did you get enough sleep or should you stay down here and rest for a little while longer?"

My husband has been much more doting since my ordeal with Coraline and her henchmen, more concerned with my well-being and welfare than I've seen him in decades. "I'm fine. No need to worry about me." I don't have the heart to tell him to stop.

We both came away from that night changed forever—me with an increased sense of self-preservation and how delicate life can be, him with a stronger need to protect and shield me. I'll never take a moment with him for granted ever again. Maybe that's part of why we've both been insatiable the past day. I wasn't strong enough when we were last together to really show him how much he means to me.

He mumbles under his breath while dressing, it sounding suspiciously close to "someone has to look out for you since you won't."

After digging for clean underwear and pulling them on, and I add jeans and a sweater, we ascend the stairs and trigger the release mechanism in the wall near the railing. The small door swings inward. In a moment, we're in the tiny bath, resetting the latch to our new sanctuary. The scent of brewed coffee and scrambled eggs trickle in past the hallway door.

"Smells like someone did a little shopping," I say.

"It was the last thing I did before meeting you at the hangar." Rafe snuggles up behind me and wraps his arms around my waist, planting a kiss on my neck. "I knew it would be the only chance I'd have. After that, I'd be lost in our 'reconnecting' for the next twenty-four hours or so."

"Let's join him before you convince me to have my way

with you again." I look in the mirror and cringe at my bedhead. "You go first. I want to wash up and brush my hair."

"Sure thing, I'll make you a coffee, too."

I finish my brief toilette and head into the kitchen, unsure of what awaits me between the two men in my life. Hopefully Rafe will be more tolerant now that he's had his way with me non-stop for hours. Jon stands over the stove, finishing up what appears to be, judging by a dirty plate at the table, a second batch of food. I take the offered mug from Rafe and settle in an empty chair across from the men's spots.

"How did last night go?" I ask Jon.

"Not bad, but not great, either," he says, swinging a frying pan from the stove and moving to fill Rafe's plate and the used one I noticed earlier. Fluffy yellow eggs slide onto the ceramic. "There have been changes in the local pack, and an issue they have demanded my help with."

I take a sip of the coffee and place my mug on the table. "Demanded? Interesting. Tell us about the changes first."

"Hector, the previous leader, is dead and—get this—it was at the hand of his alpha mate. She strikes me as a little on the crazy side. But that could just be the circumstances."

"Why do you think she's crazy? Weres in unstable packs tend to vie for supremacy quite often."

"It's not that. I think she'd have to be a little cray-cray simply for what she's doing. She's the first female leader of a pack I've ever encountered—but then again, it's not like I've traveled the world and met dozens of pack leaders, so what the hell do I know?" He shakes his head, getting up to grab the plate of bacon he left on the counter. "The insane opinion comes from something else. She fears her pack will accuse her of the recent killings in the city and wants my help to prove her innocence."

"That doesn't sound crazy. But I doubt we'll have time to help her. Why do they think she's responsible? Had you ever met her on previous visits?"

"No, I hadn't. She must not have been at the bar last year when I briefly met with Hector. She's hot enough I would have remembered seeing her. And two years ago they had a different pack leader. You're right, this pack does appear to be more volatile than most. Romeo and Elsa have held the Manitoba pack for decades.

"This new leader is named Magdelena, and she has news regarding the killings the media doesn't. The first death, the woman behind the herbal shop—she was a witch. And the wounds on the animal victim were made by something much larger than a werewolf. Oh, and get this—she's a rare type of alpha who can partially change her body, achieving an in-between state of humanoid and werewolf—a form much larger than a regular human, or werewolf on hind legs, could ever be.

"And to answer your other question—they think she did it based on the fact she can half-shift. Her hybrid claws could have easily made similar damage as what the M.E. described."

Rafe pauses in eating. "I haven't heard of this half-form trait before. How common is it?" He looks to me, wondering if I might have more data.

I shrug. "Weres and their history have never been my specialty." I return my attention to Jon, assessing him with new eyes. "But is this an alpha skill that can be acquired over time? Could you learn to do it?"

Jon stares back at me, curiosity lighting his eyes. "I have no idea. That's something I hadn't thought of. I could ask."

Rafe snorts. "Oh yeah. That'll work." His voice take on a falsetto tone. "*Sure, I'll teach you my prized secret that allows me to control my entire pack.*"

"Hey. It might work. She wants my help. I could bargain with her."

"Why does she think you'd be interested in helping her anyway?" Rafe asks, a hint of incredulity in his tone. "Did she turn up the sexy werewolf pheromones to lead you around by your dick?"

I watch Jon's reactions carefully. Before the summer hunt with lots of female werewolves at the inn, he would have jumped at the chance to seduce or play with an eligible female alpha, but now he seems... reluctant. I won't ask him about his possible recent conquests. His responses to this new situation should reveal all I need to know.

"She tried. But I'm not so sure I'm interested. Especially after she threatened to blame me for the murders."

"How? And are they even related?"

Jon nods, grabbing his coffee and taking a long drink. "Turns out Hector had an affair a while back with the witch who was killed. And the second death—if the animal wasn't an animal but a supe—would mean supernaturals were involved in both cases."

"Surely no one would think the killings could be attributed to you when you just arrived in the country last night?"

Jon cringes. "While yes, that's technically true. I have a feeling she'd twist the truth to enflame and enrage the pack further to get what she wants."

"And why do you think that?"

"Because she told me her pack members traced my scent back to where I'm staying. She already knows about you *and* this house. And... She... uh... stated I had twenty-four hours to decide to help her or she'd tell everyone I was the culprit for the animal attack and reveal your daytime location to the supes in the city."

We're all quiet for a moment before Rafe speaks up. "Well, shit. I really liked this place. It's got the escape route through the root cellar and everything."

"Dammit," I say, no real heat in my tone because the damage is done already. "Looks like we need to pack and move out." I stand and glance around the tiny space, sorry to be leaving it so soon. "And then we need to have a chat with Justin again."

"Why Justin?" Jon asks. "I'd rather have you 'talk' to Magdelena so she'll leave me alone."

"Justin is inspired by money and a job. We'll give him both. I want to hire him to help me locate Rolando. And you," I look deeply into Jon's eyes. "You could be working on getting closer to the crazy bitch to learn her unique 'skill.' I guarantee, if she wasn't born an alpha with these traits, she discovered or learned them later."

Jon looks surprised. "Really? I don't know how that could be possible. But then again, if it was a learned skill, wouldn't she tell others how to do it, too?"

Rafe glances at the shorter man with a snarl of disbelief curling his lip. "Come on, furball. Didn't you hear me before? Why would she teach her packmates a skill that could potentially help them kill her?"

"Well, if that's the case, why the hell do you think she'd teach me?"

I arch an eyebrow. "You'd be surprised what lovers share."

Jon pales in the afternoon light. "You're suggesting I seduce this woman to learn what she knows?"

I step closer to the indignant young man, a harshness coloring my tone. "No. I'm suggesting my right hand man learn a useful skill that will make him a more powerful protector of *me and mine*. Do you have a problem with that?"

Am I pushing him too hard? Can he separate his feelings for whoever he bedded in Alaska to focus on the task at hand? I've done it myself over the centuries, and would have done it again in a heartbeat before marrying Rafe, but would I do it now? I ignore the niggling in the back of my brain. There's no way Jon's recent love interest can compare to the dedication of a sixty-five year mate-bond.

Before Jon can answer, Rafe chimes in. "Did you tell him about my entanglement with Coraline before beheading her?"

Jon lashes out, "*Yes*, I heard about it. Can you really compare saving your wife's life by having to *pretend* interest in your captor, to this scenario?"

Rafe's eyes cut to mine before he responds to Jon. "You weren't there. You don't know what I had to 'pretend,' as you so artfully put it. It was a matter of life and death. I'd do anything to protect Dria. *Anything*." He glances back at Jon. "But then again, she's *my* life, not yours."

Jon jerks up from the table, his face livid with anger. "What the fuck is that supposed to mean? Are you doubting my loyalty and sincerity to Vivian? I've given up everything for her—and I will continue to do so, no matter the price."

"Take a step back, both of you." After a few deep breaths, I approach the topic another way. "Jon, do you love your new pack?" He nods, annoyance in his eyes as he struggles to keep them from turning a light golden brown, a sign his wolf is very close to the surface. "Would you attempt whatever was needed to keep them safe? Even if it brought you harm?"

"Of course, I would. You know that."

"Well then, how is this suggestion any different? Your pack is growing. One day you will have a mate of your own and maybe children, too." He's listening now, and his eyes are staying hazel, indicating he's fully in control of his beast. I resist the burning desire to ask if he found someone he could see himself having children with. It's his decision and I want to see him happy.

"Do you want to learn a skill that could essentially make your whole pack contenders against any threat? No matter where you all were, no matter who stood by you, your loved ones would always be safe."

"You're suggesting I learn this and teach the whole pack?"

I raise a shoulder and let it fall. "Why not? You've always talked about forming a network of packs, opening up communication for a system to keep people safe and informed. This could be the *thing* to entice packs to unite. You could become the lynchpin in something much greater than yourself."

My message sinks in and Jon quiets, leaning against the back of his chair, staring at the uneaten food on his plate. "And all it will cost me is my dignity—*and* it will hinge on my success to seduce a woman I don't really like."

"Not a bad price, overall," Rafe says, rising from his place and carrying his plate to the counter. "And how about with the next safe house, you don't mess up and lead people right to us on the first night?"

In a few hours we're settled in a new apartment. It's not

nearly as nice or as big—nor as convenient—staying in a basement unit under an old repurposed bank. Since it's located much farther from San Telmo where the Tribunal resides, we'll be using the car more, which could help in shaking possible tails, too. Jon will now experience the joy of staying in the bedroom next to ours—I'm sure it will drive home his mistake greater than anything else I could possible say to him.

"What's next?" Rafe asks.

"Time to question a few vampires," I say, a feral grin stretching my face.

CHAPTER ELEVEN

RAFE

I'm not happy with the immediate change in locations, but we did plan for the possibility of having to switch daytime resting places daily, so I keep my frustration under wraps. Full dark has descended as Dria and I drive from the new apartment to the Tribunal's neighborhood, the luxuriant "new car" smell seeps into my senses, soothing my annoyance. God, I love a well-made automobile.

"I know you went to a lot of trouble to build the furniture in the basement." My wife's hand slides over my knee in a soothing gesture. "I'm sorry we won't be able to use it again."

"Me, too. But hey, that's life. The new place isn't so bad."

"Nope, it's fine. Just smaller." She gives my leg one last pat and stills her hand. "We'll do fine."

I want desperately to believe her, but we're not even a few days in to searching for Rolando and plans have already been mucked up. Maybe I should contact the agent and line up another property, just in case. If I wasn't so afraid of nosey owners I'd suggest renting instead of buying. Would certainly make life easier, if not safer.

"How do you think Jon will do with the female alpha?" Dria asks, her tone strangely devoid of emotion.

"Are you worried? He's a grown man."

She sighs. "It's not that. Obviously he's an adult. But he's never tried his hand at deception. I worry he's not up to the task of seduction to uncover her secrets."

"Hmph. I'd be more worried she'll turn him down flat and then he'll never be able to get into her pants."

Despite my best efforts, Dria refuses to rise to my remarks regarding the werewolf. It's more fun to tease him when he's here. Very soon we arrive at our destination. Paranoid because of Jon's recent slip, I choose a new location to watch the townhouse's entrances, hoping to throw off anyone who might be watching.

"No need for caution, my dear."

"Why do you say that? I think I've done a pretty good job at surveillance without getting detected so far."

"I'm sure you have—but that was when you didn't have a vampire in the car with you who would trip the wizard's wards."

"Damn! I forgot about that. I should have parked the next street over."

She opens her door and waits on the sidewalk for me. "Wouldn't have mattered if we drove in or walked. The wards will still go off and they will know an unregistered vamp has crossed the boundary."

"Unregistered? Hey, could Justin use the inverse to determine if Rolando has crossed the wards, too?"

Dria slips her hand in the crook of my arm. "I have no idea.

Wizard spells and magic are not my forte. One more thing we can ask him later."

"Why are we approaching them so boldly? Aren't you worried about being recognized?"

My wife tilts her head up toward mine. "On the contrary, I'm hoping to run into one of the sentries and take control of his mind to ask questions."

"Ahh... so clever. Paul and Drew mentioned a group of four greeted them when they wandered too close, that night they came looking for us."

"Exactly."

We stroll sedately up the street, casually glancing at homes and the street for signs of movement. Dria pauses mid-step and stops. "Do you smell that?"

Taking a deep breath, I detect the slight odor of car exhaust, molding leaves collected near a curb, and the faint hint of trash. "Nope, nothing out of the ordinary. What are you picking up?"

She resumes her pace, quicker than before, tugging me along with her. "I smell vampire blood. And a lot of it."

We pass the Tribunal's main house and keep walking. About seventy-five yards ahead I spy a form lying on the sidewalk. "Shit. Is that a body?"

Our pace increases to a light jog, eating up the distance quickly. A very large man lies on the sidewalk, his throat ripped out, nearly severing his head from his body. Long gouges of bloody flesh show through his clothing. A large hole in his chest is located where his heart would be. As a vampire, there's no coming back from a missing heart and severed head. A glance at his face has me once again swearing.

"Holy shit. That's George, isn't it?"

Dria's voice comes out as a whisper. "Yes. Yes, it was."

I run a hand over my forehead and up into my hair. "Dammit. He was a nice guy."

I shake off the cloying feel of a fearful death, distance myself mentally from the horror of the moment and attempt to help, squatting to examine him better in the darkness. My eyesight is close to that of a vampire, thanks to small sips of my wife's blood every month, but I take out my phone and use the flashlight function to illuminate the wounds better.

The man's a bloody mess. The white flash of his spine can be seen through the red gore of the torn muscles and ligaments at his throat. In addition to the wounds on his torso, there are huge slashes ripped through the arm of his coat in a failed defensive move to protect the large man.

"I've never seen a vampire kill another this way, especially leaving the blood to go to waste. Nor such widely spaced slashes on a werewolf's strike—doesn't match even the largest werewolf paw I've seen. What do you think made these wounds?"

Dria takes a step back, darting a glance from side to side. "I have no idea, but I can tell you it doesn't smell like a vampire or werewolf did it."

"Really? What do you think killed him—and why?"

Concern flashes across her lovely face. "Let's get out of here, Rafe. And fast."

Without further explanation, she hustles back the way we came, restraining herself from outright running away.

"Hold up, Dria. Wait! Why are we running?"

"Because we triggered the wards when we drove into the neighborhood and George's death is minutes old. Sentries, remember? There's no way in hell I want to be here when they find the body. It's bad enough our scents will be at the crime scene for any sensitive nose to discern." She moves faster, her petite feet almost flying over the sidewalk. "Come on, hon. Move it!"

No sooner do we get back to the car when I hear raised voices sounding from behind us. We slide into the butter soft seats and buckle up. I turn the key in the ignition and execute a three-point turn, heading back the way we came. My breath whooshes out as we leave the darkened residential area and travel into a more commercial section with a few people milling on the streets outside of bars.

"Holy crap. That was a close one. Do you think the Tribunal has werewolves in its employ and they'll be able to find us?"

Dria leans her head against the window. "I have no idea. But I have a feeling Buenos Aires's recent killing spree is only going to get worse."

"Why do you say that? What do think it could have been?"

"The scary truth? I've never smelled anything like it. I have no idea what we're up against."

W e rendezvous with Jon, picking him up near the new place, explaining all that happened and Dria's thoughts on it not being anything she recognizes. She even went so far as to share the discovery of the body with him in a projected memory, ensuring he knows exactly what we know.

"So if you've never smelled this predator before, what exactly does that rule out?" Jon asks, thinking of an angle I never thought to ask.

"Hmph. A bigger list than I can recall, to be honest. It's not a type of shifter I've ever met, nor a vampire, reaper, ghoul, zombie, witch, wizard... Jesus, there's a lot of paranormal creepies out there. Doesn't smell like anything from the ocean. Demons have more of a sulfur tang to their scent, and angels—"

"Whoa. Did you just say demons?" Jon looks as freaked out as I feel. I never knew half those things existed and I was happy in my ignorance.

"Sounds to me like you've protected me from a lot during our marriage," I say, a tinge of annoyance in my tone.

Dria glances at me, unperturbed. "I'm not sure what you want me to say, honey. The amount of things I've done and been exposed to in my life... well, it's enough to fill up a library. I don't remember it all, it happened so long ago."

Jon asks, "Is that why you kept journals?"

"Not initially, no. I did it in the beginning to preserve my sanity. I'd survived so much, I had trouble handling it all. And that was way before the concept of a therapist ever existed. But after the decades started piling up, I realized I was forgetting a lot of my past. If an incident came up in conversation I would generally recall the gist of what happened... but the details?" She shakes her head. "Those very quickly fell to the wayside. I found if I compartmentalized a traumatic event, denying its existence and shoving it away in my mind, very slowly the facts as I knew them changed in my memories. My later knowledge and feelings would often color what actually happened. Making it less horrible and more survivable. Does that make sense?"

I nod, placing a comforting arm around her slim shoulders. "Yes, it does."

"So where do we go from here?" Jon asks. "We've got a

witch beaten to death, a human torn up—and now a vampire, possibly killed by the same creature that murdered the human. Are these random targets or is there significance in the victims? We can't exactly collaborate with the local authorities, so how the hell are we going to discover the connections?"

I shift my wife closer to me, pressing her side along mine to offer warmth. "I vote for contacting your alpha wolf again. So far she's the only person we know with an inside track for info on the bodies."

Jon nods, his mouth thinning a little at the prospect. "All right. She's expecting my help anyway. Let's go."

We traverse the packed streets of San Telmo to return to the Lupine Luna. The full moon is only days away and I wonder how safe it is visiting an establishment full of werewolves. "Jon—do we need to be worried about the full moon being so close?"

"Jesus, man. All these years with me and you still don't know that crap is fake? A werewolf doesn't need the moon to change. But I will concede, it does often raise instinctual tendencies—like a propensity to hunting or mating. Very hard to avoid extremes if you're unbalanced by your baser instincts."

"Okay—so there's no chance the group will turn furry and attack en masse, but they may be horny and-slash-or looking for prey. Good to know."

In a few minutes we arrive at the bar and find a parking spot off the street. Like a lot of San Telmo, the streets here are paved with cobblestone, lending an air of times past to the setting. Noises from local restaurants spill into the streets, patrons still happy, despite the local deaths, to carry the *joi de vie* of the evening into the cooler night air.

The tension brought on by the discovery of George's

corpse melts away, replaced by the magic that is Buenos Aires. I'm grateful for the change of energy, especially as we're just about to enter what could become a hostile environment.

"Is it smart for all three of us to approach the pack?" I ask, allowing my inner doubts to surface. "Would it be better if Jon handled this on his own?"

The three of us halt on the sidewalk, the sign for the bar about half a block down. "That's a really good point," Dria says. "Jon, what do you think?"

"As much as I hate to admit it, Rafe is probably right. Especially if you were serious about me trying to seduce the woman to learn her transformation secrets." He looks down the street then glances back at Dria. "If our experiences with Romeo's pack are anything to go by, our unconventional relationship of servant and vampire may not be looked at too kindly."

A miffed expression crosses Dria's face. "They already know you're traveling with a vampire, what other reason could it be for?"

Jon raises his eyebrows, a distinctly lewd expression on his face. "They could think we're lovers." He reaches an arm to Dria's waist and a not so subtle grumble begins in my chest. "Relax, man. I'm just teasing. We all know she's yours." He leans down and nuzzles her neck, pushing her hair back over her shoulder with his face.

Dria extracts herself from the shorter man's embrace. "And now you've successfully coated yourself in my scent. Clever. Was that for Magdelena's benefit?"

Jon winks. "You're catching on. If she thinks I'm with someone more powerful than her, I will make a more tempting conquest."

"Jesus," I say with disgust. "You people are more animals than I give you credit for."

The young werewolf walks away, laughter ringing out on the night air. "And you're just figuring this out now?"

CHAPTER TWELVE

JON

Despite the crazy bitch's threat to find the killer or else she'd rat out Dria, I'm taking a chance coming back here so soon. Magdelena probably expects me to fall at her feet in my eagerness to help clear her name. Slip into line like all her packmates have with her dictatorship-like rule. I've got to make her work for our help a bit more.

The sounds and smells of the bar wrap around me as I step inside. Old, stale beer—which, truth be told, often smells like vomit—smoke, and body musk, which is a unique blend of werewolf pheromones, anxiety, and frustration with daily work responsibilities. I don't sense any underlying fear, or agitation that could be associated with the recent killings. And unless someone here is responsible, they'll have no idea about the latest vampire death Viv and Rafe just discovered.

I stride to the bar, thankful the same bartender is on duty again tonight. "Hey, Manny. Is Magdelena in? I'd like to talk with her."

He smiles, but it's not a warm one, more of one filled with

condescension. "She told us to expect you." He motions with his head. "Go on back."

Weaving through the tables, I take a moment to make eye contact with any Weres looking my way. It's a motley lot at best. I see flickers of curiosity in some gazes, resentment in others, and a few break away and look down too quickly for me to discern more. Could Magdelena be telling me the truth that a large part of her pack wants to blame her?

I shake my head. If so, I can't sense it among the ones here tonight.

Striding into the back hall, I pause to knock on her door and don't wait for a response, turning the knob and pushing the door open at once. The pretty werewolf sits behind her desk, eyes on the slim computer monitor in front of her.

She glances up as I enter, her eyes flicking to the chair in front of her desk. "Why don't you come on in, cowboy. Take a seat." Her lips turn up in a soft smile of invitation. Very quickly her nostrils flare, and a look of distaste crosses her face. Good, she's scented Vivian.

"You do know that not all Americans are cowboys, right?" I say while lowering into the unyielding seat. I don't like that she's put me in a small chair and herself in a position of power behind the desk, but I'll stay here for the moment while it suits my needs.

Magdelena's smile broadens, showing me her teeth—which is either a sign of aggression or she's found my response funny. God, I hate figuring out werewolf shit. It takes way more effort than I'd care to admit.

Guilt creeps in, teasing me with its cold and uncomfortable touch. Can I really seduce her when I'm falling for Candy?

Can you afford not to when she could teach you a very valuable skill?

I block out the voice in my head, aware that it's not Vivian, but my own conscience.

"I know you're not all cowboys. I just love the imagery and felt you fit the word. Rough around the edges, confident swagger... all you're missing is a sidearm and a *Stetson*." She folds her hands on the desk, focusing all of her attention on me. "You've returned to help me find the real killer, yes?"

"I've come back to learn more. I'm not sure how much help I can be on my own, but thought we could pool resources."

"Pool resources? As in you have useful information I might need? That would be an interesting trick since you just arrived yesterday." She tilts her head. "Maybe your vampire friend has tapped into the local seethe and they want to know more about our petty issues? That group loves to live in their ivory tower and look down on the rest of us."

"I agree. The vampire community often shuts out the rest of the supernatural, preferring to be insular and protect their own."

Her perusal turns speculative. "And your vampire lover allows you to voice such opinions? I smell her on you—but you haven't had sex with her recently."

"No, we haven't," the lie I have a relationship with Vivian tripping easily from my lips. I smile, a cocky grin full of promise. "She's not here now, is she? My opinions are my own." I wink. "And we're not exclusive."

Her earlier observations about vampires in their ivory towers triggers an urge for me to speak about my dream to unite packs all over the world, but I refrain from saying anything. Especially considering it's her skill I'd like to exploit to bring them together.

"Let's get down to business," I say. "I need to see the crime scene pictures—or at least talk to someone. We need something to start on to connect the deaths and draw correlations."

"I'll see what I can do. But don't hold your breath. The police here move at their own pace, not like your American TV shows where everything happens instantly after the crime."

"You like to watch American police dramas?"

"Of course. You've witnessed our city's obsession with the *Simpson's*, have you not?" she says with a grin. "The rest of the world, including me, feels the same way about *NCIS*."

"When I first visited the city, years ago, I thought the local bars serving Duff beer from Mo's was hysterical." I smile at the memory before getting back on track. "Okay, so your cops are slower, and we might not get any pictures." I run a hand through my hair. "Can you tell me where the victims were found? I might be able to pick up a scent or follow a trail."

"Don't you think I've thought of that already? The witches wouldn't let us anywhere near where their coven member was beaten. They guard their barrio carefully. The scent trail from the man killed yesterday led nowhere. It's as if the creature appeared and disappeared into thin air. And I'd never smelled the attacker before. I have no idea what did it. But I can tell you it's not human."

Interesting. "Isn't the fact there was a scent trail at all, and it wasn't yours, enough to clear your name with your pack?"

Disgust twists her mouth, followed quickly by disappointment. "I've found in this case the facts don't seem to matter to those filled with hate. The men either resent my rule or want to bend me to their will so they can rule by my side. The women," she lifts one shoulder, "they stay quiet for the most part, unwilling to speak out against the stronger men in the pack."

"So they're essentially using the recent killings as a way to bring you down. No real motivation on their end to find out who's behind the deaths."

"Exactly."

"I bet they'd change their tune if a werewolf was murdered."

"Is that a threat?"

"Relax. How could it be? We've already established I arrived after the witch died. I mentioned it because I have news on another killing, one that hasn't made the media rounds yet." Before she can leap to the incorrect conclusion that it was a Were who was murdered, I say, "And it may bring the vampires out of their ivory tower."

"Are you saying a vampire has been killed?"

I rise and come around her desk, crowding her personal space as I lean a hip on the corner. "Yes. I am. So far you've got a witch, a human, and a vampire dead—all in different, but close proximity, locations around the city. The way to finding who's responsible is to find how they are all linked, if at all, and why."

"You're saying you don't think they were random victims, but chosen for a reason?"

"It's a possibility. Unless they are all victims of being in the wrong place at the right time. Which is plausible, but I'd still like to focus on finding a link first. Can you tell me what you know about how the witch died? What her wounds were like? 'Beaten to death' is pretty vague."

"My source in the M.E.'s office said she suffered multiple contusions to the head, no other injuries noted. No claw wounds like the victim from last night. There were no bite marks. I don't think it was a vampire, although it could have been, and obviously the local coroner would never have considered it anyway."

"Except in self-defense, I've never heard of a vampire killing a human and leaving all the blood untouched. How did the medical examiner rule the case?"

"Death by exsanguination. She bled out from her head wounds."

"And what about the victim from last night? You mentioned the injuries looked different than a werewolf's claws. Any idea what made them?"

"No, and I smelled that crime scene myself. It was no Were."

"What do you think it could have been?"

"I have no idea. That's why I asked for your help." She reaches over and runs a hand up my thigh. "I was hoping you'd have seen something like this from home, maybe have an idea?"

I grunt, but don't push her hand away. "I'm from Alaska. And before that, I spent a year in Canada. Neither place is a hot bed for supernatural killings." I think about all the recent deaths we've had at the resort. "Okay, let me rephrase that. Neither place has exposed me to non-werewolf or non-vampire fatalities."

Her hand creeps higher, her intent no longer questionable. "We could make this arrangement beneficial to us both. I can think of a way..."

I smile, the grin not quite meeting my eyes. "You mean a

nicer way, something physical—as in, instead of you blackmailing me into helping, or you'd reveal my vampire's resting place to the supes in the area?"

She looks away, a shy smile on her lips. "Oh, that. Sometimes I speak before thinking things through all the way."

I nudge her shoulder with mine. She grants me another timid smile, almost like she's unsure if her advances would be rebuked or welcome.

"I think we can come to terms we're both... satisfied with."

Magdelena straightens and moves between my legs, nestling herself close to my crotch, leaning her hips in to press against me. "Tell me about the vampire victim."

She wants to think she's in control of this interview, that she's seducing me and taking information in the process. Fine. I've got her number. I'll let her lead this scenario and I'll get what I want out of it, too.

"Not until you show me that magical hand transformation trick again."

She looks up at me through a fringe of dark lashes, and changes both hands resting on my hips, the half-shift almost as fast as my full shift. I reach down to clasp her furry hands, drawing them higher for a better look.

Her hands are larger than mine, covered in more muscle, and have long deadly claws at the end.

"Incredible!"

"Glad you like it. Do you know of another alpha who can change selected parts at will?"

"No, you're the first. I've heard of it, even seen a full transformation to a hybrid form from afar, but never up close like this."

Flush with my look of approval and acceptance, she

transforms further, altering her torso and arms. She expands before my eyes, stretching her shirt past the limit and ripping the fabric. Hints of fur-covered skin peek through the tears, enticing me to see what she looks like in her full wolfman form.

"Your physical mastery over your body is impressive." I emphasize my approval by running my hands up her sides, trailing my fingers below her much higher and fuller breasts. I'm reaching up, as her partial transformation has made her taller than me. "I bet the men in the pack love it as much as I do."

She melts within herself, returning to her normal size and shape. "Not exactly, no. I think it intimidates them." Sadness fills her expression and she turns naked, pain-filled eyes up to me. She comes on something fierce, pouring out the sexual pheromones when it suits her, but inside she's a lonely woman. Maybe even a little insecure. Unless, of course, she's playing me, and I have no fucking idea because I suck at spy games.

I cup her face in my hands and lean close. "It takes a strong man to handle an even stronger woman."

Our lips touch in a soft caress. I block out all thoughts of Candy and what my actions may mean to the two of us. It's safe to assume if I were a spy, I'd have no problems seducing an enemy and returning home to my real life at the end of the mission.

But I'm not a spy. And she's not an asset. This is not some game I'm playing. My heart burns in my chest, uncomfortable with what I need to do. This feels wrong. With no honor.

She's a fragile woman trying to lead a bunch of Weres who don't like or respect her—her only option to rule them with fear and brute force.

Her pointed tongue traces my bottom lip, asking me to open. I part my lips, sympathy and warmth easing the fist in my chest. I can do this. I can kiss her and turn my mind off. Her questing tongue duals with mine, darting away to skim over my top teeth.

My hands roam down her shoulder blades, skimming to her lower back and resting there, resisting the burning desire to grab her ass and haul her closer.

I break the kiss and whisper, "Show me again." I finger the warm skin between the torn gaps in her shirt. "I want to see you change." If I'm here to learn a skill, might as well try every chance I can get to watch it up close.

The lust in her eyes clouds her gaze for a split second, then she focuses on me and smiles, this time with pure joy. "You really want to see? You're not afraid?"

"It's not scary, Magdelena. It's beautiful, just like you are."

Her gaze doesn't stay on mine, but breaks away to look past my shoulder. I don't see her lips move in a spell of any kind, but her mind is elsewhere at the moment... perhaps calling the power up from within?

This time it's not only her torso that changes, but her head, too. Very quickly, the shorter woman expands to loom over me, her head larger and her elongated jaw filled with sharp teeth. Her skull doesn't transform into a wolf-human hybrid so much as it becomes a blend of the two, but more human than wolf.

Eager to convince her the new form doesn't repel me, I run my hands up to her cheeks again, but don't pull her down in a kiss like before. This time I stare directly into her eyes and say, "In this body your true self is represented equally. We're never fully human or fully wolf at any time, even when our outside shape reflects one. Like this, the real you is visible for all to see."

Her eyes have bled to a golden-green, looking even more alien in the mash-up of her new face. Her voice is rougher than before, but still obviously hers. "In a free world we could co-exist in our true forms." She turns her gaze within, seeing and not seeing me again. Very slowly she melts back to fully human. "But we're not in that world, are we?"

I sigh and wrap my arms around the fragile woman, so different with her walls down than when she's posturing in front of her pack. "No, we're not. And unfortunately, we have a killer to find."

CHAPTER THIRTEEN

VIVIAN

J on saunters from the bar, a slight swagger in his step. Rafe chuckles under his breath, the sound echoing through the car's interior. "He's not looking too worse for the wear. Perhaps Magdelena may have been *amiable* to his... advances."

I stomp down the uncomfortable emotions brewing inside me, the ones I'd rather not take out into the light and examine too closely. Doing so might make me tell him to stand down and not seduce the woman. Which would be bad for the three of us, not to mention Jon's dream of uniting the packs.

"As long as he's in one piece, we can face whatever the situation may bring."

Very soon, Jon stands outside the car, pulling open a door and then sliding in. "That was a productive meeting," he says, closing the door behind him. "She's agreed to no longer blackmail us and to work together. I think we're safe for now."

Jon fills us in on everything he and Magdelena covered,

including the beginnings of him getting closer to her to discover how she transforms.

"Have you ever encountered something similar in the past —two serial killers active in the same community at the same time?" Jon asks.

"Nope," I say. "Never. But then again, I was never a cop investigating murders in a large city. I bet they see a dozen murders a month, some connected, most not. As far as the magical connection, I have no idea—witches kept to themselves and so did we. Not enemies, mind you, but we didn't have cause to work together or have our paths cross often."

Rafe changes the topic. "Did you learn anything specific about the alpha's ability to change form?"

"I still don't know how she does it, but I don't think it's a trait she was born with. I think she acquired it over time." He shrugs. "Hopefully I'll figure it out soon, so I..." Jon breaks off and doesn't complete his thought.

A pang of sympathy fills my chest. "So you don't have to break her heart? I understand, Jon. Really, I do. Sometimes what we do to protect those who matter to us, means we have to hurt others. In a battle or one-on-one fight, the outcome is much clearer: win or die. But when we're going undercover, exploiting a person's weaknesses... it can be unsettling to the conscience."

Jon stares out the window, his posture and expression revealing nothing. "That's putting it mildly."

Rafe starts the car and pulls away from the curb. "I won't placate you with inane compliments and a slap on the back. It's hard. But you do what you have to do to survive."

Jon's face twists into a grimace and I know exactly what he's thinking, his thoughts projecting clearly to me, like a neon sign. *But what if you don't need to do it to survive? Does that make it better or worse?*

I turn to face front again, watching the streets carefully. It's not like I expect one of the pedestrians to be murdered, or to be jumpy and do something that indicates they could be a killer. Focusing on the mundane, the everyday happenings going on, helps to clear my head of the gruesome death George suffered. He was a nice guy. He deserved a chance to fight back.

"Where are we going now?" Jon asks.

Rafe slows the car before turning onto a narrow street. "To Justin's. He should know exactly when and where the breach in the Tribunal's wards occurred tonight. And who knows, maybe the ward is sensitive enough to pick up details of who passed and triggered the notification."

"Good idea," Jon replies. "Do we have time to stop and get something to eat?" His stomach growls in the dark interior, emphasizing his need. I hold back a snort of amusement at his predicament. "What? I eat a lot. Werewolves have a high metabolism."

I point toward a street vendor in the distance. "Stop there. We don't want our wolf hungry and unfocused."

The car glides to a halt, two of us piling out of the car. Rafe stays inside while the engine idles. "Get me the seasoned pork, would you?"

"You got it, hun."

Jon and I wait in line along the sidewalk, the smells of roasted meat wafting around us, tempting me to buy one for myself. My digestive tract prefers liquids with blood mixed in, so I resist the temptation, unwilling to live with stomach cramps and possible vomiting while my body tries to figure out what to do with the meat.

We're next in line to order when a tingle of magic washes over me. I look around, the hairs on my neck raised. "Did you feel that?" I ask Jon while trying to find the source.

He casts a wary glance up and down the street as well. "Yeah, I did. What the hell could it be? Is someone casting a spell? Could it be directed toward us?" He crouches slightly, leaving the food line, backing toward a nearby shop, his instincts to survive overriding his human side.

Our senses on high alert, we scan the nearby buildings and alleys, looking for any sign of movement. A child-sized form exits from the deep shadows of the alley across the street, directly behind the food vendor.

"Do you see it?" I ask, motioning to the misshapen creature, a blur of magic distorting its outline. Its head appears large, and it's hunched over, using an arm to assist on the ground while it walks in a shambling gait. There's a growth of some kind near the back of its neck, looking almost like a foot, leaving no doubt this thing isn't a small, pre-teen human out past bedtime.

"Yeah. Should we approach or follow?"

"Let's follow. You'll have to wait to eat." I glance quickly to Rafe and then back to the alley, opening our telepathic connection. *There's something in that alley I've never seen before, and it carries an air of magic. We're going to follow it.*

Rafe follows our gaze and sees what we intend to track. *Looks can be deceiving. Let me park the car and join you.* He whips the car around the vendor and speeds away, searching for a place to leave the vehicle. Jon and I are already halfway across the street, keeping watch on the small, deformed shape.

"Do you think it was human at one time?" Jon whispers.

"I think we should shut up and track it."

We trail it about fifty feet back, unwilling to get too close and reveal our presence. "It doesn't smell like anything I've encountered before," Jon says. "What do you think it is?"

I push my will out, slipping into Jon's mind, careful to stay on his surface thoughts and not see more than I'd like. *I think,* Jon stumbles as my voice fills his mind, *as a hunter you know better than to speak while hunting. Be quiet or I will leave you here.*

In answer, the Were coughs, stifling his awkwardness. *Sorry.*

In another hundred feet or so, Rafe joins us, already knowing not to say a word. Why can't all the people in my life be as smart as he is?

We follow it down a side street that runs behind the shops, as it makes its way through the city undetected. The tiny form slips into another dark alley three streets away from where it appeared. We hesitate at the opening, unsure of where it leads and whether or not we should follow, risking our discovery.

I look to both men, internally debating if I should open a mind link between the three of us. Jon opens his mouth to speak right when a gargled scream issues from the darkness. Without any time for deliberation, we rush toward the sound.

The short, humanoid form holds a bloody pipe in one gnarled fist, the stench of fresh blood and death on the air, a homeless man lying at its feet. The deformed creature looks up at us—a demented grin on its face, but its head almost looks like it's on the wrong way—and disappears with a blink into thin air.

"What the fuck was that?" Jon screeches, no longer seeing a need to be quiet since the killer vanished. "Tell me you both saw it disappear."

"I did," Rafe says while I nod my head. We enter the alley, the lingering aroma of magic on the air, combined with the fresh scents of death. The bloody pipe lays on the ground near the raggedly dressed form of a dark-skinned man in his fifties.

"There's nothing we can do for him. He's already gone." I turn on my heel and rush back to the street. "Search with me. Maybe whoever sent that thing is nearby."

We spilt up, each of us scanning the buildings, alleys, and sidewalks for anyone with a scent of magic clinging to them. After twenty minutes, the body of the homeless man is discovered by others, raising an alarm, assuring us the local police will be here soon and we should flee.

Rafe waves an arm to get Jon's attention from across the street, then the three of us high tail it to where he parked the car.

"I found nothing except the mad dwarf's scent," Jon says.

"Same here," both Rafe and I say together.

"What the hell was that thing?"

"Did you see how it walked?" Rafe says. "It used two arms and one leg. I couldn't see the second leg."

"I think the second leg was that growth on its back," Jon adds. "I could have sworn I saw toes. I may sound crazy, but it looked like the head was on backward, too."

"Who the hell would create such an abomination?" My mind whirls with all the details. I've never heard of anything like this thing we've just seen. I would deny its existence if I hadn't seen it myself. "And why?"

Rafe beeps open the car doors and we climb inside. "I think we need to visit the only person we know in the city who does magic and ask him."

Within moments we're driving the opposite direction, far away from the food vendors.

Jon's stomach growls in the silence of the car. "And maybe if I'm lucky he'll have food at his place, too."

J ustin opens the door, a guarded look on his face. "What are you guys doing back here so soon? I haven't been back to the Tribunal yet, so there's nothing new I can tell you. Rolando wasn't in when I called, either. No way I can set up a meeting."

I push past him, not waiting for an invitation, Rafe and Jon follow.

"Geez, just come right in, why don't you." The wizard shakes his head at our rudeness and shuts the door. "To what do I owe the pleasure?"

Unwilling to waste any more time, I reach out a hand, resting it on his wrist, while pushing the image of the creature into his mind. "Tell us what you know of this thing."

Justin jerks, trying to rip his arm away from my clinging clasp. His eyes widen with recognition and shock covers his face. "Holy shit. Where did you see that?"

I let go and step back. "Over in Centro, quite a few blocks from here."

"Why did you come here to ask me? You don't think I had something to do with it, do you?"

Jon stalks closer, his expression menacing. "Why don't you tell us, wizard for hire?"

"Back off, asshole." He moves into the small living room and plops into a chair, looking stunned. "I might be a wizard for hire, but I'd never have an *invunche* working for me."

I focus on the unknown name. "An *invunche*? What is it?"

"I've never seen one in real life. Just a drawing in an old spell book. Didn't know for sure if they really existed. Centuries ago, it's believed magic practitioners used them to guard their caves. And you know it was a long time ago because no one would voluntarily work in a cave these days."

"Could someone summon one to kill a target?" I ask. "Or perhaps use it as a personal hit man?"

"You mean like a magical conjuring? I suppose that could be a possibility. A hit man?" He shakes his head. "I doubt it. Like I said, these deformed dwarves were used as guards. Why?"

Jon prowls back and forth in an angry pace from the hall to the living room and back. "Because we just saw it bludgeon a homeless man to death."

"What the hell? No way! I don't know anyone in the city who would do such a thing."

"Do you have food?" Jon growls. "I'm really getting hungry."

"Jesus! Is that a threat you're going to eat me?"

Rafe's deep tones wash over the room, doing for them what he often does for me. "Calm down, gentlemen. Justin, he's hungry for food, not you. Care if he raids your kitchen? He's got a high metabolism." At Justin's nod of approval the disgruntled wolf lopes down the hall looking for the kitchen.

Within seconds we hear him rifling through cabinets and opening a fridge door.

"The first death this week was a young witch over on Belgrano." I say. "According to the M.E.'s report, she bled out due to multiple head contusions. And we just saw this thing beat a man to death with a pipe."

"You're thinking this thing could be what's committing the murders? But what about the man who was attacked by an animal? The invunche doesn't have claws—and the wounds would be lower due to its height. The latest news cast tonight reported the claw marks may be that of a large cat." He raises his voice so Jon can hear him over the clanging of plates. "That means werewolves are off the hook."

Jon grunts from the next room and Rafe replies with another question. "Argentina doesn't have any large predator cats, does it?"

"Deep in the jungles you can find jaguars and their black cousins, but they wouldn't come into the city. What about a werejaguar?"

Familiar with the Weres he's asking about, I answer. "I've met werejaguars before, it's the wrong scent. Doesn't match what I smelled at George's death."

"George who?" the wizard asks.

"He was a sentry at the Tribunal."

"You don't mean G.J. Marko, the really big, soft-spoken guy?"

"The one and the same," Rafe says.

"What happened? I really liked him. He was a stand-up guy for a vampire."

A sigh spills out of me over the useless death. "We found

him tonight. Throat and heart ripped out. Long slashes, made by claws from a hand if I had to guess."

The young wizard pales. "Holy shit." We're quiet for a moment, allowing the shocking news to sink in. "And you say it wasn't a werejaguar? And you're sure it's not a werewolf but a cat of some kind?"

I nod.

"The only other thing I can think of that could make large cat-like slashes would be something I read about a long time ago. An *hombre gato*, which literally means a 'man-cat.' But those are old legends and fairy tales—they aren't real."

"You're a wizard—you've got a vampire in your living room and a werewolf in your kitchen, and yet you don't think fairy tales could be real?"

"Come on, there's a difference. Almost every culture has old stories centered on people who can shape shift into wolves, or other scary stories about blood drinking creatures of the night. And magic?" He shakes his head, looking rather arrogant in his surety. "You can't look at any ancient society where magic didn't have some sway in everyday life. It may have gone by a different name, but magic has always been with us."

"Okay, fine," Rafe says. "If you can believe those things, why is thinking an invunche or hombre gato so impossible? Aren't they local lore? Seems to me local beliefs would remain strong no matter the time that's passed."

Jon joins us, a big plate of food balanced in one hand. "You'll need to do some shopping, man. 'Fraid I cleaned you out of most edibles."

The wizard throws his hands up. "Why don't you guys just

move in?" At Jon's speculative look he hastily adds, "I was kidding! Eat and leave. That's what I'd prefer."

"As if you have a choice," Jon says between bites.

Justin delivers a scathing death stare to the Were shoveling food into his mouth like a prisoner afraid someone else will take it before he finishes. He shakes his head and then looks back to Rafe and me. "Are you guys suggesting we have someone 'calling' these creatures from local myths and legends into reality to somehow... what? Kill people for a hidden agenda?"

"Well, that's the first idea we've been able to come up with," my husband says. "Can you think of anything else?"

Before Justin can reply, I jump in with another train of thought, the one we were originally headed here to discuss. "Right before George's attack, there was a breach in the Tribunal's territory wards tonight. Did you sense it?"

Justin nods. "Yeah, I wrote down the time in a log and called them with a warning, but they already knew—thanks to an alarm I installed that's associated with the spell."

"Can you tell us the time? Did any other details come through with the breach, like who or what may have triggered it?"

The wizard checks his phone. "It was at ten thirty. And that's all I know—oh, and that the person who triggered it was not human and not a vampire tuned to the spell, meaning an active member of the vampire community in the city."

"That's the extent your ward can register?"

"Think of it as an early detection system for possible threats. It's not foolproof and not as advantageous as a closed circuit camera system. But those can be tampered with and a spell can't." The young man shrugs. "It's got its uses."

"Agreed," Rafe says. "Especially if you only need a warning and can send out sentries to investigate."

"Which is what their protocols called for. I did my job," he says, a touch of defensiveness in his tone.

"Justin," I say, deciding to go with my gut. "What can you tell us about the magical imbalance that's created when a wizard does magic?"

CHAPTER FOURTEEN

RAFE

A cagey look crosses Justin's face. "Where'd you hear about that?"

"We have a witch who lives on our property in Alaska," Dria continues. "She told Jon a little of the basics that define witch magic versus wizard magic."

"The difference is slight, no matter what the witches would have you believe. They were born with a gift, we were smart enough to harness it even without their advantage. The imbalance you mention—it doesn't exist if you perform the ritual directions correctly with an acceptable offset.

"We like to think of it as paying tribute to the magic. For every spell, there is a price to even out the natural imbalance the use of the magic leaves behind. The best 'payment,' if you will, is the wizard's own blood.

"Witches act like the use of our blood as payment makes our magic dark or evil, but that's not the case—and I've seen a few witchy hypocrites using their own blood on a spell, too.

"Magic is inherent in the world around us—it's not defined

as good or evil. It just is. How someone uses it is what defines the magic as safe or dangerous."

Dria's brow furrows in thought. "Do all wizards use their own blood in spells? Or can they use someone else's?"

"I know of a few practitioners who use animal blood—from a butcher, not an animal sacrifice," he hastily adds. "I haven't heard of any imbalance issues with the substitution. The wizard usually infuses the blood offering with herbs and other additions to make it a more 'worthy' payment. But I— and I learned this from the wizard I trained under—stick to using my own blood. It's always on hand, and I never run out." He adds the last with a grin.

"These other wizards you mention, who use animal blood, could they be attempting more powerful spells that require a higher payment—and the animal blood isn't enough?"

Justin shakes his head. "I'm sorry I can't be of more help. I haven't heard of any wizard who created an imbalance they didn't fix. It's been drilled into us so much I doubt anyone would make the slip."

"You said 'they didn't fix,'" Dria says. "What does that imply? They could feel the imbalance?"

"Well, yeah, unless they've been knocked out or something. I don't know how they could not feel it."

I think back to the tingling sensation Dria and I have both felt in the presence of a spell activating. I wonder if that's what he means or if it's something greater.

"Have you ever sensed an imbalance after a spell?" I ask.

"Nope. Never."

"Then how do you know it can be easily felt?"

Justin shakes his head, his shoulders slumping. "That's a

very good point. If I haven't felt it, I have no idea how subtle or powerful the sensation is. Sorry I can't be of more help."

"Can you give us the names of the wizards who use animal blood? Maybe we can start there with asking if they've had any issues with spells lately."

Jon sets his plate aside, the ceramic clean. "How many wizards in the city are for hire? I never would have thought there'd be so many we'd need to make a list."

Justin puffs up, pride for his craft showing. "Hey, magic is big for protecting what you want to keep safe. All the supes in the city hire us. We don't have a guild or anything like that, but we each have specialties and refer business out to others if it's a field we're not as experienced with. Like me—I work primarily for specialized client needs. The vamps. Not really a magical specialty, per se, but they are a persnickety bunch. I'm not the only one they hire, especially with all the vamps here in the Seat of Darkness. But others work for weres, shifters, the occasional human, even witches."

"Why would a witch hire you?" Dria asks. "Can't they do it on their own?"

That arrogant grin is back again. "Not every witch can master every aspect of elemental magic. And some of the really old ones refuse to teach a witch not born with their same affinity, like if they specialize in earth magic they might not teach what they know to another witch who is better with fire. On the whole, they can be a catty bunch.

"A wizard doesn't have that issue. We're only limited by the knowledge we possess. Occasionally an air witch will hire a wizard more proficient in water magic to get a specific job done. But I'll be honest, they don't hire us much as they can normally find an expert in another element right in their own coven."

Dria sits on the couch, near the wizard's chair. "Have you ever heard the phrase 'never turn a witch'?"

The young wizard contemplates her question before answering. "No—what's it mean? Never turn them into a... what, a frog?" He shakes his head. "That doesn't seem very clear."

"Never mind, just wondered. Could a witch call up these ancient creatures—the invunche and the hombre gato?"

"I don't know. But if a wizard could, I bet they could, too. On the whole, they don't really like to share knowledge with us —like I said, too many think the use of magic by people not born with the gift is 'bad,' and that's a crock of shit."

"Well, a witch was the first victim. Maybe we should try and talk to the local coven."

"*The* local coven?" the wizard says with raised eyebrows. "Try the half-dozen local covens. This city is a hot bed for the supernatural."

"If that's the case, then why are we surprised creatures are appearing out of thin air and killing people?"

"Whoa now—did you say the invunche you saw came out of thin air? That sounds very odd. Not like he came through via thinning of the barrier, near where the imbalanced spell was worked. The legend said the invunche were guards to a wizard's cave. Maybe since we're not in caves anymore the creature hides near the wizard's home? Like in alleys and doorways. Where did you guys say you found it?"

"In an alley, off of Nine de Julio Avenue."

"Hmm... I know a wizard who lives in that area. I wouldn't

think he'd create an invunche to protect his spell lab, but anything is possible."

Jon raises a hand to halt the conversation. "Am I the only one who doesn't know what the hell he means by 'thinning of the barrier'?"

"It refers to the imbalance we spoke of before. If the imbalance is not corrected, then the barrier between our world and 'beyond' is thin, allowing whatever's on the other side to pass into our world."

"What's in the 'beyond'?" Jon asks.

Justin shrugs. "I don't even know if that part is true. It's just something I remember from my training. We've already established I've never felt an imbalance when I've worked a spell, so maybe I'm not the best person you should be talking to."

"Give us the name of the wizard who works near Nine de Julio."

He snorts. "Yeah, that's not going to happen. So you can charge over there and question the guy? It *may* be him—there's no certainty, and I sure as hell won't be the whistleblower that got the guy in hot water for no reason."

"All right then, let's try a different track. Is he the same one you know who uses animal blood in his rituals for payment?"

"No, he isn't. That's Bart, short for Bartholomew. He's older than me. Not sure by how much. He knew my mother."

"Your mom? She's a wizard, too?"

"Was. She got me started on the path when we moved here from the States, taught me most of what I know. She died six years ago."

"I'm sorry for your loss. Is it common for wizards to pass on knowledge to family members?"

He shrugs. "I don't know. Can't vouch for what others do, only what my mom did. She was a practicing Wiccan for years. But only when we moved here did she get involved with strong magic. Before that, she'd created a few herbal potions and tinctures, not 'real' magic, if you know what I mean. Once she discovered how to control real magic, through intricate rituals and payment of blood, she was like a sponge, absorbing everything she came into contact with on the subject."

"And how did she die?" Dria asks, concern in her voice. "She couldn't have been too old."

"She wasn't. We think a spell backfired. Officially the police ruled it as a kitchen fire."

"How horrible! Was she your only family?"

"In the area, yes. I haven't seen my brothers or father for almost two decades." He shrugs, clearly accepting of the loss after so many years. "Wouldn't even know where to start looking for them."

"Where does Bart live? We'd like to talk to him about his magic and see if there's even a slight imbalance when he casts."

After much back and forth, reassuring him we weren't going in to kill the old guy, Justin finally gives us both addresses—Bart's and the one to the wizard who lives near where we saw the invunche.

My wife raises another topic before we leave. "One last thing—we want to hire you."

Surprise crosses the wizard's face. "Me? Why?"

"You can make a tracking spell, right?"

"Yes, practically in my sleep. Who do you need to track?"

"Do you really need to ask? The same person we asked you to arrange a meeting with: Rolando. Rafe hasn't seen him enter or leave the Tribunal in the past weeks and we need to find him."

"Do I want to know what you'll do to him when you find him?"

Dria's face shuts down. "No. You don't."

Justin sighs. "Normally I wouldn't take a job like this. I find it much safer to stay out of personal vampire feuds. But..." he drags the word out. "I owe you after the shit Coraline pulled with using me to abduct you. Don't tell anyone in the Tribunal I did this for you, okay? I'd rather not piss off my best client."

She nods once, agreeing to his request. "How much?"

"Would you consider an ounce of blood?"

"Whose?"

"Yours."

"Done." She extends her hand for a shake. No doubt or hesitancy when she agrees. "I'll give you the ounce when we find Rolando."

"Fair enough. Give me your cell number. I'll get started on the spell and call you when it's ready."

We travel to Bartholomew's and stand silently on the empty street for a few minutes. Before we left, Justin gave a final suggestion to try listening near the older wizard's home, using the same senses that 'heard' his ward spells near the Tribunal. It's a stretch and we aren't sure the idea has any merit, but Dria did sense the invunche before we saw it, so we give it a shot.

All three of us stand on the sidewalk, looking like we're

waiting for a sign from God. It's days like this I wonder what the hell we're doing with our lives.

When we finally ring the man's doorbell, it's near midnight, and I think we're all a little frazzled. Probably me the most. A short, stout, wrinkled man opens the door. Thick glasses perch on the end of his nose, and he's wearing mismatched clothes with clashing patterns. I'd say he reminded me of Mr. Magoo, but he has a more important air about him, despite his shabby appearance.

Before any of us can say hello to the round little fellow, a laugh bubbles up my chest and spills out. Dria shoots me a glare, and Jon raises an eyebrow while I stifle my amusement at looming over the frail old man.

"Can I help you?" the man asks in a heavily accented voice, a loud sniff of insult aimed my way. He sounds like he could have lived or grown up in Russia or one of the newer Slavic nations.

"Are you Bartholomew?" my wife asks him.

"Yes. Bart for short. What's this about? Are you looking to hire?"

Quick on her toes, my wife replies. "Yes, we are. We'd like to ask you a few questions first, may we come in?"

"You think I'm inviting a vampire, a werewolf, and a rude, large human into my home who I don't know? You've got another think coming."

This time Jon laughs. Glad it's not just me having a hard time keeping it together.

"Dude," he nudges me. "He called you rude and large. Nailed it in one!"

I resist the urge to shove Jon. It's difficult, but I manage.

Dria extends her hand in greeting. "I apologize for the

intrusion and any fear our appearance may be causing. We've been referred to you by a wizard named Justin, who has done extensive work for the Tribunal of Ancients." The older man takes her hand and shakes. "We came by to ask for your expert advice on ritual magic, blood payment, and a possible magic imbalance from various causes."

Bart looks up and down the street, a nervous look on his face. "So, no job, eh? Come in, come in." He stands aside and ushers us in. "I try not to talk about this kind of stuff within earshot of a neighbor. Wouldn't want to give them a reason to hate me even more. Even though it is late enough that most of them are asleep. "

We enter his cramped dwelling, making me wish immediately we were back outside in the clear night air. Choking incense fills the small cluttered space. I feel like a bull in a china shop, one wrong move and I'll knock over a glass jar or run into a piece of furniture. Bookshelves and flat surfaces full of items covered in dust make my nose twitch worse than the overpowering odor.

Jon sneezes. "Man, that's a lot of patchouli you've got going on in here."

The small man doesn't respond, but rushes past us to another room deeper in. "Come in, come in. The kitchen is where I prefer to do business."

We follow him to a room that doesn't look like it's in the same house—bright, airy, open, organized, and the air smells clean and odor free. If I hadn't walked the short distance myself, I'd swear it was two different homes.

"The front room is a decoy, isn't it?" Dria asks. "Nice illusion."

Bart nods and climbs up onto a high stool next to the

kitchen island. "It works wonders at helping to preserve the doddering old-man persona. Most guests leave within a few minutes, overwhelmed by the clutter and stink."

"Smart." Dria joins him at the counter, taking the only other stool. Jon and I exchange a glance and remain near the doorway.

"If I didn't know better," she says, "I'd say this was a witch's home."

Bart bobs his head, glancing around at the copper pots and row upon row of books. "Yes, it would easily pass. They might not admit it, but witches and wizards are like cousins in the same family." He sniffs again, this time in derision. "Although they make us feel like dirty whores for taking jobs they deem beneath them." He motions around him. "Magic is magic—whether you have it in your blood, or you study for years and learn to harness that which is not freely given."

"Speaking of work—you're still a wizard for hire? I would have thought after a time you'd retire."

"Hmph. You sound like the local coven. Retiring means dying." He looks her hard in the eye. "What would happen to you if you stopped taking blood?"

"Are you saying your magic keeps you alive, like blood for a vampire?"

"Not really the same way, but after a fashion, yes. When I use magic, it enters me, too. Preserving the shell of my body a little longer. I'm one hundred and forty-seven years old. Don't look it, do I?"

Jon coughs, a sure sign he's going to say something he probably shouldn't. "If you mean you don't look dead, then no, you don't. But dude, you look wicked old."

"That's enough helping, Jon, thanks," Dria says. "How about I talk with Bart for now?"

Jon looks at the floor, clearly annoyed at being chastised.

"So you keep working to have a longer life—got it. When did you start using animal blood instead of your own?"

His face scrunches up. "Damn Justin. He told you that part too, eh?" He folds his arms over his chest, and slumps. "He'll see what it's like someday... to lose..."

"Yes?" my wife prompts, eagerness in her tone that we might be getting somewhere.

He shakes his head, a faraway look on his face. "When you do too much magic, when you don't shore up your soul and sense of self... well... eventually your blood isn't enough payment. You've diluted it with your greed. Then, you have to seek purer blood, blood untainted by magic usage. I use animal blood because I refuse to harvest from humans like they used to do in the old days."

"I would think such a practice would be frowned on nowadays."

"Oh it is, you bet your pretty little head it is. But that doesn't mean someone, somewhere, isn't doing it."

"Do you think another wizard in the city is using human blood to pay the price? And if they were, would that cause an imbalance?"

"Ahh... so that's where you're going with this. You think a magical imbalance could have caused the recent killings I've seen in the news. Now that's a thought, young lady. Normally I'd have said no, especially if you're looking my way," he says with a wink. "But there have been a lot of strange things seen lately."

This is the first we've heard of seeing strange things, and Dria leans forward in anticipation. "Sightings like what?"

Bart looks under his bushy eyebrows at her, well aware he's got her on the hook now. "I heard of a witch beaten to death. My first thought would have been one of your lot," he gestures to Jon, "but the witches who found her were positive it wasn't a Were. And honestly, I wasn't sure they were barking up the right tree." He looks to Jon and grins. "Pun not intended. It doesn't take a supe to beat someone to death. Just strength."

"Agreed," my wife says, her expression showing deep thought. "That was the first murder, as far as we know, but not a sighting like you mentioned a moment ago. Did the witches see something and tell you?"

"That's not my story to tell, you should ask them direct. Here," he says, grabbing a scrap of paper and jotting down a name and address. "This is the name of a witch I'm glad to call a friend. She's the one who helped me perfect my formula for using animal blood over my own."

"And how did she do that?"

"I use blood purchased from the butcher over in Monserrat. The animals die for a use, rather than being wasted to serve only as fuel for a spell, but because of that, the 'weight' or value of their collected blood isn't strong enough to be a true payment. If I infuse the blood with certain herbs, add blessed water, and perform chants of power, the blood becomes something more. It transforms into exactly what I need it to be: payment for a spell, with no life lost."

"Why don't the witches utilize the practice for their spells, too? Why would they need to hire a wizard?"

"Some witches do—or else I never would have had one who could teach me. But it's harder than it sounds. I made the ritual sound easy, in reality it's quite time consuming, taking a few days to complete. And most magic users want instant results. Even witches. If they have the contact and can get a wizard to do a task for less or faster than what they would charge, they'll do it."

Dria looks down at the paper in her hand. "Gwendolyn will talk to us? And it's not too late to see her tonight?"

"Yes. I'll call her when you leave so she can expect to hear from you."

My wife rises from her seat, extending a hand to Bart. "You've been a terrific help. Thank you."

CHAPTER FIFTEEN

JON

We hustle out of the strange little man's stinky house and make our way to the car. I'd offer to drive, but one look at Rafe's face tells me there's no way he'd agree. Man, he's looking tense and anxious. Too bad the basement apartment of ours is so tiny, I'm sure the couple could use some alone time to work off that stress.

Who am I kidding? If they decide they need to rip their clothes off to release stress and sexual tension, they will, whether I'm behind a paper thin wall or not. I swear, it's like they've got no respect for the sidekick.

My mind drifts to Candy and our last night together. She was so sexy and carefree with stating her desires. It's refreshing to be with a woman who knows what she wants and isn't afraid to ask for it.

And yet, I'm risking it all by dabbling with Magda to *possibly* learn how to half-shift. Could I forgive Candy if the shoe was on the other foot?

Dria opens her car door and slips into the front seat,

tension vibrating from her body. If I had to wager a guess, I'd say she's bottling up a lot of frustration over our inability to find Rolando on our own, and this current distraction of figuring out who is responsible these killings isn't helping.

"Do you really think it's possible someone is behind these murders or could they be more random?" I ask the couple when I join them in the car. "This whole magical imbalance crap seems rather convenient."

Rafe pulls away from the curb while answering, "Finding the right connection is what we need to do. So far, we've got two South American mythological creatures who sprang into being and started killing people—for no apparent reason. Or a reason we're still unaware of." The car speeds down the silent streets. "Were those people targets or victims of bad luck?" He takes multiple turns, not needing a map since the two know the city so well.

"I vote for a killer behind the deaths," I say, happy to play devil's advocate.

"I think it's this magical imbalance we've heard of," Vivian says.

"Really? And these things just poofed into existence?"

"We *saw* it 'poof' into existence, Jon," Vivian says, irritation showing in her tone. "And then kill. Were they summoned by a spell? Did the victims have an item on them that made them a target?"

I edge forward in the backseat to angle myself closer to the couple in front. "So either way, we're thinking the deaths are related to magic, right? No chance it could be another supernatural occurrence, like a curse has been triggered, or a bunch of individual incidents?"

"All happening within the tight timeframe of a few days?"

She shakes her head. "It doesn't make sense. I know we've got at least two different causes of death for four victims. Rafe is right, the next logical step is to discern how they're related."

"A curse?" Rafe asks. "That thought never occurred to me. A magical curse put in place, who knows when, and recently triggered? What do you think, liebling?"

"I have no idea. But if that's the case, it's still fueled by magic, right?"

"I would think so," I say. "A witch, a delivery man, a vampire, and homeless man. One beaten and died of blood loss, two ripped apart by sharp claws, and one we saw bludgeoned to death by a freaky little person known to protect wizards. Without questioning the witches, we can probably assume their witch was killed by the same thing we saw today, right?"

"I don't know," Rafe says. "You know what they say about assuming."

"Well then," his wife chimes in, "is it safe to assume a wizard is behind the deaths?"

"Why couldn't it just as easily be a witch?" I say. "Wouldn't it make sense to deflect suspicion elsewhere by summoning an invunche to do your killing, knowing the magical community would pin it on a wizard?"

It's quiet in the car for a moment while we all ponder the last statement.

Rafe clears his throat. "We haven't discussed motive yet. What would be the reason to kill a homeless man? How did he hurt anyone?"

Vivian says, "Could he have witnessed something he shouldn't have?"

We pull to a stop on a quiet street, a calico cat slinking

down the sidewalk. "We're here. Time to find Gwendolyn and see what the witch knows." Rafe opens his door and steps out, leaving Vivian and me alone in the car for a moment.

I lean closer, my breath moving the long red hair by her ear. "You can get into their heads, can't you?"

Vivian nods. "Yes. But I won't risk it."

"Why? Wouldn't it make this interview go *a lot* faster?"

"And what if they have a charm to alert or block them to such manipulations? Beginning with force won't garner any trust, and then they'd shut us out. We'd be back to square one."

We exit the car and join the hulking man on the sidewalk. The streets are empty, leaves swirling in darkened doorways. "This place is like a ghost town, what gives?" I ask.

Vivian closes her eyes and breathes deeply. She looks like she's concentrating, perhaps doing that thing she does in Alaska that allows her to connect with the resort and all the people on it. Think she calls it extending her consciousness.

We stand patiently beside her for a minute before Rafe breaks the silence. "Anything, darling?"

Vivian opens her eyes. "Nothing. I can sense life in all the buildings, but nothing beyond that. They could have protective wards in place we triggered with our arrival, or traps waiting behind every door. I didn't feel a tingle like we did at the Tribunal, but their defenses could be different. I have no way of knowing."

"Swell," I say, taking point and striding to the first home. "How about I lead, so I take the brunt of damage if anything goes sideways?"

Neither of them complains or raises a disagreement, so I knock on the door. It opens instantly, as if the attractive young woman stood on the other side, waiting for us. Even at our late hour, she's dressed in a long flowing dress, cinched at the waist. Her long brown hair is braided and drapes over one shoulder. I stifle my surprise at her quick answering of the door, and clear my throat, ready to launch into an introduction.

She jumps in before I have a chance. "My, my, my... a werewolf, a vampire, and a great big human... What a pleasant surprise," she says in a voice that holds no surprise. She steps to the side and ushers us in. "Please, come in. Bart called and told me you were coming."

I glance back at the deserted neighborhood, mouth open to question her about a promise of our safety in her home, when a firm hand shoves me between the shoulder blades, directing me to enter.

I shoot Rafe a dirty look as I step over the threshold. She should have said "big dumb human" instead.

The full-bodied woman snorts through her nose, my annoyed gaze meeting hers as she smothers her amusement. Once we're all inside she closes and locks the door behind us, making me feel like I'm Hansel and I've just entered the witch's home in the forest with my sister, Gretel. I shake off the macabre thought and try my best to look calm, cool, and collected. If I'm acting as the muscle in this trio, I should look it.

"So, master vampire. What brings you here with your mate and your werewolf? I don't think I've ever had one such as yourself in my home before."

"I thought you said Bart called you," I say. "Wouldn't he have told you why we were coming?"

"He was curt on the phone. Just told me to expect you."

Vivian arches an eyebrow, her only physical reaction to the

witch knowing exactly who we are. "Why don't you tell me why we're here?"

Interesting ploy. She's using the witch's knowledge against her to see what she has assumed or learned on her own, just by us being here.

"If I had to guess, I'd say it's related to the vampire who was slain a few hours ago in the Tribunal's neighborhood."

Vivian answers with another question. "Would it only be the vampire's death that concerned us?"

The witch looks surprised. "Why would your kind worry about Sophia's death? We already cleared vampires as the possible murderer."

"And who do you think killed her?"

"More accurately would be 'what,' but we're getting ahead of ourselves. Please, come in and sit. Have some tea."

She directs us to the dining room table in her cramped home—all the houses in this section of town being small—where we all take seats. Mugs already sit arranged on the tablecloth, a teapot in the center. I get a creepy vibe watching her pour the tea slowly into her cup. I have no intention of drinking anything this woman offers me, no matter what Vivian says.

It smells okay, but I'd rather be safe than sorry.

Vivian smiles at the witch's show of hospitality. "We're fine. But thank you for the offer." She folds her hands on the table in front of her. "Tell us about the strange sightings."

"Ahh... that's what brought you here then. Nosey old wizard." She crosses her arms over her chest. "They're nothing. Just whisperings."

"Whisperings of what?"

"Legends come to life. Poppycock if you ask me."

It's strange hearing the old phrase come out of the young witch's mouth. Then again, maybe she's not as young as I think. Vivian doesn't look a day over twenty-five.

"The sightings wouldn't happen to be of a misshapen dwarf, using his arms to help walk, would it?"

She snorts, uncrossing her arms and reaching for the tea. "I believe the PC term these days is 'little person.' I would have expected more from a master."

Vivian ignores the dig and keeps going. "Should I take that as confirmation?"

"I can't confirm or deny something I've not seen myself. Would be rather presumptuous of me."

"Can you tell us who claimed to have seen something? Maybe we can ask them ourselves."

Sorrow crosses the witch's face, indicating she isn't as unmoved by our questions as she cares to pretend. "It was Sophia who told me she saw something. Right before I sent her out for more herbs."

Her attitude makes sense now. It's a front to cover up her guilt. She fears she may have been the one to send the younger witch to her death. I glance at Rafe and Viv, their eyes searching out each other then mine, possibly to confirm we all share the same suspicion.

"Tell us what you know of the witch's death."

"Not without payment."

Another smile, this one cold and calculating. "What do you want?"

A bold look crosses Gwendolyn's face. "Your mate's blood. Not much, just a small amount."

"Not a chance."

The witch raises a shoulder. "Couldn't hurt to try."

"Gold?" Vivian asks, eyebrow raised. She looks confident, like she knows exactly where this game is going to lead.

"I have no need for gold. The wolf's blood?"

I squirm in my seat, uncomfortable that Rafe and I are being bartered like yesterday's bread.

"No, again." A peaceful look steals over the vampire's face. "How about mine?"

"You would grant me your blood, vampire? Over theirs?"

Vivian raises an elegant shoulder. "I know you intend to use it in spells. I also know if you try and use it to control me in any way it will backfire on you, leading me straight to you. And make no mistake—you try that and I'll kill you."

"Well done." The witch smiles, showing all her pristine teeth. "But why not give me theirs, over yours?"

"Because I can thwart any attempt to become your puppet or have magic used against me. They may not be able to. I won't risk their safety. Even at the expense of my own."

"Bravo." The young woman leans back in her chair and examines Vivian more carefully. "A vampire with a heart and a conscience. You must not be from around here."

"I was. A long, long time ago. Way before your time, Gwendolyn."

"Since you know my name, why not tell me yours?"

Vivian tilts her head to the side, a calculating gleam in her eye. "You may call me Vivian. This is my husband, Rafe, and Jon, my vampire servant."

"Quite a strong contingent to visit one little ole witch, wouldn't you say?"

Rafe speaks, frustration in his tone. "You've already established that we're an odd group to show up at your door. What do you intend with my wife's blood?"

"Nothing you need to be worried about, I assure you. I want it to work a few powerful spells." She nods at Vivian. "And none of it will trace back to your lovely wife in any way, shape, or form."

I recall something Bart said. "I thought witches considered using blood beneath them, and that's why you guys look down on wizards."

"Not exactly. We may use blood as an ingredient in a ritual to bind and fuel the spell. A wizard uses blood in every spell, no matter how simple or intricate, to *pay* for the imbalance their use of magic causes. Since they can't command it like we do, they rip it from the earth and air around them, forcing it to their whim. Such a practice extracts a toll on the world around us—thus the payment in their blood."

"How was your witch beaten to death behind the herb shop? Was she that vulnerable all alone or was she set up to be vulnerable?"

"Based on other witnesses, we think the killer was an invunche—an ancient creature not seen in these parts for over a hundred years. Traditionally they serve wizards, but we're not ruling out other spell casters just yet."

She's mirroring exactly what we discovered with Justin already. But that last bit has me speaking up. "Other spell casters?"

"You've heard of fae, haven't you? Humans aren't the only ones who wield magic to their advantage. We're just the most prominent users in the city."

Vivian nods, asking another question. "Do you think someone called the invunche to attack her on purpose?"

Gwen shakes her head. "It doesn't seem likely. She was a

novice, new to the coven, out running errands. Too young to have made any enemies in the community yet."

"What about the coven she was a part of—could they have an enemy who targeted their group directly, and she was an easy target?"

"Again, I don't think so. On the whole, the witches in town work together. There's no place for killing your equal with magic based on nature."

Rafe leans forward, pouring himself some tea, brave bastard. "What about the fae you mentioned. Would they have a reason to target Sophia?"

"The fae prefer to stick to the woods. We don't interact with them enough to warrant an attack."

Vivian tries another track, one we keep circling back to. "We heard your coven has hired wizards in the past. Could one of them be unhappy with payment and seeking vengeance?"

"It's true, I know of witches who've hired wizards for tasks they felt were too staining to their aura. But I have no idea if any of them are disgruntled or unhappy with the arrangement."

"Stain their aura? We haven't heard that before," Vivian says. "What do you mean?"

"All magic, no matter who is wielding the spell, leaves a taint. If your aura is strong, you can easily absorb it to offset the 'cost.' But some useful spells are a little darker and require more cleansing to use them safely. In that case, a busy witch may hire a wizard to do the spell to avoid the extra work."

"What does that do to the wizard's aura? Wouldn't the darker spell cause them harm?"

"Not when they are using their own blood in payment."

Vivian watches the witch closely. "Why wouldn't witches use their own blood?"

"Like I said before, we do—just very sparingly. Casting with your own blood comes with risks, too. And a smart witch avoids risk to live longer."

"What type of risks?"

A heavy sigh comes from the witch. "Your blood better be worth all this. Because of the magic in a witch's blood, we can't add it to powerful spells without the blood changing the core of the spell."

"Wouldn't that mean the spell won't work properly?"

"Yes. And doesn't that defeat the purpose of doing complex magic in the first place? If you're going to go through all the damn trouble, it better work out right."

A few things slip into place for me. "So what you're saying is—mixing a witch's blood into a spell to pay for it, could actually mess it up? That must be why you guys hire wizards. Their blood is pure of magical taint and makes better payment."

A scowl crosses the young woman's face for an instant. "I wouldn't call it a taint. But I have noticed if I'm doing earth magic, which is my strength, and add my blood as a binder, it doesn't always come out right."

"I have more questions about the young witch's death," Vivian says.

"Let's not forget payment, night-walker. Don't make me get mean."

Vivian reaches into her pocket and withdraws a silver-bladed knife. "Do you have a suitable container?"

The witch scurries into the kitchen. In a moment we hear cabinets opening and closing.

"Is this wise?" I whisper to Vivian.

She shoots me a glare and answers in my head. *Never fear, I know exactly what I'm doing.*

The witch returns with a small clay pot, two inches high, two inches across, with a cork in the wide-mouthed opening. She places it on the table in front of Vivian.

Without hesitation, the vampire draws the pot to her, removes the cap, and slices the sliver blade across her palm. Blood spills out of the wound, cascading into the jar. Power punches me in the gut, expanding to encase the entire group. "May my blood be used only for good and never against me and mine."

The witch's face scrunches up a bit, unhappy over that last bit. "Tricky vampire. I gave you my word."

"And I don't know you. Your word means squat." Blood wells in the cut, but doesn't close, the wound resisting immediate healing due to the silver in the blade. The redhead stares at the witch, deep into her eyes and issues a command, "Open your mouth."

Caught off guard, the witch's mouth opens. Quick as a wink, Vivian dips a finger from her opposite hand into the blood in her palm and raises it over the other woman's mouth. One drop falls into Gwen's open maw before she's aware of what Vivian's doing.

The moment the blood hits her tongue she jerks, snapping her mouth shut, face livid in anger. "You tricked me!" She spits on the floor, eager to dispel the vampire blood from her system.

Vivian sits back in her chair, completely unperturbed. "Now we're bound, you and I. You try to go against your promise and I'll know immediately."

"You've linked us! How dare you!"

"As I said, I don't know you nor do I trust you. You have my blood. Any harm that befalls me will befall you as well."

Won't the bond wear off in thirty days? I hear Rafe's voice through my connection with Vivian, she must have opened a mind link to the three of us.

Yes, but she doesn't know that.

"Goddamn, vampires!"

CHAPTER SIXTEEN

VIVIAN

Due to our new connection, I feel the anger and fear rolling off the witch, but I ignore it. Did she honestly think she could take my blood with no price? Fool. Information is not worth my blood, only a witch would think it was.

"Now, let's get back to business," I say, placing the stopper in the jar and offering my palm to Jon to lick. His werewolf saliva will help the healing process despite the silver blade that caused the wound. "Or would you rather I take my blood and leave?"

His silky tongue rasps over the cut, drawing my eyes to his. I hope it's not enough to make him drunk with a flood of new power. We need him focused.

"Conniving bloodsuckers! That's why we never do business with you people. A simple exchange of information for blood and you take it too far."

I rise from the table, the blood vial in my hand. "Okay, we'll see if we can get the rest of the information we seek elsewhere."

"Fine! Fine." She thrusts her hand out. "Give me the blood and we'll get started."

I return to my chair, careful to keep the blood vial in front of me until we're done. "Who has your coven hired within the last week?"

"You're referring to right before Sophia was killed?"

"Yes."

"We hired at least three other supes that I know of—one was a local wizard named Justin for a specific task. I don't know his last name. He's good. He's done work for us before and has never been a problem. Another job went to Bart, whom you already know. And a third job was hired out to the local werewolf pack. That was for an upcoming security job for the winter solstice."

The three of us go silent at the mention of Justin. It takes me a minute to recover, and in the interim, Rafe jumps in.

"What did Justin do for you?"

"Same thing he does for the Tribunal. He specializes in protective wards to surround our neighborhood. It ensures none of our witches are harmed."

A tingle creeps across my flesh. None of us felt anything when we drove through the ward. Which might mean the ward is down now. Either through tampering or it failed.

"The ward didn't work too well for Sophia, did it?"

A frown forms on Gwendolyn's face. "She was beyond the ward when she was attacked."

"Was there anything different about Justin's casting that day?"

"I have no idea. I wasn't there."

"Can you find us someone who was?"

"No. I won't subject anyone else to being bound to you."

I smile. "You play with fire, Gwendolyn, you're going to get burned. How about the job you hired Bart for—what did that entail?"

"He has an affinity for animals. I think this time he came in to cast health and pain nulling charms for the animals we're planning to sacrifice at the winter solstice tomorrow. He was cheaper than the vet and faster than us doing something similar."

"Purifying and improving the health of your sacrifice, and removing their coming pain, sounds like something a witch would want to do on her own, not hire out."

"Not when you've got an entire flock of chickens and a small herd of goats to prepare—and the spells you're using must be cast individually over every animal. Bart was a better choice."

Gwendolyn reaches a shaking hand out to her tea mug, taking a sip to fortify herself. "I've told you everything I know," the witch scowls again. "I think it's time you all leave."

I slide the blood across the table to her. "Thank you."

"Hmph." The witch snatches up the ceramic pot.

"My blood is very strong. Use it sparingly in your spells and it will last you a while."

We leave, the door slammed unceremoniously behind us.

"Your blood seems to be a popular request lately," Rafe says.

"Of course. Whenever you deal with magic users that's a given. But I never give without protecting myself first. They're idiots if they think anyone my age would hand over that much power with no constraints in place. One drop and they're bound for thirty days. Not a bad bargain in my mind. They have to use the blood before it spoils."

"Now what?" Jon asks on our way to the car.

"Now, we face the uncomfortable fact that Justin is our primary suspect."

The phone in my pocket rings. I don't recognize the Argentine prefix, but answer it anyway.

Justin's desperate voice comes crackling over the line. "I need help. I think I'm the source of the imbalance. My neighbor is dead and the cops are swarming outside."

"We're on our way."

Our mad dash through the crowded streets amps up the tension level in the car.

"How the hell could we have missed that he's the source?" Jon asks. "I know the guy is cocky and arrogant, but come on... it didn't occur to either of you?"

I grind my teeth and stare straight ahead, annoyed with myself for thinking Justin was more capable than we thought. "He hid his weakness well. Confident, arrogant swagger... he had the all-powerful mentality down pat."

"Jesus, Jon," Rafe barks from the front seat. "If we knew, don't you think we would have stopped him immediately? Do you think we would have hired him?"

"How the hell should I know? Vivian has a way of jumping into the fray whenever it suits her. And you just blindly follow her, never stopping to say no."

My anger pulses under my skin, making me wish I could lash out and humble the out-spoken Were. But I don't. He's right, but I'll be damned if I tell him. While I have been more impulsive the past few days, in my defense, all this crap is not something I deal with on a regular basis. Will that matter to the hotheaded Were? Probably not, so I keep quiet and let him vent his frustrations.

Rafe grips the wheel tighter, also refusing to rise to Jon's comment and start a fight. "If you'd like to go back to Alaska, we can arrange it."

"No way in hell! You really think I'd walk away and leave her to your protection again? That worked so well last time, didn't it? She was almost killed while you were on the job, asshole."

"Enough!" I screech across the car, loud enough to echo back at us. "In the end, no one is responsible for my safety but *me*. It would be best if you both remembered that. Jon," I say, turning in my seat and facing the agitated young man. "I know this crap from you is coming out now because of what happened to me recently.

"But one thing I didn't tell you about my torture and why I almost didn't pull through—I thought Rafe was dead. *Taken from me forever*. At the moment, my pain was so great I had no desire to continue fighting. I was ready to die. I hoped my death would reunite me with him.

"My love for you, the resort, our lives... none of it mattered in the end. Rafe is what keeps me sane and solidly in the here and now. Without him, I didn't want to face another moment of pain and torture. I know it's hard to hear, and even harder to accept, but when the day comes for me to die, it will be a day of my choosing and no one else's. Not even Coraline could have taken from me what I was unwilling to give."

Jon looks shocked and hurt. "But if I was here you never would have been in that position. Never would have had to make the choice of life or death."

I smile, hoping he can see what I can't put into words. "We don't know that, Jon. It all happened very fast. We were taken in our bedroom, minutes before sunrise, in a place where we'd been promised no harm would come to us. You don't sleep with us. You wouldn't have been there to stop it."

Rafe makes the turn onto Justin's street and stops the car with a hard braking to avoid the police cars. "Shit. We'll have to park on the next street over and come in through the back."

"I could have found you faster, saved you from the pain."

"Dammit, Jon!" My anger getting the best of me. "It's the past. Let it go."

Rafe turns the car around and in a minute we're parked and spilling out into the darkness of the deserted street. We scan the narrow road and Jon points toward the opposite end. "Down there. I see an alley. We can move quietly between the houses and make our way over to Justin's street."

We walk briskly toward the alley, unwilling to call attention to ourselves by running, just in case anyone is looking outside. The alley is more of a narrow side street between the older homes. We scuttle over the older pavement, on the lookout for anything out of the ordinary pursuing us.

After much slinking and avoidance, we make our way to Justin's back door. One light rap and he opens it, hustling us inside his kitchen. The lanky man looks shaken, his demeanor completely changed from earlier. His gaze shifts over our shoulders, to the darkness beyond, as if he's searching for someone or some *thing*. The door closes behind Jon with a thud, blocking out the sirens on the street. I think I hear an ambulance arriving.

"What happened?" I ask, my voice soft and reasonable, hoping it helps to reduce his distress.

He runs one shaking hand through his hair, shoving the longer strands back. "I... I don't know. I was following the steps for the tracking spell like I always do. But when it came time for payment, my blood was... I don't know... rejected. It turned to dust when it hit the ritual bowl. Ruining all the ingredients. That's never happened before."

"Did you feel anything happen around you? Like that tingle we feel when we cross a charmed ward?"

"No. Nothing."

"You didn't sense a disruption of any kind, but you still think you're the source?"

"My blood turned to dust! Did you not hear that part? That's fucking freaky and—just wrong! There's no other word for it. Wrong." He paces, hands on his hips, head down. "And to make matters worse, I think I saw the invunche leaving my neighbor's house. It's here. That creepy little fucker is here!"

"Okay, man," Jon says, his hands moving in a slow-down gesture. "You're good. No need to freak out."

"No need to freak out? Are you fucking kidding me?" He faces the unflappable werewolf, looking a bit like he's about to burst a vein in his head. "Something I did may have caused the death of five innocent people! How much more serious can it get?"

"Six?" the wolf offers, with an unsympathetic look on his face. "Come on, dude. You fucked up. We'll help you fix it."

"Can you save my nice neighbor who used to bake cookies for me, or bring those other people back to life? No! You can't."

"Beat yourself up over it on your own time. Right now, we need to concentrate on stopping whatever is killing people."

My husband isn't much better than Jon. Rafe looks like he wants to smack Justin. Instead, I step in and rest a hand on the frantic wizard's arm. Cool, tranquil energy flows from my touch over his skin. Instantly, his face loses tension and his shoulders release from the bunched-up position around his ears.

He looks at me, surprise in his eyes. "Whatever you did, vampire, it worked. I don't feel like I'm going to run out of the house screaming anymore."

"Who would have guessed you were the panic and run type," Jon says teasingly, trying to get the wizard back to normal. Or at least I hope. With Jon you never know.

Rafe's deep voice booms across the kitchen, bringing us all back on track. "If you're the cause, what does that mean? You never sensed an imbalance."

The young man shrugs, the lost look from earlier threatening to creep back into his gaze. "My blood was refused. The payment wasn't accepted." He swallows. "My blood is no longer strong enough to work magic."

"Isn't that what Bart said happened to him?"

Justin whips his head up to look at Rafe. "That's why he uses animal blood? His own blood is no longer valued as payment to work a spell?"

I remove my hand but stay near the on-edge wizard. "From what he described, it may not be a permanent... shunning... for lack of a better word. He mentioned ways to restore or shore up your aura from the draining that using magic can take on a wizard."

"Is it that meditation and chakra balancing crap? He's mentioned it to me before." His shoulders slump in defeat. "But I was too sure of myself to listen."

"It's never too late, Justin. You can recover from this."

"Never too late? I should be in jail for the people who died."

"Did you intend to kill anyone when you did your job?"

Rafe asks, his voice detached and clinical.

"No, obviously."

"Did you even know the homeless guy or the delivery man?"

"Nope. But would their families care that I didn't know them, or intend to hurt them? Would a court of law?"

Rafe steps forward, getting into Justin's face to get him to listen. "Don't kid yourself, Justin. Even if you're responsible because you inadvertently caused the magical imbalance that brought those creatures to this plane, there is no judicial system that could persecute you based on the evidence."

"Do you think that matters to me?" He steps back, unable to meet Rafe's gaze. "I know what I did."

"Then you must work to make amends," Rafe says, "instead of placing blame on yourself. Even if it takes you the rest of your life to pay restitution. Be part of the solution. Not the problem."

"What the hell is that supposed to mean? I was the problem, man."

"It means," I butt in. "Those *things* are still loose in your city. What do you intend to do about it?"

Justin straightens, a determined look finally replacing the despondent one. "We have to hunt them down and kill them."

"Starting with that deformed little person who lives outside a wizard's cave," Rafe says.

"Did you see where it went when it left her house?" I ask.

He nods. "To the storm drain out front. Right where the cop car is parked. And don't kid yourself. They're going to be knocking on my door any minute to ask me if I saw or heard anything. I'm lucky they haven't made it here yet."

Rafe nods, glancing toward the front of the house.

"Probably still processing the scene for evidence."

A thought occurs to me. "You haven't been to her house recently, have you?"

"No, thank God. At least I won't have physical evidence tying me to the crime scene."

Rafe motions him toward the spell ingredients on the table. "All right then. You clean up the remains of your spell casting and get ready for your guests, and we'll slip out and hunt down the invunche. Hopefully he won't have gone far."

"Would you like me to stay and help?" I offer. "You need to redo the tracking spell, right?"

"And how will I pay for it?"

"With my blood, of course." I smile, trying to reassure him. "And the good news? You'll need much less than you think."

We watch as Justin clears away the ruined herbs before setting up the new ingredients. "I'm not taking any chances on the previous spell. I'm starting from scratch."

"What happens if the cops knock while he's busy?" Jon asks. "Can you stop in the middle?"

"Good point," I say. "Why don't you two go out the front—let the cops see you. You can pretend to be residing here or visiting, but manage to reveal you saw nothing and waste their time while you're at it."

Rafe nods. "And then when they're done, Jon can track the invunche and destroy it."

"Am I going after it alone?" the Were asks.

My husband walks toward the front door, calling over his shoulder, "Is the big bad wolf afraid of the deformed little person?"

Jon cocks his head to the side. "When you put it like that, how can I possibly say yes and keep my balls?"

CHAPTER SEVENTEEN

RAFE

Jon and I spend the next twenty minutes outside the front door, slowly answering the police's questions, feigning we don't speak Spanish, which delays the officers more. When they're sure we have no information of any importance to relay, they leave us, moving on to the next house.

The Were casually walks to the nearest storm drain, pretending to pick something up from the ground, and takes a deep breath. He looks back at me and nods. He returns to my position, speaking out of the side of his mouth. "It's down there all right. What do you want to do?"

"Let's go back to where the car is parked, get into the sewers there, then track back here."

Jon's face scrunches up. "That was what I was afraid you'd say. Shit. It's gonna be messy."

"Look on the bright side," I say.

"Oh yeah, and what's that?"

"These are storm drains. Not sewage lines."

He snorts. "Yeah, big difference—and yet, I'm still going to be covered in filth. I can almost guarantee it."

"Quit your candy-ass bitching, pretty boy. Time to get dirty."

"Spoken like the man who's staying up top."

"If I was a small as you, maybe I could fit down there."

"Hah! Didn't realize I was working with the Hulk. However do you fit your huge head through the average door?"

I shake my head at the nervous banter. "Sideways, asshole."

We hustle to the other street, avoiding police on the way.

I pry up the closest manhole cover and motion for Jon to proceed me. "All yours."

"Seriously, you're not coming to help?"

"You really think you need help with one little invunche?" I know questioning his ability is the best way to ensure he'll boast he can do it himself.

"Nah, you're probably right."

"How about I watch the exits in case he makes a break for it?"

Jon nods and drops into the man-made hole. "Frakin' dark down here," the Were says, using his old favorite "swear" from Battlestar. Despite the job he has to do, he still aims for humor. Gotta love that about the guy.

"Use your other senses."

"Yeah, I know how to hunt. You can shut up now."

I close the lid and move to the nearest drain, listening for sounds of the werewolf. To Jon's credit, I don't hear so much as a scrape of shoe or foot shuffle in the dark. He's gone into wolf mode rather quick.

I extend my senses, just like my lovely wife has taught me,

hoping to catch a mental trace of the furball. I walk down the street to a nearby alley, staying close to the storm drains. After a few useless minutes, I admit defeat. I'm not mentally connected enough to Jon to sense him or his movements. I'm sure Dria would have no problem, but I'm out of luck.

Best bet might be to return to the drain outside Justin's house and see if there's any noise coming from there. I make my way past the police cars to an open stretch of street. It appears the big push of investigating is done, there's only two cars remaining on the block, and the ambulances are gone.

I stand next to a lamppost and wait, mere feet from the storm drain closest to Justin's front door. After a time, I wonder if Jon's okay down there. It's been quiet. Surely a big, bad werewolf can take care of one hunched and deformed little person, right?

It's way past two a.m. All the homes on the street are dark, despite the excitement since midnight. Checking right and left to make sure I'm not seen, I sit on the curb next to the drain. I relax, taking a deep breath, and extend my senses out and down into the darkened opening.

There! I sense something. Movement, a shuffle of some kind. Before I can blink, there's a blur of a small form creeping out of the storm drain. Dammit. Looks like the creature is quietly slipping away from Jon.

The streetlight shines down on its deformed head, with what looks like a small leg poking out from behind its skull. I draw back my fist and slam it forward against the creature's head, forcing it to the pavement and momentarily stunning it.

I grab the slight form and pull it the rest of the way out of the drain. It's light, probably weighs under a hundred pounds. I know I'm supposed to kill it, but pity washes over me. Who brought this kind of thing to life in the first place? Why twist a little person to become... this. I flip it over on its side and drag it away from the opening.

I hear metal scrapping behind me and whirl to face what made the sound, while still keeping the unmoving invunche in my sights. A manhole cover in the center of the street slides open, and Jon pops his head out.

"You got it?"

I nod, motioning to the creature. "It seems pretty harmless."

"You're forgetting we saw it kill a guy with a pipe earlier tonight."

"Yeah, but why? Has anyone tried to find out why it's doing what it's doing?" Pity and compassion well up inside me. "Is it even aware?"

Jon jumps out of the sewer and returns the manhole cover to its original position. He walks to the creature and squats down near its head.

"Hey, little guy, can you hear me?"

The thing's eyes open and it launches at him, a knife clutched in its right hand. A guttural grunt erupts from its mouth, but no words. Jon reacts lightning fast, deflecting the knife and breaking the invunche's arm in one fluid move. With one powerful punch straight to its head, Jon crunches the invunche's skull with a sickening crack. The creature collapses, blood on its deformed face, but not flowing like a head wound normally would, indicating he's killed it with one blow.

"Hell," I mutter, while looking back and forth on the street carefully. "Right here in front of Justin's house. Really? What if the cops come back out?"

Jon doesn't hesitate, he scoops up the inert body in one fluid motion, tossing it over his shoulder. "Let's get moving." He takes off at a jog, heading back down the alley to an access gate that will get us to Justin's backyard.

Everything happened so fast, I doubt a full minute has elapsed since the thing started crawling out of the sewer. Jon vaults the fence, hopped up on adrenaline from the brief encounter.

The moment he lowers the body to the ground outside Justin's backdoor, the creature turns to dust. Both of us stare at the remains in disbelief.

"Did you have any idea that would happen?" Jon asks.

"Not a clue," I say, running a hand over my head. "This shit is weird." I step over the dust and knock on the door. "Maybe Justin will know what the hell is going on."

"Uh-huh, sure. The guy who didn't know his blood was not up to par for making spells. Yeah, he'll be a big help. We should go back to Bart. At least he's lived a long enough life to *have* a freakin' clue."

Justin opens the door, a relieved look on his face. "You've got him already? Just like that?"

I motion to the pile of dust. "Not exactly. That's all that's left of the little guy." Justin comes out to investigate the remains and I step through the door into his kitchen, eager to make sure Dria is okay.

She sits at a small table in the corner, looking over the ingredients Justin has assembled. "*Little guy?* Sounds like you feel sorry for the invunche. What happened?"

Jon answers from behind me before I can. "Nothing to report really. He was hiding down below, came out when I got too close. Rafe stunned him and when I approached it attacked me with a knife. I broke his arm and hit him hard, one punch to the face. It crushed his skull. End of invunche."

"Not a worthy opponent," I say, still feeling uncomfortable with killing the deformed creature.

Dria rises and comes to me, placing a small hand on my arm. "It was a 'he' at one time?"

I nod. "As far as we could tell."

"And you're feeling bad because of its size?"

Justin interrupts us, coming back in and grabbing a garbage bag from under the sink and a large plastic serving spoon from a drawer. He sees us looking at him and pauses before heading back outside. "The remains could be valuable for a spell. No way am I wasting that."

My stomach turns and Dria sends a soothing wave over me, halting the worst of the nausea. "I found a book with local lore in Justin's collection," she says. "You're correct, that invunche was a little person at one time. They often took humans of smaller stature or pre-teens. Over many years it was deformed by magic and turned into what you saw.

"Its sole purpose was to guard a wizard's cave and kill whomever came too close. It may not have looked like much, but never underestimate the element of surprise. From what I read, it couldn't speak, and there was no longer any remains inside of the human it once was. They lived for hundreds of years, often longer than the wizard who created it."

"Doesn't make me feel any better for killing him."

"I killed him, so don't worry your pretty little head about it." Jon sounds like he's taking joy in throwing my words back at me.

Justin returns with the full bag and my stomach lurches. The callousness disturbs me.

"Waste not, want not." Justin shrugs. "Don't judge me, dude. It's hard to be a wizard for hire."

Jon chuckles. "You mean used to be. With dust for blood, you're out of business."

The tall wizard looks at my wife. "Not with her help, I'm not."

Dria lets go of my hand and returns to the table. "I'm helping with only this spell, Justin. After that, you're on your own."

"What about the blood you promised me in payment?"

"And how long will that last you? You have a bigger problem, my boy. One you need to figure out how to handle or your wizarding career is over."

Justin shrugs, unwilling to admit to the horrible bind he's in. "Bart uses animal blood. Maybe I can, too."

Dria motions to the spell components. "Let's get back to the locator spell and find Rolando. The rest will take care of itself."

Justin puts the bag of invunche remains in a large bin under his sink and focuses on the task at hand. "It'll take me an hour to complete all the chants and add all the ingredients again at the appropriate times. Vivian's blood will act as the catalyst and payment all at once."

"Okay," Jon says. "So you don't need us for the next hour, right?" He looks my way and nods. "We should go after Cat Dude while his scent is still fresh near the Tribunal."

"Fresh? That's been hours," Justin says, at the same time Dria says, "Cat Dude?"

"Not for a werewolf—it's still fresh," Jon replies, then smiles wickedly at my wife. "Yup, Cat Dude. Aren't I clever?"

"Uh-huh," she teases back. "Yeah. Like a brick."

"I'll go," I say. "But I want to be back here when the spell completes. You'll call me, right?" I ask of Dria.

"You got it, hon. Go, do what you need to do. I'll keep the wizard safe."

We leave through the backdoor as the spell incantations begin. I glance at the gray, powdery remains left on the cobblestones and dead grass, a shiver stealing over me. "That's just wrong. On so many levels."

"Do you think the same thing will happen when we kill Cat Dude?"

"I have no idea," I say, striding away from the dreary leavings. "Guess we'll find out soon enough."

We drive to the Tribunal, unsure if Jon's werewolf presence will trip the magical wards or not. Are they even working anymore now that Justin is unable to renew them from the last alert? I have no idea. This magical shit is way over my head.

Jon and I park the car as near to where I can recall we found the body. The second he steps out, he reacts. "Oh man, there's no doubt that thing is a cat. I can smell it from here."

"Great. Can you track it, too?"

"No problem." Jon takes off down the street, the opposite direction Dria and I approached from earlier. "Can you keep up, old man?"

I don't answer, but follow close behind, unwilling to rise to any taunts while on a job. We lope down side streets and main thoroughfares, surprise growing inside that the hombre gato didn't kill again when it traveled so far—and that it could get this far undetected. The trail twists and turns, venturing into side yards, parks, and finally into an abandoned building.

Dead dogs litter the alley leading up to a side entrance. Leaving a message to keep out even a non-supe can figure out.

"Looks like we've found its lair."

"Let's do this."

Jon cracks open the door, listening intently before moving. He pauses to sniff, then his air of expectancy disappears. "There's nothing inside."

"Dammit. Are you sure?"

"Positive."

"You know what that means then, right?"

"That it's out looking for prey."

"Yup, that's what I was thinking, too."

We travel up and down the alley, then circle the building, looking for an exit trail that might be fresher than the one that led us here. After a few minutes of searching, Jon finds a lead.

"I think it's heading into the heart of San Telmo. Where the pack resides. I've got to let Magdelena know."

"Can you call her?"

He shakes his head. "Never thought to ask for her cell."

I let out a deep sigh as I check my watch. "All right, we've been out here a while. Let's hustle back to the car. I'll drop you off and get back to Dria. I don't want her to activate the tracking spell without me."

"You suspect she'll go after Rolando on her own?"

"In a heartbeat. She's headstrong and always willing to put herself at risk to protect me."

"At least she's predictable."

Within twenty minutes I've dropped off Jon at Lupine Luna and made my way back to Justin's. After he and Magdelena get the hombre gato, we have just one more person to track down: Rolando.

CHAPTER EIGHTEEN

JON

I linger outside the bar, unsure about entering. Yes, I need to warn her of the possible danger and get going after Cat Dude, but I'm all mixed up with how I feel about this woman. Guilt weighs on me for what I hope to steal from her. Betrayal burns in my gut for what I'm doing to the "us" that is building between Candy and me.

Call her, my conscience whispers in the back of my brain.

Geez, should I? Should I tell Candy what's going on? How would I react if I was in the same position with something she was doing? I shake my head, indecision plaguing me.

The cell phone in my pocket feels like a leaden brick, mocking me for not manning up and talking to her about what's going on.

Okay, what's the worst that could happen? She could hate me for what I plan to do and dump my ass. Yikes. That's one option—but another could be that she'd understand and accept why I have to do it. There could also be a middle ground, of which I have no idea the results.

Without waiting for my insecurities to talk me out of it, I dig out my phone to call her. I wander a few doors down and sit in a closed store's doorway, making sure there are no eavesdropping Weres around first. Anxiety coils in my gut, making me hesitate before I press the send button.

After a few rings, she answers the phone in my cabin. "Jon? How's it going in wintry Argentina?"

"Good." The automatic response leaps out before I have a chance to realize it's not accurate. "I mean bad. Damn..." I drop my head, comforted by the sound of her voice. "I mean things have gotten mixed up."

"Tell me what's going on."

I fill her in on everything that's happened since we got here, unsure if Viv will be pissed I've said anything to someone back home or not. Or, more accurately, to someone she doesn't know exists in my life and is staying in my home. God, this is so messed up. I'm not good at deception. There's no way I could be a spy.

She listens to all of it and focuses on what I've revealed about Magda. "This half-shift trait you mentioned, it sounds fascinating. Would she be willing to teach you?"

"You see, that's the problem. Rafe thinks she'd never teach me, and Viv is pushing for me to learn it by whatever means necessary."

"What does that mean? It's not like you can threaten to kill her to get her to reveal how she does it. Sounds like her secret is powerful enough to kill you on its own."

"No, not by threat. Viv wants me to..." I trail off, uncomfortable voicing the vampire's suggestion even though it was why I called.

"Yes?"

"Oh God, this is hard." I let out a deep sigh. "Vivian wants me to seduce Magda and gain her trust. Get close enough to her to figure out how she's doing it so I can learn the skill and teach others."

Candy's quiet on the other end of the line. Perhaps processing what I've said, perhaps debating on hanging up on me, I don't know. All I know is my heart feels tight—like I could explode any second now.

"Jon," she says in a soft voice. "Do you remember when, for my safety, I said I hid, disguised as a man in your old pack?"

"Yeah..."

"You also remember I had... relations with a few of the female pack members."

"Uh, yeah. So?"

"At first, I came onto the women so I'd fit in. It was expected, you know, to bed hop, to look for your potential mate. I knew I preferred men. I used women to keep myself safe—at least that's what I told myself. But it wasn't the truth."

"No?"

"No. I came to like those women, a lot. I liked getting close to them, I liked their warmth and affection, and let's face it—as a man, I couldn't 'fake' an erection, so I knew the attractions I was feeling at the time, which was mainly a combination of like and lust, were real.

"It was a difficult situation to come to terms with. I was acting in my own best interests, not theirs. I was dishonest when I approached them as a male werewolf, one they thought they might have a potential mate with.

"The betrayal of their feelings, their wishes and dreams... it felt awful. But I had to do it to survive. And if I was completely honest with myself, I enjoyed it at the time. I felt something toward the ladies, even if I had dishonorable intentions and was misleading them."

"You're right," I say. "You had no choice at the time. You had to fit in to survive."

"Did I? Did I really? I could have gone off on my own. I could have pretended to be gay—although, with a few of the homophobic males in the pack, that might have been a dangerous choice.

"The point is, I did it. And I can't change it now."

"Why are you telling me all this, Candy? It's your past. I have no right to judge or get angry over what you did before we met."

"It may not be the same, but I've felt what you're feeling right now. It's tearing you up, isn't it? The desire mixed with the guilt?"

I let my head drift back to the glass door behind me, the cold and isolation mirroring what I'm feeling inside. "Yes. It is."

"If you can forgive what I did, how can you not forgive yourself what you must do?"

"But we weren't involved when you deceived them. I'm very much involved with you now. It doesn't feel right."

"It's not about my approval, Jon. Or about right and wrong. It's about your acceptance of what you need to do."

I'm quiet for a moment, letting her words sink in.

"I've gotten to know you these past few weeks. You're a man who values integrity—which is a good thing. So let me ask you—are you fighting to seduce this werewolf because Vivian suggested it, or are you afraid of what doing so will mean to your honor?"

Her words twine deep within me, forcing me to see what I

didn't want to admit to. Maybe my issue really is protecting my sense of morals, what I feel is right and wrong. But surviving, as Candy pointed out before, is about doing what must be done, honor be damned.

I clear my throat, the chill from the night stealing my voice. "So after all that, you still think it's a good idea?"

"To learn a skill that could unite the packs? Yes, without a doubt. To tear yourself up for feelings and emotions building about a woman you must ultimately deceive and leave? No. Let it go."

Candy goes silent for a moment before speaking again, perhaps sensing I'm still on the fence. "Let's look at this from a different angle—you've not made her any promises have you?"

"No."

"She knows your Vivian's servant, right?"

"Yes, she knew it the night she sent wolves to track me."

"And wasn't that to blackmail you so you'd do what she wants?"

"Yeah."

"This woman isn't expecting long term with you. She's looking for a good time. And for you to help clean up her city. Do what you need to do and leave the guilt behind. It's okay to enjoy it. It's okay to feel. I know in the end what you're having to sacrifice to do it, and I'm still here. I'm not going anywhere."

"Damn, Candy. You're making this too easy."

She laughs. "What were you hoping for? Tears and screaming? Damning you to hell for cheating on me, when've we've made no commitments to each other and have only known each other a month?" I can almost see her shaking her head at me in frustration. "The bigger picture, Jon. Keep focused on the bigger picture. Life is not a game, it truly is about surviving. And what she knows will help you—will help *us*—to survive."

"Thanks. I needed that."

"Good. Now do what you need to and come home to me."

We end the conversation and I feel lighter. I may not have a lot of experience with relationships, but I made the right choice in calling her. Pushing up from the cold concrete, I stride toward the bar, determined to do what must be done, and leave the guilt behind.

"I didn't expect to see you back so soon," Magda purrs from her seat behind the desk. She rises and approaches me, arms extended in greeting.

The alpha wraps her arms around my neck, snugging her soft curves against me, and rubbing me with them in a long, languorous stroke. I'd have to be blind and stupid to not see what she's offering—a good time with no strings attached.

"Do you want to tell me where you live so I don't have to keep coming to the bar to find you?"

"I practically live here, so this is the best place to find me six nights out of seven." She leans in and takes a deep breath of air close to me, her nose brushing the hair near my ear, a sigh of anticipation escaping her.

I slide my hands down to cup her ass, hauling her closer and planting a kiss on her neck. Should I match her sexual assertiveness move for move and try to seduce her? Or should I stick to safe topics, like what I know?

"I have news on your killer."

Yup, I went for safe and easy. Lame-o. I can almost hear Rafe's laughter and Vivian's disappointment in my head.

Despite my determination, I'm not used to approaching seduction with an end goal other than sexual satisfaction.

She draws back and peers up into my eyes through her lashes. "Really? What do you know?"

"Buenos Aires has a cat problem. An hombre gato to be exact."

"Hombre gato? I know what those are. But, they haven't been seen in South America for centuries. You can't even call them shifters."

"Rafe and I took care of the invunche that killed the witch and the homeless man. Then tracked Cat Dude out of its den. We think it might be headed this way."

"An invunche? I don't even know what that is. And you say the gato is headed toward San Telmo? That can't be good. From what I was told, they're more like human and animal aberrations created by magic. Man-like beast with huge claws, a cat head, and not necessarily a human brain behind the mask —if I'm recalling the stories correctly."

I nod. "The invunche is a creature from legend, too. Also created by magic. They were usually guards for a wizard—and we have no idea what brought it here, either. And you're exactly right on Cat Dude—or at least that's what it sounds like from what we've been able to dig up. We think that could be what made the fatal wounds on the delivery man and the vampire. Would its magic prevent a vampire from healing the wounds?"

"I don't know. Like I said, there's been no sign of them in Argentina for well over a hundred years. The vampire could have died because the attack happened so fast. If the heart and head are removed before a defensive retaliation, you could very easily kill a vampire without there being time for healing."

She runs a small hand over my chest, reaching the open neck of my shirt and tentatively touching me with her warm fingertips. "But the creature would have to be *very* fast to surprise a vampire. If that's the case—meaning the gato is magically supercharged—we'll have to be very careful when we hunt it. The wounds it inflicts on us might have the same effects."

"Good point." I squeeze her firm bottom one more time. "Glad I've got the super alpha on my side."

She smiles, happy with my admiration of her special traits, thrusting her hips to grind against mine in response. "Let's hope we'll be enough to take it down once and for all."

At a loss for words, I lean down and trail kisses up her neck again. Candy likes it when I do this, maybe she will, too.

Jesus! I can't think about Candy while trying to do this. Is this even a good time to seduce her? Aren't we supposed to be out tracking the gato? What the hell was I thinking coming on to her now? How do spies go home at the end of an assignment to the people they're involved with and not feel guilt?

Because dead people don't feel guilt, you fool. And those alive value life and love when they have it, doing what must be done to protect it.

The voice of reason is my own conscience, although I wish I could attribute it to Viv or Rafe. Can I do this? Candy's quiet voice of support fills my head, and I know I can.

I think back to the skill this woman possesses, and what it could mean to shifters all over the world if I could share it and unite packs with the knowledge.

You can do anything you set your mind to.

Magda moans softly, arching into my embrace. The air in

the office fills with sexual pheromones, triggering all my alpha tendencies to respond in kind, to take her like she wants to be taken. My body reacts to the delectable aroma filling my head, arousal growing whether I'm ready for it or not.

The pretty, dark-haired alpha feels my physical reaction and rubs her pelvis against mine, encouraging me further.

"Are you eager, my little alpha?" I whisper against her smooth skin. "Do you want me to give you pleasure before we hunt?"

I reach a hand to her front, cupping her mound through her thick pants. She whimpers, thrusting her heat fully into my palm.

"You need it, don't you?" I move my hand to her waistband, intending to slip underneath to touch her. "Is there no one from your pack you can trust in your bed since Hector?" I skim past the fabric, my hot fingers delving down, creeping toward her center. "Can you be quiet so they don't hear?"

Apparently, that was exactly the wrong thing to say. Or the right thing, depending on how you look at it.

Magda steps back, gently easing my hand from her pants. Desire smoldering in her dark eyes. She licks her full lips and glances down at the bulge in the front of my pants. "As much as I hate to admit it and stop what I want to happen—you're right, this is not the time or place. We have a killer to catch. And I have no desire to put on a show for all the Weres beyond the door."

I nod, strangely relieved things didn't go further. I can do this. I can screw a woman to get what I want. A woman I care nothing for when I'm involved with someone else I really like. Even if the alpha's not as crazy a psycho bitch as I claimed.

Damn, this is difficult.

Best to push it all away and pretend it's not affecting me. That's the guy thing to do.

I reach for my shirt hem, deciding to go with the flow and take the necessary steps to disrobe before shifting to my wolf form. "We need to get going then. Like I told you, it's on the move. No telling if it's out to kill again or just going for a stroll." I pull the fabric over my head, revealing the tight washboard abs Candy was raving about earlier in the week.

Magda runs a hand down my chest and then lower, over the taut skin. "Make time for play when we're done. I will have you, Jon."

I smile, hoping I look sexier than I feel. And considering I feel like a cornered slab of meat she intends to eat, that's not very sexy. "And you will, Magda. You will."

I relay the location of where we last scented the Gato and explain how I'd like us to go there with me in my wolf form to track it better. She'll stay as is and change to her hybrid form if needed. I've got to figure out how she does it before this adventure is over or enduring her attentions will have been for nothing.

Enduring. Who are you kidding? You like it. Like that a powerful woman wants you. Wants to—

Cutting off the unhelpful diatribe running through my head, I chuck the rest of my clothes and change into a wolf, the transformation happening so fast it's like a blur of the light. Her eyes widen in surprise before sparking with interest. "You're fast. Very fast."

I wink. *Not in all things, I swear.* Realizing she can't hear my internal thoughts, I turn toward the door, indicating it's time to go.

She opens the office door and I'm off like a shot, forcing her to hurry to keep up. Loud cat calls and hoots follow us, her pack having no idea what we've planned. If they had, I wonder if they'd join us to help or hold on to denial a little too long, more content to blame Magdelena for the deaths and remain blind.

Ignorance is funny that way. If you're happy with the status quo, you've got no reason to seek what's behind the curtain. And let's face it—some people are happier wrapped in hate. It's a sad state to be in, but there it is. People do it every damn day.

The moment she opens the outer door to the street, I spring into the night air, feeling truly alive. It's been a while since I took on my wolf form. The urge to run past the paved streets and tall buildings is strong, almost overwhelming, but I resist, promising my inner wolf we'll be able to run free very soon.

Without worrying about the pretty alpha keeping up, I race down the darkened streets.

The fragrant night air billows past me, my lungs consuming huge gulps as I allow supernatural speed to course through me. The location we last tracked Cat Dude isn't far, but on a hunch, I lead her toward the den Rafe and I found in the abandoned warehouse.

Tempting food odors—simmering pork, roasted beef, marinated chicken call me to stop and savor all the city has to offer. There'll be time later. Now, I'm on the hunt. My body vibrates in eagerness to rend and tear, to pin down my enemy and feast upon its flesh. I snort through my nose, hoping to dislodge the visceral imagery mixed with all the food smells.

Whatever Cat Dude is, human or big cat, I doubt it's on

my preferred meat list. Parked cars fly past me in my haste, the forms of a few late night walking pedestrians a blur of color. I know they won't see me too clearly when I pour on the speed like this, and that's a good thing. The city has enough to handle with the recent deaths, no need to make matters worse by thinking they've got a large rabid dog running through San Telmo, too.

Within minutes I'm back at the abandoned warehouse, nose to the ground, scenting for recent signs of the hombre gato. If this thing is summoned by magic, what happens to it when it's not killing? Does it magically disappear like the invunche did after we saw it kill? Or does it have a sentient awareness and it hides until it needs to feed?

I breathe deeply near the doorway, allowing the fumes from old oil stains, cat urine, and garbage to enter my olfactory senses. Nothing. I rear up and slam a paw into the half-closed door, forcing it to open wider and allow my large wolf frame to pass.

Stepping into the dark space, I still and focus on my senses. Stale air, small rodents who've taken up residence, and the unwashed stink of a large predator who's been covered in blood come at me from all directions. Like before, I don't sense the creature here now, but by the smells it seems he's been here since we tracked it earlier. Could that mean it's killed again recently?

I trot into the darkness, nose down, looking for more clues to relay. In a few minutes I hear Magda join me. She enters the old building without fear.

"Long gone, is he?"

Not as long as she may think, but I chuff out a breath of air to indicate my agreement, continuing my investigation. Back in a dark corner, I find where he sleeps. A rank pile of newspapers, cardboard, old food containers, and scraps of cloth. And judging by the amount of territorial urine scenting he's done, there's no doubt in my mind this creature is a male. The original hombre in the name alludes to a male, but still, it doesn't hurt to be sure.

There's a narrow second door, one we didn't see the first time we discovered the location. I trot toward it, my gums pulling back to reveal sharp teeth as I realize the cat scent is fresher here. This must be his preferred means of exit. I look over my shoulder, a low rumble of sound erupting from my chest. Magdelena pauses in her examination of the gato's sleeping quarters, an eyebrow raised. "Found something?"

She joins me, leaning closer to see the slim, closed door. "Ahh... another way out. Let's see where it leads." She opens the door and sounds rush in. This exit leads to a much busier street, even at this hour, located on the opposite side from where we came in.

"Crap. He could be anywhere." She sticks her head out, glances side to side, and then back down at me. "Any way you can make yourself less conspicuous? I doubt a dog your size will go unnoticed."

I stare straight at her, unsure what the hell she expects me to do. I'm a freaking wolf. Changing back into a man—a naked man—will draw even more attention our way, I'm sure.

"Cat got your tongue?" she says with a crooked grin. "Just kidding. Okay...." She looks over my large frame. "How about we have you walk really close next to me, like you're my pet? That might work."

I cough once in agreement and we step into another alley, this one closer to the busy restaurant district than I'd like. We follow the trail onto what would be the thriving streets of a Buenos Aires's shopping district. But at this time of night, approaching dawn, the sidewalks are empty of patrons, only delivery trucks and end of shift workers present.

How did Cat Dude travel unseen? Does it have some type of obfuscating abilities—meaning whoever sees it doesn't see what's really there?

With no way to voice my questions, I keep my head down and try to look innocuous as I track the old scent of the gato. After one block the creature strays away from the activity on the streets and takes another dark alley. We continue tracking for several blocks and soon find ourselves near the area where the witch coven lives.

Despite the bragging their magic is superior, could they have triggered the imbalance that allowed Cat Dude to come to life? I snort, happy with the thought. Would serve those stuck up bitches right to have caused all the problems the city is having, especially after they were so quick to place blame on another supernatural group.

Magdelena's soft fingers weave through the fur at my neck, grabbing and gently tugging on the scruff. "What do you think, Jon? Has the trail gone cold?"

A small whine escapes me, indicating my frustration. She's right, the scent markers have dissipated. But the ones here were fresher than any I've come across. Could the beast have another den he hides in? With that thought, I backtrack, breaking her hold on me, and retracing the last hundred yards. Come on... there's got to be something here.

Magda catches up, her eyes scanning the dark roads, the infrequent street lamps our only source of illumination. She nudges me with her knee. "How about there?" She points to a partially visible basement window, deep within shadows. "Want to check?"

I trot over and sniff the sidewalk out front and then the old window casement. Nothing. I look back toward her then to the window, twice, almost shaking my head, to indicate negative.

"The damn thing didn't disappear. It's got to be around here somewhere."

I think back to the invunche. It seemed quite at home within its cave-like sewer hiding spot. Could that be a possibility for Cat Dude, too? I move to the closest sewer and lower my head.

The scent of molding leaves, water runoff from the street, including gasoline, oil, and dirt, rush to fill my senses. No smell of the cat creature. Crap. Another dead end.

Magda picks up on my idea and points down the road to a subway sign. "How about the trains?"

I pick up my pace, trotting quickly to the stairs leading down. This time I smell something cat-like mixed with a man. Bingo. My ears perk forward and my tail goes up, a clear indicator to the female alpha that I've found something.

She rushes to my side and weaves her hands through my fur. "Good work, Jon." She peers down the steep stairs and then looks up and down the street. "Let's check it out."

CHAPTER NINETEEN

VIVIAN

"Are we finally ready to activate the spell?" I try my best to keep the frustration out of my voice, but since his neighbor was found dead, Justin hasn't exactly been very focused.

"Yeah, give me another minute."

Rafe opens the telepathic link between us. *He's been saying that for the past thirty minutes. I wish he'd finish already.*

You and me both, dear. A little longer, that's all. I lay my hand on his and squeeze. *I thought for sure I'd be on the road before you two found the invunche.*

I just bet you did. You'd have left me to track him on your own, wouldn't you?

I look to my husband and raise one eyebrow. *Why ask if you already know the answer?*

He cuts off our connection, his annoyance showing clearly on his rugged face. I'm not going to lie to him. If the tracker spell had been activated and he was not here, I sure as hell would have gone without him, and he knows it.

Justin's agitated voice breaks into our silent standoff. "Okay, I'm ready for the spell's binding and payment." His dark blue eyes seek mine. "That means your blood, Vivian."

He hands me a ceremonial knife, the hilt carved of bone and the blade wicked sharp. "The blood should go in the center of the other ingredients. No need to mix it, it should trigger at once."

"How much do you need?"

"Depends on how strong your blood is." He shrugs. "For me, I'd use about a teaspoon. But that was before. When my blood was worthy. Now I have no idea. Maybe five or six drops?"

I examine the blade carefully, sniffing it to make sure it hasn't been covered with a poison or other substance. Justin scowls at my actions. Like I give a damn if I insult him. This is my life and my risk, the fool.

Pricking the end of one finger with the knife tip, I watch the thick blood slowly pool, forming a large drop. When enough gathers, I let it fall into the wooden bowl. A poof of magic wafts up from the bowl, dimming the light in the room for an instant.

Justin's mouth drops open. "I've never seen a spell bind to activate *and* accept payment with only a drop before." He looks to me, something akin to greed in his gaze.

Rafe clears his throat. "And don't get any ideas, wizard. I'd kill you before I'd let you exploit my wife's blood."

Justin shakes his head. "Whatever, man. Don't go thinking the worst of me. You don't even know me."

"I call 'em like I see 'em. What I know so far doesn't impress me too much."

The wizard mumbles something under his breath that sounds suspiciously close to *fucking bastard*, but continues assembling the last of the spell. "Sure, just forget I'm the one who helped you save your wife three weeks ago. Nice."

"You pointed me in the right direction, saving me time. But you did not fight by my side. Don't confuse the two." Rafe rises from the table and goes into the living room. He says to me, "Let me know when you're ready to leave."

I sit quietly while the wizard assembles the activated ingredients into a leather pouch, unwilling to make matters worse with questioning him further on what he's doing. In a few steps, Justin is done. He hands me the soft leather pouch, similar to what I've seen witches use for herbal talismans or to hold chakra stones.

"How does it work?"

"You hold it and think of the one you seek. Face a direction and when you feel the bag heat slightly, you're on the right path."

"Seems tedious and slow. Are you sure it will work?"

A scowl forms on his unlined face, disappearing as fast as it appeared. "Thanks for the doubt and back-handed insult. Yes, I know how to do my job. And I do it well. It will work."

This is also the guy who wrought such a magical imbalance in the city we've had two mythological killers appear in a week's time. But I refrain from pointing the obvious out. "Thanks, Justin."

"Not so fast, lady. Don't forget my fee."

"The agreement was for *after* we find Rolando."

The young wizard looks like he's ready to argue, but quiets

down soon enough. He nods sharply and starts to put away the unused ingredients.

I staunch the tiny feeling of dishonesty creeping up my spine. What the witch and Justin don't know is I plan to remotely nullify my blood in a day's time. Despite the reassurances I gave earlier, I have no intention of giving anyone unsupervised access to the power in my blood—maybe I'll send payment in gold when this mess is all over.

One of the perks of being a master manipulator is divine connection to everything my blood infiltrates. Including the spell contents of the bag, which should make using the pouch to play a supernatural game of "hot and cold" much easier.

Rafe appears in the kitchen doorway. "Are we ready to roll?"

I nod and rise from my chair. "Thanks for your assistance with the tracking spell, Justin. We'll keep you posted on what's happening."

"And will Jon let me know when they catch the gato?" Uncertainty clouds his expression, no doubt wondering how his whole livelihood could, literally, go up in a cloud of dust like it has.

"Sure thing," Rafe answers, hustling me toward the back door. "We'll make sure you're notified."

A thought occurs to me as we're leaving. "And let us know if this latest spell left any type of imbalance—we don't want another killer on the loose."

Justin grimaces. "I'll try, but I didn't know when the imbalances occurred previously. Everything felt fine, just like during my other spells."

The door shuts behind us and as we walk away I hear the wizard turn the lock. I wonder if it's normal for him to not feel an imbalance when he completes a spell, assuming he created one by making the spell to begin with. That doesn't seem right to me. How could a magic user be expected to correct the problem if they didn't feel it come into existence?

"We've got a few hours until dawn, hon. Let's get a move on," Rafe says, one hand on the small of my back easing me forward faster. "I'd love to track that bastard down before the sun rises."

"Is that so you can question him when I'm indisposed?"

A surprised grunt sounds next to me. "What, do I look stupid? He's older than you. He may not need to sleep until close to noon, if at all—and if that's the case, only an idiot would confront a cornered vampire."

We journey to the car and slide inside. "Where should we start?" I ask. "The pouch doesn't have a feel to it yet."

"Hmm... maybe you should get out and hold it in your hands while facing different directions."

Feeling dumb with the action, I comply, climbing out to stand on the sidewalk. Turning slowly, I pause at each cardinal direction, hoping the little bag will point me the right way. I allow my thoughts to center on Rolando and how much I want to find him. I wait a breath before turning again, hoping the extra time will help.

After a complete circuit, I'm annoyed. The leather feels the exact same—cold. Should I barge back in and call out Justin for his ineptitude? "Some fucking wizard," I mumble under my breath.

Rafe lowers the passenger window. "Have you tried connecting with the blood in the charm yet?"

"No," I answer, feeling foolish I hadn't tried. Bitching is so much more productive.

Heeding my husband's suggestion, I close my eyes, preparing to expand my awareness through my blood. Like my connection to the resort, I can trace my life source anywhere, and reach out beyond the sphere of it to whatever it connects.

I slow my breathing and wait. When I've cleared my head of all the negativity and disappointment from the charm not working instantly, I begin to feel something in my hands. My blood does indeed connect all the ingredients together. Combined with my desire to find Rolando, a reaction starts to occur.

I turn to the right once more, attuned to any change in the leather pouch. This time, I sense the components of the spell working. Heartened with the change, I turn again and wait. Before I have a chance to let my breath out, the leather warms in my hands. Bingo.

"This way," I gesture, with the bag still cupped in my grasp.

"Toward the Tribunal's neighborhood. I should have guessed."

I return to my seat and buckle up. "Could mean anything. That direction covers a lot of the city, not just the Seat of Darkness."

"Hmph. We'll see."

At every intersection I hold the bag to the right, left, and center, to see which triggers a reaction. Very soon, we're turning back onto Independence Avenue, approaching the Tribunal's townhouse from a different direction, one that will require us to pass all the other homes on the street first. The security ward doesn't send a tingle over me, making me think it must still be down after George's death earlier tonight.

"I knew it," Rafe says. "I knew that son of a bitch hadn't left."

We pass the second townhouse, still many doors down from the main house, and the pouch goes cold in my hand. "Wait!" I shout. Rafe slams on the brakes. "I think he's in a house on this street, but not the headquarters. The bag just got cold. I think we've passed him."

Rafe pulls the car over to park. We unload and walk back the way we'd come. The leather heats up again. I hold the pouch out toward the walkway of the next house and the heat eases. I turn to face the opposite side if the street and the charm turns hot. "Okay, he must be in that house."

"Or behind it."

I glance at my husband. "Good distinction. Should we approach from behind to make sure?"

Rafe looks up and down the street. "There're no alleys between the homes on this end. Access to the rear must be through a secondary street running behind the houses. Let's go to the front door and see who's inside."

"Just knock on the door?"

"Yeah, and if no one answers we break in."

"Okay, let's do it." I hold back a snort of uneasy humor, triggered by my nervousness. Amateur sleuths we are not.

Rafe's fist pounds on the door. A tingle of sensation runs over me.

"Crap," Rafe says. "Did you feel that, too? What was it?"

Recognition of tripping another ward cascades through me. "Dammit! Kick in the door. He may be trying to escape after the ward went off."

My husband steps back and delivers one solid, powerful kick to the door, sending it crashing inside to bang against a wall. Before we can cross the threshold, a mini explosion goes off, sending smoke out the door to blind us.

"Wait!" I hold Rafe back by the arm, unwilling to have either of us barrel in when we can't see where we're going or what awaits us on the other side.

"He's going to get away! We've got to get in there."

The smoke rises, still blocking our view, but leaving the area near our feet clearer. "Look," I say, pointing down to the yawning blackness just on the other side of the door. "Isn't that the same kind of trap door Paul and Drew described when they were captured?"

Rafe pauses with his foot in mid-air, ready to rush in despite my warnings. "Dammit all to hell—it is! Who in their right mind uses trap doors as a deterrent against break ins?"

"Paranoid old vampires, that's who." I wave my arms to dispel the rest of the smoke. The hole beyond the door is about four feet wide. "We can jump it." I nudge his shoulder. "Go ahead."

Rafe flashes me a look that says *why the hell am I going first?* and jumps. Without waiting to see if I follow, he races deeper into the dark house. I gracefully leap over the expanse and follow, slower than him as I check for signs of Rolando.

"Come on, Dria!" Rafe's voice drifts to me from the rear of the house. I hear him wrenching open a backdoor. "I see him! He's running down the back alley toward the other end of the block."

Right toward the Tribunal's main house. Before I have a chance to tell him to wait for me, he's out the rear entrance like a flash.

CHAPTER TWENTY

RAFE

My feet miss the stairs completely as I launch myself off the back porch. I sprint down the small yard and leap over the back fence dividing the property from the narrow alley in the back. A dark shadowy form, which I assume is Rolando, has about a hundred yard head start on me.

The man races past the next few houses, eventually turning into the backyard behind the largest house on the street—the Tribunal's headquarters. I follow, sure I've got the bastard now. I slow down at the turn, running through the painted gate and toward the stone steps of the backdoor.

"Wait!" Dria yells from behind me. "That's not him."

I stop, chest heaving from the mad dash. The townhouse sits quiet, not like someone has just pounded on the door and demanded to be let in, and yet, no one is lingering in the shadows, either. "What the—"

My wife waves the locator charm pouch. "The bag is cold. That wasn't Rolando."

"What the hell is going on?"

"I think it might have been a decoy spell."

"Jesus. Right when I think I know what the hell is going on, we throw magic into the mix. A decoy spell, really?"

Dria stands by my side, looking back the way we came. "Stop and listen to your senses. Do you smell a fleeing, anxious vampire? Do you smell any recent trace of vampire besides me?"

"Crap, you're right." I run a hand over my head, pushing my hair back off my forehead. "Damn Justin. He could have warned us he'd made the man a decoy spell."

"Justin isn't the only wizard for hire in the city."

"You're right, he's not. He might not have known. Shit. Where to now?"

She holds still, turning her attention to the bag still firmly in her grasp. "He was at the house, or else the spell wouldn't have led us there. I think he got out the moment he sensed us, or the protective ward revealed us, and the decoy spell was set off sometime after we entered."

Dria walks back toward the alley. "Come on, he couldn't have gotten far. Let's retrace and check for his location again."

"Yeah, okay." My mood sours as I join her. Can't believe he got away that easily. I feel stupid. Another thought occurs to me as we jog back to the house. "He could have a car and drove away."

"Good point. We didn't hear one, but the explosion could have hidden the sound. You go through to the front and drive our car back here." She points to the end of the alley two houses down. "I'll meet you there." Sensing my bad mood she smiles. "He can't have gotten far, honey. Buck up. We'll get him."

I nod and take off for the front, running back the way we

originally came, leaving all the bastard's doors wide open when I exit, too. I smile, an evil grin if there ever was one, maybe he'll get robbed.

I reach the car and drive to the rendezvous point Dria indicated. She climbs in, a determined look on her face.

"I already checked, he went that way." She points in front of us. I pull away from the curb, slowing as we reach the next intersection in case the charm indicates we need to turn to follow Rolando.

"Are we sure the spell is accurate?" I ask.

Dria pats my thigh reassuringly. "It led us here, to where he was. I doubt it would start malfunctioning now. Have faith."

I open my mouth to respond, and snap it shut when I realize I'm not being helpful. I have faith. Faith in us, not some damn spell. I swear, when I find that man... my fists tighten on the steering wheel. When I think about what he did to my wife...

"Hey now, you okay, Rafe? I feel you getting really angry and upset."

I take a deep breath, loosening my grip on the leather-covered plastic. She's right. I can't let this situation get to me. "I don't like all this running blind shit. I prefer to strategize. This mess feels like disaster unfolding."

Dria jerks slightly in her seat. "You're right. That's exactly what this is. Contrived chaos. Pull over."

"What?" I ask, while scanning the upcoming street for a place to stop the car. It takes fifty yards or so, but I find a clear curb and swing the car in. I shift into park and turn to my wife. "What're you thinking?"

"I'm not used to taking into consideration the possible

ramifications of working with magic." Her hand reaches toward her face, one slim finger tapping her lips as she stares through the windshield. "If you were smart enough to set a ward to predict when an enemy approaches, a trap at your door, and a decoy spell to lead pursuers away... then wouldn't you have thought about the next steps? Like how to hide your escape trail successfully or not to be tracked at all?"

I lean back in my seat, using the headrest and shutting my eyes. "I have no idea. All I know is I'm tired. Tired of tracking the people who mean you harm, killing the ones who tortured you, and trying to figure out—and then stop—the creatures killing innocents in the city."

The warm hand on my thigh starts to move, stroking up and down in a soothing gesture. "I wish I could change what's happened, but I can't." When I hear my wife turn toward me, sliding sideways in her seat, I open my eyes. "I understand your frustration. I'm right there with you. I haven't been the same since that night."

Without a word, I know the night she's referring to—the night I had to save her from her fellow vampires. A night she'd feared and worked hard to avoid for over five hundred years.

I reach a hand down to cover hers, offering a little bit of comfort while she continues speaking. "I'm experiencing doubt. And worry. And occasionally I'm feeling fear." It's quiet in the car for a moment when she pauses. I keep silent, anticipating she's not done. "And I don't like it. Not one damn bit."

"What do you intend to do about it?"

"I need to regroup and meditate. We're reacting, instead of acting first. We won't find him chasing our tails like this. Like you said, we need a plan."

"Let's return to the apartment. Get our heads on straight."

"Agreed."

I turn the car around and drive to our temporary home. Determination fills the air in the confined space, a sign neither of us is giving up any time soon.

W ithin thirty minutes, Dria and I are on the couch, dawn less than an hour away. The guilt of abandoning the hunt too soon washes away, replaced by the contentment of a full stomach. We stopped at a late night food vendor closing up for the coming morning, the remains of the feast spread over the coffee table.

"Let's look at this from another angle," I say, eager to get a plan in place before sleep overtakes me. "Think back to when you were an enforcer. If Rolando was a rogue you'd been sent to track, how would you approach the assignment?"

Dria's hand slides up my thigh, similar to the touch in the car, but with an entirely different intent. Her hand stops at the top of my thigh, her fingers snug against the swell of my shaft.

"I'd follow him for a while, discern his habits, decide on a location I could get him alone to take him out with the minimum amount of fuss and lowest chance of discovery."

I shift slightly in my seat, scooting closer to her hand, silently encouraging her absent-minded explorations of my anatomy. "Uh-huh. That makes sense. But what if you didn't have any way to track him? What if the rogue was crafty and elusive?"

My wife scoots tight to my right side, turning so her body presses to mine and hiking her right thigh over mine near the knee. "I'd get a lay of the land, uncover the ins and outs of the territory, determine where he'd go to feed and stake out various locations to find him."

Her hand roams over my growing erection, fueling more blood to rush to my genitals. "Now you're on track." I snort at my own double entendre. "Think like a hunter to take down your prey."

The rasp of my zipper lowering has my breath hitching in my throat. Sex is certainly one way to work off stress and frustration. And who am I to complain?

Her cooler hand snakes through the opening, cupping and stroking my heated flesh. Even though she's arousing me, she hasn't forgotten our original topic. "You can also set a trap for your prey—like bait if they're hungry, or a situation too good to resist."

"Like drunken college kids at a packed bar?"

She removes me from my pants, stroking me to full height in the dingy basement room. "For some, yes. For others, the most irresistible scenario could be as simple as a blood drive with lots of busy volunteers."

I smile at the image she paints, settling back into the soft couch to savor her touch. "So what really matters here is how well you know Rolando. Let's apply those ideas to him. What would he find," my breath hitches as she strokes faster, "irresistible?"

Without a word about what we're doing, she removes her hand and slowly starts to undress me, working on my shirt. "He's older than me, and like me, probably wouldn't prefer to feed in a crowd—too vulnerable. And besides, he's been here for centuries. He'd have plenty of established blood donors to choose from."

Eager to help, I slip off the sleeves of my shirt and toss the garment aside. Before an appropriate response to her statement can form in my sex-addled brain, I'm reaching for her sweater, tugging it over her head. Her full breasts press against the bra cups, clearing my mind of any intelligent response I could add to the conversation. "Uh-huh."

"I'd also track who he socialized with—if he was a member of a seethe, I'd start there." My talented, multi-tasking wife stands and shoves off her pants and underwear, then straddles my hips. She reaches behind her back and unhooks her bra, spilling her breasts free as the straps and fabric slide down her body.

I reach for her soft flesh, cupping the globes in my hands, unable to offer more insights on hunting a rogue. I rub the pads of my thumbs over her hardening nipples, aching to take the pretty, dark pink tips into my mouth.

"Oh, yes—that feels good. And if he wasn't in a seethe, I'd check property records to see if he owned a residence suitable for secure daytime sleeping."

Her breath hisses out in a rush as she runs her fingers through my hair, pulling me tight to her generous cleavage. My hands slide down to her hips, unable to wait any longer.

"Maybe the best bet would be to offer bait he found irresistible. That would draw him out of hiding."

A trickle of dismay zips through me at her suggestion, but my mind can't hold onto the unease and it's quickly squashed by my need to make love to my wife.

I pull away from her breast, run my hands up to grip her hair, and draw her head toward mine. "No more talking."

Twenty minutes later, my wife collapses on top of me, soft and pliant for the first time since we last made love.

"You are all I need," she whispers. "You are all I will ever need."

I swallow, my throat parched from the loud yell. "Ditto."

She chuckles and snuggles closer. "You're so good with words."

"Yeah. I know." I sigh and wrap my arms around her slender back, hugging her to me. *I may not be good with words,* I send to her through our telepathic link, *but I love you with every ounce of life inside me, and will do anything to keep you safe. Anything.*

She smiles against my chest and nips me lightly. *For someone claiming to not be very good with words, you did all right.*

I squeeze her tighter for an instant. *We'll get through this. I have no doubts.*

CHAPTER TWENTY-ONE

JON

"Well, at least the subway doesn't stink of human waste," Magdelena says. "Could always be worse."

I don't respond, but nudge my furry shoulder against her thigh, hoping she gets the hint and keeps quiet. This would be a good time to have Vivian's telepathic ability.

We edge forward, continuing down the quiet train platform. The place looks in good repair, with little to no graffiti or trash. Not what I expect from the four-hundred year old city. The founding fathers of Buenos Aires may state that's how old the city is, but people of all persuasions lived here much, much earlier.

The place isn't called the Seat of Darkness for no reason. It's been credited with where the undead originally organized, more years back than anyone is telling, where they became a unified body with governing elders ruling acceptable behavior and practices among humans.

I focus on the silence around me, unwilling to let my mind wander in a direction that won't help us catch the gato. I hear a steady in-and-out breathing from Magdelena, the repetitive drip of water from somewhere in the distance, and the occasional scurrying of a newspaper caught in the drafts from the tunnels.

My nose is overwhelmed by the scent of trains and the passing of thousands of humans, making it near impossible to pick out anything else. A trickle of unease flows over me, with the feeling this venture may not have been the smartest move. Together we creep across the empty subway platform, not surprised to find the place deserted when it's close to dawn on a Thursday. Magda's hand releases the scuff at my neck, before she says, "It looks clear. You want to go ahead?"

I trot forward, nose held close to the floor for traces of the cat scent. After a few minutes of searching, I pick it up and follow it to the far end of the station to the edge of the platform. It's so close to the mouth of the tunnel, that I highly doubt the creature entered a train, but probably jumped down to the tracks.

I glance over my shoulder at Magdelena, and then back toward the waiting blackness beyond the ledge. Sure she can grasp my intent, I leap to the tracks below. In a moment, I hear the scuff of her shoes and the loud thud of her landing as she follows me.

Sound inside the tunnels is distorted and magnified, making the fur on my neck stand with awareness. We'll see and hear the trains before they reach us, but the far off noises could distract us from determining what is happening closer.

Head down, I quickly pick up Cat Dude's trail, following it deeper into the two-lane tunnel.

The alpha's soft voice reaches my ears. "Do you think he's hiding down here, or has been sent this way to find his next target?" My ears flick back to indicate I've heard her, but obviously I can't respond verbally. After a moment she snorts at her own absentmindedness. "Not like you can answer me right now or anything. Ignore that last question."

She continues to speak aloud, presumably because she thinks our prey is nowhere close. "I'm still of the mindset that someone has purposely unleashed these creatures on the city. Not that it's an accident or something, like a thinning of the magical barrier you mentioned. I wouldn't put it past my own pack to have dreamed this shit up just to get rid of me." The sadness such a statement brings laces her voice with despair. "Why do I even bother? They don't want me as their leader. Maybe I should consider moving and starting my own pack in another city."

Panic grips my heart for a moment in fear she may ask to join me in Alaska. That sure as hell wouldn't work. I feel sorry for her, and I can't deny I'm attracted to her, but I sure as hell don't want her to move to Alaska.

"What do you think of Brazil? Not far from here and I have cousins in Sao Paulo. It's worth a shot."

Tension drains out of me as I grunt my approval and continue forward in the dark. Thank God she has another viable option. Between Vivian and Candy, I really don't need another woman on my hands.

A rumble starts in my feet, indicating a train is heading toward us. No lights yet to show us which track it might be on. Perhaps there's a bend in the tunnel up ahead' blocking the view.

I pause, waiting for a sign to determine which track is safe. Magdelena joins me, both of us still, staring in opposite directions, just in case.

"What would happen if two trains were coming at once—in different directions?"

A whine escapes my throat. Two trains would not be good.

Headlights appear ahead and slightly to the left. I confirm nothing is approaching from the opposite direction and move to the tracks on the right. Magda leans into my leg as we wait for the oncoming train to pass. The lights rush toward us, seemingly like they are on a direct path, and it takes all my will power to stand still and wait.

The train doesn't slow as it approaches the platform behind us—it must not be scheduled to stop this pass. Dozens of tons of steel carries a strong wind in the confined space, pushing us back slightly as it speeds closer.

Magda curses and falls, the shape of something large riding her to the tracks in front of the oncoming train, a familiar scent thick on the air. I leap, diving toward the stench of the unwashed Cat Dude as it pushes her down. A growl rips from my throat as my strong jaws clamp down on the filthy fabric covering its back. Before the train crushes her, Magda rolls toward the far wall of the tunnel, opposite from where I am.

An ear splitting yowl issues from the man-cat as it arches its back and twists to swipe one long-clawed hand at my side. Pain lances through my left flank, sharp and brief. I release my hold and leap away, eager to face the creature head on rather than in a tangled heap.

The agile cat creature lands lightly on its feet, two huge, furry hands with razor-tipped claws aimed my way. Flickering light from the passing train illuminates its cat head—large eyes, broad nose, whiskers, golden fur, and a gaping maw issuing a hiss of anger—revealing no sign of human intelligence in its gaze.

Whatever this thing is, it's more animal than anything else. It lunges toward me, swiping at my vulnerable eyes and nose, reminding me all too clearly why dogs don't mess with cats. Especially cats bigger than them. I duck to avoid the blow, countering with a bite to its left thigh.

I resist my instinct to clamp down, knowing a blow with those wicked claws is coming my way. I let go as the last train car passes, another whoosh of air buffeting us, and the cat-man's strike slides through my fur, inflicting no damage. With a strangled scream, Magdelena returns to the fight, leaping over the tracks to reveal her magnificent half-turned form. She's a tall mass of fur and muscle, her clothes in tatters, what remains hangs tight to the rigid planes of her wolfman physique.

She towers above Cat Dude, having gained at least eighteen inches in height when she transformed. Her face appears more wolf than human, but there's no mistaking the gleam of the woman I know in the golden-green eyes.

Her reappearance startles me for an instant, which the gato takes full advantage of, landing a flesh-gouging tear along my right side, slicing deep enough for the claws to snag on my ribs. I howl in pain and anger, twisting away to let Magda have a clear path to the creature.

"This way, you furry bastard!" she yells, her voice low and guttural, distracting his attention from me as I slink to the wall, sheltering my wounded side.

Cat Dude roars a challenge, leaping toward her through the air, one arm forward, one back, preparing to land a crushing blow. Magda's longer reach, thanks to her increased size, enables her to go low and launch upward, underneath his guard. She sinks her clawed hands into its stomach and chest, then drops down backward, throwing the creature over her to land in a heap.

Her attention darts to me for an instant. "It's coming," she says in a rough whisper. "Can you hear it?"

Unsure what she's talking about, I stare back at the cat-man, watching it rise from the tracks, unfazed by its wounds—wounds that aren't dripping any blood I can smell.

A horn blasts in the distance, signaling another train is headed our way, this time from the opposite direction. That must be what the pretty alpha meant.

She dances around her opponent, drawing its attention to her, turning the beast so its back is to the distant train. Is this thing the same as the invunche? Can it be killed if it doesn't bleed?

Magdelena backs up, letting the gato think it has the advantage, while she's clearly leading it where she wants.

"Jon!" Her deep, gravelly voice sends a tingle over me. "Lie down between the two tracks."

Not sure what she intends, I listen, creeping carefully behind the beast to not draw its attention.

She holds her own, delivering blow after blow to the angry, cornered cat. But the cat-man goes round for round with her, long slices on her furry torso sending the pungent scent of werewolf blood into the air.

Magda drives the beast toward my location, and understanding fills me. I brace for the upcoming weight, listening closely for the approaching train. Again and again, the creature slashes at her. Swipes and punches are exchanged with fluid grace, her moves and counter moves seeming to blur in the stale air of the subway tunnel.

Lights from the oncoming train illuminate the pair in stark

relief. The transformed alpha doesn't look tired, but her blows have slowed a little as she concentrates on positioning him where she wants him.

"Now!" she screams, while jumping up, landing two feet solidly in the cat-man's chest. I rise, bracing my legs in anticipation of the extra weight, but still crouching, ready for my one and only chance. The creature stumbles toward me, the back of its legs connecting with my side. It loses its balance to fall backward as I press upward, launching the creature over me and into the path of the approaching train.

The timing is perfect. Cat Dude sails overhead, landing on the tracks to be dragged under the speeding train. A poof of dust billows up as the steel dragon roars past, pushing me farther from the rails with its gust of angry air.

Neither of us makes a move as the train barrels by, both waiting to see if the creature is truly gone.

"What happened?" Magda says, peering through the dust and debris kicked up by the train. "Did he get away?"

I change back into a man, to not only heal my wounds but to answer her. "No. Did you see the cloud of dust?" My voice sounds raspy, even to my own ears. "I saw this before with the invunche. When it died, it turned to dust."

"Wait a minute—the thing didn't bleed and yet I'm supposed to believe it can die and turn to dust. Just like that?"

I twist, examining my skin, checking for damage to my hip and ribs. No trace of the stinging injuries remain. "I don't know how and I don't know why, but there it is." I glance back and forth in the darkened tunnel. "He's gone and that's all that matters."

I walk toward the platform where we entered the tunnel,

the cooler temps causing me to shiver, gooseflesh rising over my body.

Magda looks me over, head to toe, taking her sweet time checking me out. "How about I call someone from my pack to pick us up? You aren't exactly able to walk home like that." She glances down at her own tattered clothes. "And neither can I." A smile splits her face. "Oh, and I have no money, so a cab is out, too."

"Who do you trust?" Before the distant light from the subway platform can land on me, I change to a wolf, the transformation more of a shift in thought for me than anything else. It took a while to master the skill and to force myself to alter faster, but it was worth it.

"Jesus! I still can't get over how fast you change. It's incredible. Okay, back to your question—that's the problem. I'm not sure who to trust."

We jump up to the landing and make our way across the empty platform, grateful no one is here waiting for a train. What a sight we'd make. A large wolf—or what many would see instead, a huge dog—and a woman who looks like she's lived underground for a week.

I huddle close to her side as we travel up the stairs to street level, the light of dawn seeping between and over the buildings from the east to light our way.

"It's not far," she says. "We could've taken a train, but the next stop is almost the same distance past the bar as if we'd walked from here." Her fingers hold onto the scruff at my neck. "Might as well keep on like we are. There doesn't appear to be anyone around to wonder at our appearance."

The silence and freshness of the coming day hangs in the air, making our recent ordeal in the tunnel seem unreal. If I hadn't been a part of it, I might doubt the whole incident happened. Perhaps it's the letdown after the adrenaline rush. Maybe it's remnants of shock. No need to pick it apart and analyze it to death, suffice it to say, it feels weird.

"You know what? I forgot the bar is closed at this hour. How about we go directly to my place? I live in an area where a lot of the pack resides." Her voice drops to a deeper, sensual tone. "Now that the gato is gone, you and I have unfinished *personal* business to attend."

I wait for the anxiety to hit me. The sense of betrayal for what I'm planning to do to my new relationship with Candy. Nothing. I feel normal. As normal as can be expected after a quick battle to the death with an opponent who might have killed me had I faced it on my own.

"I live two blocks farther than the bar," she says. "Not far. That's why I practically live at the Lupine Luna. I own the business but not the building. One day I'll buy it. Until then, I keep my own place."

I can tell she's nervous, babbling about small details to fill the silence.

"Have you ever thought of your future, Jon? And I'm not asking because I'm hinting to have you move here, I know your allegiance lies with your vampire." She sighs, the cool morning air making her breath fog before us. "Your arrival—how I initially felt toward you—made me think of all I'm missing. All I've endured since taking over the pack. They hate me. Pure and simple.

"Each of them may have had their own issues with Hector, but they knew him and put up with his dominance because they had to. The known evil and all that. He forced the women to sleep with him when their husbands were away and couldn't protect them,

233

and the husbands were afraid to retaliate when they returned, knowing they couldn't challenge him one-on-one and win."

Her words seem to soothe her, despite my inability to respond in kind. I nudge her thigh to show I'm listening. Sometimes, all a woman wants is to know her words are heard and understood.

"I tried once to organize the unhappy males, get them to rally behind me so we could overthrow Hector together. He was a poor leader in other ways, too. But it didn't work. Hector found out and beat me to a pulp—first, and last, time he ever hit me. Claimed he needed to show me my place. That's when I discovered..."

My ears perk forward. Is she about to say what I think? Is she referring to when she learned how to partially shift?

"Well, let's just say, I learned how to take care of myself after that." Her hand tightens in my fur. "I never had to worry about him laying a hand on me in anger again."

I quicken my pace, eager to arrive at her place so I can pursue this topic further in human form. It sounds like she discovered the ability to transform on her own, out of necessity. Is it only a question of wanting it badly enough? Being pushed into a dangerous situation? Or is it about focus? Could there be a ritual involved, like with magic?

Magdelena lengthens her stride to keep up. "My, you seem in a hurry all of a sudden. We'll turn up ahead, at the lamppost. The entrance is off the street."

I note the location, lifting my head when the wind changes, bringing the scent of Weres to me. I hesitate, slowing to sift through all the smells and what they mean. She did say she lives on a street with other packmates.

"What's wrong, Jon? We're here, let's get inside and warm up."

I stop and she walks ahead, sure of herself and her surroundings. I issue a low growl to get her attention. Maybe I'm just being paranoid. She halts at the mouth of the narrow side street. "The door is back here, come on," she says, motioning with her head. Concern fills her eyes as I wait, poised for action. Paranoid or not, something feels off.

Maybe it's your mind's way of making sure you don't have to sleep with her.

Geez, that's a dumb thought. Wish I could tell my head to shut up.

"Jon?" Magda asks, stepping toward me. A man reeking of werewolf musk steps out from the alley and grabs her arm, pulling her into shadows the rising sun hasn't had a chance to scatter.

I bolt forward, hackles raised, ready for retaliation. I round the corner and slam to a halt, seeing Magdelena surrounded by four very angry Weres.

They're all bigger than the slight woman, and all look tired, like they've been waiting a long time for her to arrive. The men are dressed in dark colors, as if they expected to take her by surprise in the night. I've not met three of them, but one familiar face stands out—Manny, the bartender from Lupine Luna.

Magda tears her arm from the man's grasp. "What the hell is this all about?" She turns to the bartender. "Manny?"

"We know you're behind the killings, Magdelena," Manny says, stepping forward to confront the smaller woman. "Another body was recently discovered—beaten to death in her home—right around the time you left with your pretty wolf-boy for a late night run."

Wolf-boy? Are they referring to me? I step closer and growl, the sound unmistakable in the quiet alley.

"It wasn't us! I swear it. We were tracking down the real killer. It was an hombre gato. We killed him in the subway, just a little while ago."

One of the others steps closer, menace in his face and voice. "An hombre gato? Now you're making shit up. They haven't been around in hundreds of years."

"Are you calling me a liar?" The angry woman's voice sounds deadly.

Manny breaks in, his voice heated. "This is bullshit. Where's the body? If you killed it, I want proof. Take us to it."

The unsure alpha's composure slips for a second, and the heated Weres see it, like sharks picking up a drop of blood in the water. "It turned to dust when we killed it. There is no proof."

Manny's laughter spills into the deserted side street. "Isn't that convenient? Or it's just another one of your lies."

"Lies?" Magda draws herself up, her slight frame seeming to expand as she stares them down one-by-one. "What lies have I told in the past?" She steps closer to the one who doubted Cat Dude was real. "Did your wife lie when Hector took her against her will? Do you lie to yourself every day when you look in the mirror and think *you* are the one who stopped her torment?"

She turns toward the next man, this one younger and slimmer. "Or did your sister lie, Diego, when she cried rape?" She pivots to face the last man I'd not met, the youngest of the four. "Orlando, did you lie when you said you saw Hector abuse your mother after your father died?"

While she's talking, her body has been slowly changing, growing larger, sprouting fur and claws, in anticipation of a confrontation. "You people make me sick. I stopped a man from abusing those you love. And all you see is this—" her face, the last to change, transforms before our eyes into the fierce wolf-human mixture I saw in the subway tunnel. "I will take your ridicule and scorn no longer!"

Without warning, she whips around to the last Were, Manny, and delivers a lightning fast swipe from his neck to his waist, slicing him deep with four razor sharp claws on the end of her transformed hands. "I trusted you to run my business!" Her left hand swipes upward, reversing what her right hand just did. "I trusted you to have my back!"

Shocked for a split second, the other men stand frozen, then burst into action, tackling the transformed woman from behind. The five go down in a blur of fists and kicks. I leap forward, tackling the one she called Diego, driving him to the ground with a snap of my jaws at his face. I have no desire to permanently harm her packmates, but these bastards have gone too far.

Diego yields to my retaliation, looking away and lowering his chin. I snap my teeth at the air in front of him again to drive home my point, and then leap off him to take down another man.

Despite their odds, the men are not able to hold their own against the enraged woman. She's tearing huge chunks of flesh from them now, her anger a force to be reckoned with. "No longer!" Her rough voice doesn't even sound winded as she lands continuous blows on the charging men. "No longer will I tolerate this bullshit!"

I dive at Orlando, sinking my teeth into his shirt when he twists to the side. The fabric rips as I drag him down, climbing onto his back before he can right himself. I clamp my sharp teeth over the back of his neck, tightening my hold and slamming him to the pavement below. Knowing I'm one step away from breaking his neck, his body falls limp in defeat.

Manny stands, swaying on his feet, blood pouring from a dozen different wounds on his body, but still, he doesn't relent. "You are an abomination! No one should have the ability to half change like this. You are either wolf or man, not both."

I growl as I let go of Orlando's neck, conveying my desire he should not move. Shifting positions, I move to stand by Magda's side. She doesn't sway under his harsh proclamation, she stares him down. "You're an ignorant fool, Manny. This," she says with a gesture toward her body, "this is the truest representation of our two halves. Like this, I am wolf and woman."

I raise my head in pride, her sentiment is exactly what I said to her earlier.

"You, you pitiful man, are stuck between one or the other —never able to fully benefit from both halves of your soul working together. And you," she snaps around to address all the men who attacked her tonight, her gravelly voice a deadly caress in the still morning air, "are no longer welcome in *my* pack. Get the hell out and never return. If I see you again, I'll kill you." She tilts her head up, exposing her throat toward the pink of the dawn sky, and lets out a long, sorrowful howl.

CHAPTER TWENTY-TWO

VIVIAN

U nwilling to wait any longer for Jon to return, and hoping he had better luck tonight than we did, Rafe and I retired to our small basement bedroom shortly after dawn. I felt uneasy closing my eyes without Jon here to watch out for us, but Rafe soothed me into sleep, convincing me to relax with his agile fingers and sweet kisses.

It's well after noon when I awake, only to find Jon has still not returned.

Sensing my unease, Rafe reaches for me in the dark room, drawing me close before speaking. "Maybe he got lucky and Magda let him stay at her place."

"I can check easily enough."

Rafe smothers a yawn. "Then why don't you?"

I shrug, not sure how to put it into words. "It doesn't feel right to barge into his privacy. I know, some sense deep within me, that he's fine. Therefore, pushing into his head to double-check seems like overkill." I sigh and relax into my husband's arms. "I just have to trust him. He'd contact us if he needed to."

"I agree. How about we get up and start formulating a plan? I haven't been comfortable with this run-around-and-put-out-fires crap we've been doing since you returned to the city." He sits up and leaves the warmth of the bed, rummaging through his bag for clean clothes. "I love this city, don't get me wrong, but these killings aren't our problem. I understand we initially feared Magdelena might reveal your daytime resting place or somehow try and blame the murders on Jon, but that's behind us now."

"How about because it's the right thing to do?"

"I disagree." He pulls on clothes, while I watch from my comfortable cocoon of warm blankets. "The local alpha and Jon seem to have an understanding between them now. He didn't mention she's still tossing out threats or anything like that. We need to focus. I was discouraged last night after we lost Rolando, but overall, I know we'll flush the bastard out soon."

My husband finally looks my way, one eyebrow raised. "Don't make me pull the covers off you. Get your cute butt out of bed and get dressed."

I smile, loving the commanding edge to his voice. "Yes, sir. Should I crawl over and suck your cock, too, to prove how in charge you truly are?"

He snorts, enjoying my teasing. "We had plenty of that this morning. Seriously though, get up and join me in the other room. I need to make breakfast."

"I'm going to shower first. I'll be there in a minute."

Rafe leaves as I snuggle deeper into the covers, debating if I could get away with pulling them over my head for five more minutes of luxuriating in his warmth and scent left on the sheets.

The sounds of cabinets opening and pots banging reach me, ensuring I'll never get a chance to pretend the day hasn't started.

"Get up!" he calls. "Don't make me bring in the wet rag."

What happened to the sweet guy from yesterday asking me if I needed more rest?

Rafe reads my mind and calls from the kitchen, "He was subjected to your demanding lovemaking and knows, without a shadow of a doubt, you are completely healed." I hear the water run and see the image of the wet dish towel in his hand. Bastard is going to come in here and shock me with the cold water if I don't get up.

"That's right," he says with a chuckle.

I toss back the covers and stalk into the bath between the two small bedrooms. In less than a half hour, I've showered and dressed, and pulling my damp, freshly-combed hair off my face into a ponytail. By the time I get to the tiny table and chairs in the space between the small kitchen and living area, Rafe has finished eating.

"I've been thinking," Rafe says, his hand curled around a steaming mug of coffee. "These killings, these *distractions,* could be more than we originally thought."

I pour myself a half-mug of black coffee and take the seat across from him. "What do you mean?"

"You mentioned last night that the decoy spell and the trap door could all have been a set up to allow our prey to slip away."

"Uh-huh, do you disagree?"

"No, on the contrary. What if everything we've encountered this week has been for an ulterior motive?"

"By whom? And for what purpose?"

"At first, due to the rumblings Jon reported in Magdelena's pack, I wondered if maybe the local pack could be involved. But now I don't think so. And I wouldn't think they'd kill a vampire on purpose, especially right in front of vamp HQ. They'd have some sense of self-preservation to know better than attack the undead."

"It's true, with all the vampires in the city, the pack wouldn't stand a chance. Are you saying now that you don't think Justin is the cause for the magical imbalance that brought the legendary creatures to life?"

He shakes his head. "Honestly, I don't know what to think. It's all too convenient. But what if he is responsible for it? What does that mean in regards to the rest of us? That his blood happened to be rejected the very week you're scheduled to return into the city?"

"But no one knew I was coming back, let alone that I'd left to begin with."

"Your moves were logical, your retreat to heal a wise move."

I bristle at the use of the word "retreat" and the implication of weakness it conveys. "So, essentially we're back to our original idea—that someone is calling these *things* into being. A magical conjuring of some kind. But to what end? To cause havoc in the city? Is it a diversion from something else that's happening that we've failed to notice?"

Rafe sets his mug down, a speculative look on his face. "Now there's an idea worth following. If this was a redirection, what did it divert us from?"

"The assumption there is the distraction was aimed at us. But what if it wasn't? What if it was aimed at someone else?"

"Like who?"

"Like a group—the local pack, one of the various covens in the city, or even the Tribunal. Could they have an enemy who conjured these magical creatures with the sole purpose to distract and cause harm? And if yes, what harm has been done? We've been so focused on finding these things we haven't thought of what else we could be missing."

My cell rings from the other room. I rise to get it, thinking it has to be Jon or the inn calling, as no one else has the number besides Justin. Digging through yesterday's pockets, I find the phone and answer it, Jon's name flashes on the screen.

"Hey," Jon says. "Just wanted to let you know I'm all right. I didn't wake you did I?"

"No, we're up and discussing theories. Where are you?"

"I... uh... I stayed at Magda's and crashed on her couch."

My eyebrows go up at the mention of her couch. Wonder how that happened and he didn't wind up in her bed.

"I've got a lot to fill you in on," he says. "First and foremost, the hombre gato is dead."

"Glad to hear it. And you're all right?"

"Thanks to Magda, yeah." I hear cars in the background of wherever he's calling from. "I'll fill you in on the rest. I'm on my way home now, via the subway to throw off my scent."

"You left already?"

Jon chuckles. "Yeah. Crept out while she was still sleeping. Seemed like the smartest move."

"Yeah, for a thief in the night maybe. You should have said goodbye."

"That was something I was trying to avoid." He sighs.

"Look, it was a long night, didn't end 'til after sunrise, and I still had to trek back to the bar to get my clothes and phone. I was in no mood to rehash it all and told her I was wiped out, which was not a lie. Thankfully she was exhausted, too. I'll catch up with her later. When my head is on straight."

"Uh-huh."

"We've got more important things to do. Find Rolando, right, Dria?"

By the tense tone and his use of my real name, I can tell he doesn't want to talk about it anymore. I don't blame him. "We'll see you soon," I say, disconnecting the call.

Rafe wandered in to lean against the doorjamb, and heard both sides of the conversation. "He didn't sleep with her, did he?"

"Nope. But he may not have to seduce her to learn what he wants to know. I'm inclined to let him handle it. If he can't find out what he needs to know before it's time for us to leave, then I'll pay the new alpha a visit and rip the knowledge out of her head."

"Why wouldn't you have made that offer first, rather than put him through all this?"

"Because it's his pack, his desire to lead it, and his aspiration to unite all the packs with this knowledge. It should be him who makes the sacrifices to uncover what he needs to know."

"Won't you be defeating all that if you take the knowledge for him?"

"If he's unable to finish what he's set out to do and unable to extract what he needs to know, it doesn't change the fact that him knowing the skill will make him a better protector and stronger right-hand man for us. I'd rather take whatever he needs to accomplish those goals than sit around and watch him flounder—but that doesn't mean I don't give him time first. He may be able to pull it off in the end."

"Okay, fine. Come back to the table. I've just thought of another way to approach this."

"Really? How?"

"With a city map. Let's mark what we know and where it happened, and see if we can find a center point where the magical conjuring could have originated, or perhaps an overlap of distances that could relate to a commonality."

"And if we do all this work and it still leads to Justin?"

"Then a duck is a duck. I won't fight it anymore. But something seems too... easy in blaming Justin and a magical imbalance. And the timing is too coincidental."

"Ahh... is this where you start quoting TV to me again?"

"You do remember!" Rafe smiles and draws me into a big hug. "'Rule thirty nine: There's no such thing as coincidence.'"

"God save me from TV quoting men and performance anxiety werewolves."

"Hah! You think Jon's anxious about his seduction of Magdelena? That's a good one!"

"Don't tell him, though. He'll get all defensive and loud, and start posturing. And really, how much testosterone is one woman supposed to take before she gags on it?"

My intentional double entendre draws loud laughter from my husband as he pulls me in his arms for a kiss.

Within the hour, Jon arrives and fills us in on his long night hunting the gato and their early morning confrontation with the men from Magda's pack.

"She banished them, Viv," Jon says, sorrow in his eyes. "Like they meant nothing to her. Not bothering to try to communicate with them, come to an agreement, work it out... nothing. Just kicked their disloyal asses out to fend for themselves."

I hold back a sniff of derision, thinking she did better than I would have. "I probably would have killed them. But hey, that's just me."

"What does it mean to a werewolf to have no pack?" Rafe asks.

Anguish colors Jon's soulful hazel eyes. "It means to run without protection, to fear being discovered by a pack and deemed a threat—hunted down and killed for infringing where you don't belong. It means being alone. Forever."

Rafe asks, "Or until the lone wolf finds another pack, right?"

Sensing this goes deeper for Jon, and maybe touches on his own hidden doubts in leading a pack, I ask, "What would Romeo have done?"

"Perhaps she tried talking things out with them in the past?" Rafe suggests at the same time.

"You're right, she could have," Jon says, answering Rafe. "I don't know. She might be the strongest in the pack due to her special abilities, but that doesn't mean she's a natural leader—or a true alpha. As far as Romeo?" Jon shrugs. "Any number of things, I think. He'd definitely have tried talking to them before things became so hate-filled and out of control. Maybe he'd have had to kick a few asses... but honestly, I can't see him banishing anyone from the pack. Hell, we fought all the time and he never did that to me, even tried to get me to come back, through Elsa, after I stormed out all those years ago."

"How could Magda have been mated to Hector and not be a true female alpha?" I ask.

"You remember me telling you about the past disagreements Romeo and I had, even when we butted heads this summer at the resort?" Rafe and I nod. "I knew I had to leave his pack, even though I knew going out alone was an even scarier idea. I was evolving into an alpha, showing the signs and strength—the first of which was how fast I could change.

"I was born with the potential to be an alpha in my genes. No matter when I was bitten, those traits were already inside me. But for other alphas?" He shrugs. "Sometimes they evolve out of necessity. It can be a good fit or a bad fit when a wolf battles for the alpha spot in a pack. If they're a natural leader, things run smoothly. If they aren't... well, dissension can rise in the pack."

"And what's your impression of this pack?" I ask.

"Based on what you told me, that they change leadership often, and what I've seen myself, I'd say this pack has been held by very weak alphas. Ones that became what was needed through necessity, and not through actual power and the ability to lead with diplomacy."

A grimace forms on Rafe's face. "The strength to take the lead doesn't always mean the conqueror is the best candidate for a leader, just the best fighter."

"Exactly," I say. "And what would that mean to this pack if Magda didn't have this half-form to keep them all in line?" I straighten in my chair, glad we're getting back to what I want to know. "Speaking of which, how much closer are you to discovering how she does it?"

Jon shifts in his seat, then rises to fill a plate with whatever is left on the stove. "She revealed a few personal things last night when I was in wolf form. I wasn't able to pursue the line of questions I had in mind, but plan to when I see her next."

"That doesn't answer my question, Jon."

Jon becomes stiff when he sits at the table. "I'll get what you want, not to worry."

I back off, pleased to see he's showing some backbone.

"Good," Rafe says, looking eager to change the topic. "When you're done eating, I'd like your help with this map idea I have."

Jon finishes eating and cleans all the dishes. The next few hours are spent with them marking up a city map and drawing circles all over it, fanning out from crime scenes, residences, and jobs we know Justin has taken.

In the back of my mind, I recall a detail we may have missed. "What about the address of the wizard Justin gave us, the one close to the second invunche victim?"

"We never did talk to him. Do you think it would help?"

"Not sure, but I'll find it."

I rifle through my clothes from yesterday and find the information. After I add it to the map, I can't see it will make a difference. It's only half a block from where we saw the homeless man beaten.

"All right, that looks like a dead end."

Jon nods, but continues to stare down at the map. "Unless we find something else pointing toward this other wizard, I say we leave it alone. We've got enough data on the map already. Rafe, what do you think?"

Pleased to hear the two of them working together, I sit back and sip my cold coffee.

"I agree." He stares at the map, his finger tracing the

overlapping circles. "What's in this spot, Dria? Anything look familiar to you?"

I lean forward, looking to where he's indicating. He's pointing to one of the few green spaces in the city, the Plaza de Mayo.

A chill seeps over me as I recall a fight I had there centuries ago, when the city was still forming. "You're right." An icy chill slinks down my spine. "All along, these distractions, these killings... they've been set up with one purpose in mind."

"And what's that?" Rafe asks.

"To draw me out."

CHAPTER TWENTY-THREE

RAFE

"What the hell?" Jon says. "That can't be right."

I nod, feeling lighter now that my fears have been confirmed. "It makes sense."

"What do you mean it makes sense? The killings started before she even got here."

"That's my point, furball. No one but us knew exactly when she would return. What better way to lure her back than to start killing people and drawing attention to the supernatural in the city?"

"Why would that work?" Jon asks. "That's a stupid theory."

I move to my wife's chair and drop an arm around her shoulders. "Because whoever did this knows my wife well. They knew she couldn't resist doing the right thing."

An annoyed look replaces Dria's shocked expression from a few moments ago. "You make me sound like some paranormal Dudley-Do-Right."

I squeeze one shoulder. "Come on, hon. Admit it. You hate

to see the underdog lose. You *always* look out for the little guy."

She delivers a harrumph of annoyance. "I do not. What a load of horse shit."

Dawning lights Jon's face. "You're right, she does."

"Come now, this is ridiculous."

"No," Jon says, his voice gaining enthusiasm as his understanding increases. "No, it's not. You do fight for your beliefs. And you don't walk away from a perceived wrong. I see it now. Rafe is right. These attacks were all aimed at drawing you back into the city, and involving yourself in local matters that shouldn't concern you.

"George was the lynchpin. Justin's neighbor was just in case you started to wobble, and it was a poke at you. By that point, thanks to your bold visit to the Tribunal with Rafe, he already knew you were here. The killings would continue until you figured it out."

My wife pales, what little color she has fleeing in an instant.

I pat her shoulder. "Look at the timing, Dria. Rolando has planned this every step of the way."

"I don't believe it. We've already accredited the magical imbalance to Justin."

"Just this morning we discussed it might not be him. Denial doesn't suit you, my dear."

She pushes back from the table and storms from the room. "I like living in denial quite nicely, thank you very much."

Dria slams the bedroom door, and the two of us are left alone, staring down at the map.

"That didn't go over well," Jon says. "What next?"

"Next, we convince her she has to walk into his trap and

put an end to this deadly charade once and for all." I jab my finger on the map at the Plaza de Mayo. "He wants her here. We just have to figure out when."

After a half-hour cool down period, I venture into our shared bedroom to see if Dria is ready to talk. Much to my relief, she's doing a complex yoga pose. I know she's aware I've entered, no matter how deep in thought she is, she's always *aware*, so I stand quietly, waiting for her to naturally finish the pose in her own time.

She needs the exactness of the move to still her thoughts. Something she seeks out regularly to remain in control of her mind, and not to become overruled by her emotions.

When she's finally upright—standing perfectly still with bent arms in front of her chest, palms touching—her chin dips as her lips move, then she lifts her eyelids and her face, focusing her attention on me.

"You won't be going without me," I say, laying my determination out there early so we can get past it.

Her lips turn up at the corners. "Understood. Did you really think I'd face them without my Wolf Killer by my side?"

My heart swells at her acceptance. She hasn't been herself since we escaped from Coraline's clutches. And frankly, neither have I. I would have started a knock-down-drag-out-fight if she tried to exclude me now. I'm done letting her handle it all. Last month proved, without a doubt, we can both be taken against our will—anytime. And I intend to shore up our defenses any way I can.

"Do you know when?" I ask. "That's what you were

pondering in the back of your mind, through your moves, right?"

She gives me a sly smile, her eyes crinkling at the corners. "Maybe. Can't say for sure what's working in my subconscious." She softens, the lines of her face smoothing, the most relaxed I've seen her in ages. "That's the point of meditation. To ease your mind, to accept what is. To see, with clarity, the best life-route to bring happiness to you soul." She becomes more solemn, walking toward me. "And to understand when you might have to darken your soul for a while with a choice you have to make. To know your soul will be happy again, soon, as long as you are careful not to let too much darkness taint you."

I open my arms, inviting her into my heart with the motion, reassuring her she is not alone, she will always have me by her side. I run my hands down her spine, letting her feel my touch.

She presses her lips to my shirt in a kiss. "He'll be there every night, waiting," she says, referring to Rolando at the Plaza de Mayo.

"The nights are long this time of year."

"And he won't want to waste all of it on waiting for me to figure out what he's doing. He'll limit his time in the plaza."

"To when?"

"Well past sunset, but before midnight."

"How can you be sure?"

She shrugs. "I can't. But it's what I would do. Especially if I had to plan more magical mischief that night."

"You're right, the murders all happened after sunset, but well before midnight."

"He'll then wait for me where I fought rogues who'd tried

to destroy the Seat of Darkness. It was a bloody day in the city's pre-history. Not one I'll ever forget."

"And why would Rolando know this day would stick out for you? Was it one of your worst battles?"

"No, not by a long shot. Thankfully though, when I look back, the details seem more like I'm watching an historical reenactment show on the History Channel, not something I really did. But to answer your question—he would refer to that night because he fought by my side."

"Interesting."

"Not really. We had both been enforcers for the Tribunal at one time in our long undead lives. I'd sparred with him before, knew he could fight."

"Was it significant in any other way for him?"

She cocks her head to the side, a thoughtful gleam entering her gaze. "Yes. I hadn't thought of it until you mentioned it. He was offered a position in the inner circle after that."

"Who initiated the discussion for his nomination?"

A bright smile shines across her gorgeous face, lighting her green eyes with fire and determination. "Persephone."

We fill the hours of the early evening with more food and even more planning. We're sure Rolando wasn't acting alone all this time, and the group consensus is Persephone has been working with him. What would the ancient gain by involving herself in this scheme? Dria is unsure who originally turned Rolando and made him a vampire, and I'm inclined to think perhaps he has a deeper connection to the distant ancient than we were previously aware of.

It's almost eight when we decide to leave for the Plaza de Mayo. Jon paces with nervous energy. "I'm still not so sure we should be going with just the three of us. I could call Magda, see if she's willing to join us."

My wife smiles, the sentiment softening her lines of worry. "I appreciate the thought, Jon. But there's no way in hell I'm bringing anyone else into this mess. Truth be told, I'd rather go alone."

"Not going to happen," I say. Jon's forceful "hell no" sounding at the same time.

"I know, I know. We talked about it. You guys are both coming." She shoots us an annoyed glance. "Doesn't mean I have to like it."

"What are you expecting will happen?"

"Could go several ways. Rolando wants to finish what he started last month, and plans to question me further. And possibly kill me when I can't reveal any information about the Atlantians or more manipulators.

"Or he plans to kill me outright. Although, I'm less inclined to believe that one. He's proven he could've come after me anytime this week if that's what he wanted."

I break in with my thoughts. "I don't think he's after you for information. If that was the case, he'd have been in that room while they tortured you."

"What else could he want?"

"To meet you on neutral ground?" I suggest. "When you're not tracking him with the intent to kill him on sight."

"That was never my plan, and you know it. I'd always intended to question him before I killed him. What good would it do to end him without knowing if there were others plotting to come after me, too?"

256

Jon's pacing stops. Hands on his hips, he glances back and forth between us. "And what about weapons? Are we taking any? Should I go as a wolf or man?"

"There's a martial arts equipment shop over in Monserrat," I say. "I wouldn't mind bringing a bo staff and throwing knives."

Dria shakes her head. "Whatever you bring could be used against you by a powerful vampire. I wouldn't risk it."

"Nothing?" Jon asks. He sees her shake her head again. "Dammit. I feel naked enough as it is. This sucks." He shoves his hands into his pockets and stares down at the map.

"Am I walking in as bait, with you two watching from the sidelines?"

Jon's head whips up. "Uh—another resounding *hell no*. We go in together, a united front."

My wife sighs. "I was afraid you'd say that."

By eight-thirty we're parking a couple of blocks away and walking into the well-lit Plaza de Mayo, scanning every face we pass for signs of Rolando or Persephone. I flank my wife's right side and Jon is on her left. The plaza isn't very busy this time of year, with the trees bare and the grasses looking lifeless and flat. Palm trees tower above us, bracketing the brick sidewalks, the fronds rustling in the chilly winter breeze.

Dead ahead lies the pristine Mayo Pyramid, a stone monument made in 1810, and the *Casa Rosada*, or Pink House, sits behind it. A lone figure leans against the black fencing around the monument's base, staring toward us. Slicked back dark hair, tall, slender build, impeccably dressed as always.

That's him, my wife says through our telepathic bond. *Stay sharp and watch for Persephone.*

We continue our approach, angling toward Rolando's position. He straightens as we get closer, stepping away from the fence, hands spread wide. "So good of you to finally join me, Alexandria. I wondered how long it would take you to figure it out."

"Was it worth it? To kill all those people?"

"We had to be sure you'd come back to the city."

"You could have called me."

He smiles, a deadly expression that doesn't reach his eyes, which remain flat and emotionless. "And would you have listened? Would you have come to meet me?"

"Considering you helped torture me, probably not."

He nods once, his suspicions confirmed. "Exactly as I thought. You never would have believed I was there to keep you safe. To make sure they didn't go too far and kill you."

My wife tilts her head to the side, narrowing her gaze on the suave vampire. "And I don't believe you now. Why would you have tried to help me?"

He motions a hand near his feet, and out of nowhere, two black puppies appear. Rolling and tumbling on the ground in play.

Dria freezes, mentally screaming through our bond, *Protect your mind! Lock it down tight!* And with that, I sense an emptiness that wasn't there a moment ago. My wife cutting off all mental contact with me.

"Because, my dear," Rolando says, his voice dangerous and low. "I'm exactly like you."

Shock slams into me as understanding hits me in the face.

The puppies aren't real. He's casting an illusion, a physical illusion so strong, even Dria can see it. And to prove my point, the puppies disappear.

The older vampire smiles again, this time with a hint of superiority in it. "That's right. I can see you've all worked it out. I'm a manipulator, just like your lovely redhead."

Without warning, a shimmer of movement, like heat dancing in the air over a summer street, appears at his side. Slowly it takes on corporeal form, revealing the tall, lithe body of Persephone.

Her voice travels the short distance between us to dance up our spines, like the icy fingers of death on a cold Alaskan night. "And if we'd wanted you dead, you already would be."

CHAPTER TWENTY-FOUR

JON

A bead of sweat forms near my temple, despite the cold, and slowly trickles down the side of my face. Every muscle in my body is poised to fight, to leap forward and smash my fist into the detached faces of the vampires before us.

But I hold still, very aware they could kill me between one heartbeat and the next—with just a thought. The sounds of the city swirl around us, the scents of the distant food vendors and chatting tourists reminding me we're not as isolated as it seems.

"Why?" Vivian asks. "Why did you do all of this? Why the elaborate plan to draw me back in?"

"We had to be sure," Persephone says, slipping her hand into the crook of Rolando's elbow. "Sure you were uncorrupted by the power. Sure that you would not reveal what you knew, even under extreme circumstances."

The redhead snorts. "And you thought torture was a good way to determine that?"

One slim shoulder rises. "It worked. As did the means to get you here, exactly where we want you."

Viv gestures with her arm, "Here? In the Plaza de Mayo?"

A crafty look passes over the ancient's face. "Is that really where you are? Are you certain?"

Slowly the sounds drift away, as does the breeze and the smells it carried. The monument shimmers in the background and dissolves, the distant Pink House and palm trees a memory. I feel a rush, like my head is spinning from a carnival ride, and hear a whoosh inside my mind, like the shutting of a door on a strong wind. All at once, an extravagant living room appears around us, a home I've never been in before.

Creams and browns dominate the space, with touches of color here and there in a pillow or piece of artwork. The adjustment to another view of reality sways me and I reach out a hand to steady myself.

Vivian's colder hand finds mine, and she squeezes it once in reassurance.

"How the hell did we get here?" I ask, proud to hear my voice sounds steady and doesn't reveal how freaked out I'm really feeling.

"I slipped into your minds the moment you left your car. You walked here under my direction, while thinking you were at the plaza." She gestures to the brown couches. "Please, take a seat."

Vivian steps forward, pulling Rafe and me with her. She doesn't speak through our mind link, but I understand instinctively we can't make a move until we know what the hell is going on. All three of us sit on the sofa facing the fireplace, leaving the love seat and chair for Rolando and Persephone.

The evil couple follows us, sitting close on the shorter couch. With a flick of her fingers, the fire lights in the hearth, flames springing up instantly to lick the logs laid on a metal grate.

Vivian sucks in a breath. "You! Not Rolando. You were the one who created the magical creatures that killed all those people. There was no imbalance and thinning of the barrier between worlds. You did it and let Justin take the blame."

"He took the blame all on his own, thanks to your meddling. He drew an incorrect conclusion based on the information he had. As you all did. Not my fault."

"But you aren't denying you killed those people to get me here?"

She looks over the three of us, her face an unreadable mask devoid of emotion. "We did what we needed to do."

"And George? Did you cast a binding spell for the gato to kill him easier?"

"An unfortunate death," the ancient vampire shakes her head. "But we knew you cared for him and it would lead you where we wanted."

The air seems to leave Vivian. She slumps into the cushions behind us. "But why? I don't understand what you want from me. You two obviously knew I was a manipulator, and have for some time."

Rolando answers, moving to the edge of the love seat, leaning toward us. "Because we want you to join us. We want to unite all the manipulators on the planet, to rise up and seize control, to ensure we're never hunted down like prey ever again."

"Is that why Coraline came after me? To make sure your dream never came true?"

"In part, yes," Persephone says. "She'd always hated you.

Once there was a whisper of manipulators surviving, she was convinced you were one and behind it all."

"And you," Vivian says to Rolando, "pretended to be a part of the group, ferreting us out so you could save us for your cause?"

He nods and my stomach turns. There's so much wrong with this scenario, I don't even know where to begin. Good thing I don't have to say anything and can sit quietly while they hash it out.

Rolando's suave accent paves a path of anxiety inside me. "We'll never regain what we lost all those millennia ago. But maybe we can build a new Atlantis here in the city."

A new Atlantis? This guy is freaking nuts. I look to Persephone to see her face mirrors the crazy-light of a true believer as well.

"Give me a chance," the ancient says, extending a hand to Vivian. "Let me show you what we once had, let me explain what happened and how we came to Buenos Aires, long before it was ever called that."

Seeing that Vivian isn't reaching across the space to take her hand, Persephone drops it, returning it to her lap. She looks collected and in control, despite the stench of adrenaline that's bound to be pouring off me, coiling my muscles for an attack.

Rafe drapes one leg casually over the other, letting them know he's not cowed by their brute show of mental force in getting us here. "Go ahead. You brought us here for a reason, and it obviously wasn't to kill us. You've made it clear we can't stop you, so you might as well get on with it."

Rolando smiles. "I knew I liked you for a reason. See?" he

says, resting a hand on the ancient's knee. "I told you he would be an asset."

Vivian doesn't react, and I hate to admit, but I'm torn on what the hell to do. They aren't attacking us, and yet I feel like I'm stuck in a trap with no way out, my death at the end a surety.

"I sense your tensions and misgivings. All of you," Persephone says, while staring at me. "But I promise you, we won't hurt you."

Yeah, unless we don't do what you want. Then all bets are off.

"It'll go much faster if you lean back and relax."

Sounds like my last prostrate exam. The doctor said something similar then, too. Bastard.

Vivian reaches for my hand, locking it in a tight grip. *We can't leave until she lets us.* She projects into my mind. *Protect your deepest thoughts and allow yourself to see what she wants to show us. Then we'll figure out a way out of this hell.*

I squeeze her hand to show I heard, letting myself sink back into the cushion next to her. *This is going to be one freaky-ass ride,* I send back to her.

Without a doubt.

A look of consternation crosses Persephone's face. "How about we cover a few things before we begin? Might help you all to calm down. Did you know Atlantis was considered the birthplace of vampires? All breeds of supernaturals visited and worked there, but it was primarily populated by humans and vampires. It was a very big island, around the size of New Zealand, truth be told. And the whole society was ruled by manipulator vampires. It was the true Seat of Darkness before we came here."

Rolando shakes his head slowly, dismayed over all that was lost. "Stories have twisted over the centuries, 'til most people think the island never existed. It's a shame, really. Almost like the lost library of Alexandria, the possible knowledge it contained a myth more than reality."

"Really?" Vivian says. "Not everyone believes there was a real Atlantis originally ruled by vampires? Go figure."

I squeeze her hand in support. Although, right now, the idea of a big island and all the vampires in the world are stuck there doesn't sound like a bad idea to me.

With a long stare at seemingly nothing, Persephone ignites the candles on the low coffee table between us. I stifle a shudder at her carefree use of magic.

Vivian is right, the bitch could easily kill us. How do you relax your guard when you don't trust the person you're with?

"That's a no brainer," Persephone says, answering my question without me vocalizing it. "You don't. But what you can do is listen and keep an open mind."

"Are you messing with my servant's head?" Vivian says, bristling in agitation. "I don't like it. Leave him be."

I feel a pressure course through me, and harden. Vivian's powerful mind expands to encase mine, like she's erecting a shield around Rafe, her, and myself. After the recent display of strength from the ancient, I'm not so sure her efforts, or mine, will make a difference.

She shrugs one elegant shoulder. "That's life, Dria. You had to know you wouldn't be the proverbial 'king of the hill' and the most powerful vamp in the room once you shared space with an ancient."

Vivian snorts in false bravado. "I've known you for centuries, and yet you've never revealed to me that you were a manipulator."

"I understand your frustration. How about we start with the basics. You're aware of manipulator vampires—but have you heard of elemental vampires?"

Thanks to our new connection, I feel Vivian's immediate responses as if they were my own. Curiosity for another species simmers below the surface, eager to perk up and listen to what the woman has to say, and it overrides her instinctual fear of Persephone.

"That's a new one," Viv says. "No, I haven't."

Persephone nods. "I thought not. There's an old phrase that's been handed down from one turned vampire to another, 'never turn a witch.' You're familiar with it, yes?"

"Of course. I don't know its origins, but I can easily follow a simple direction."

The ancient looks relieved, as if she was glad Viv wasn't a rule breaker in that regard. "Good. An elemental vampire starts as a human witch turned into a vampire. It's not a safe combination. I've meet several vampires in my time who didn't follow the advice. I had to kill them and the vamps they turned."

"Why?" I ask. "Did the new vamps go crazy or something?"

She stares into the fire and then looks at Rolando briefly before turning her attention back to the three of us. "No. I almost wish they had."

Shock colors Vivian's mind. "Why would you wish insanity on a new vampire? Think of all the destruction they could do."

"Ah... my lovely Dria. A crazy vampire is easily spotted and stopped, especially by the one who turned them. But this... this is something much different. And much more serious." She takes Rolando's hand and motions to the room around us with the other. "I'd like to show you, if you're willing."

CHAPTER TWENTY-FIVE

VIVIAN

"Hold up now, just like that?" Rafe asks. "You're ready to share the memory?"

She nods again, this time with a mix of excitement and sadness on her face. "Once I share the memory with you, as it was shared with me a very, very long time ago, it will be yours. That way others can see the truth if anything happens to me in the future."

"Do you think there's a chance of that?" I motion to Rolando with my chin. "The inner circle out numbers the ancients four to one. With their protection, how much safer could you be?"

"That's not what I mean," she looks at me slyly, "and you know it. Our existence as manipulators is a free license to kill among our peers. None of my fellow ancients suspect what I am. It's been a secret I've kept for over two thousand years."

Shock spills through me. "You mean to tell us you're older than Christ?"

"Technically, yes. But does the son of God have a real

age? Or is he timeless and has perhaps walked this earth before, in another human form?" Her face takes on a faraway expression. "So much is unknown to us, and yet at times it seems like everything is possible—every interpretation, every legend, every belief. If someone thinks it, it has power. The more who believe, the more power the idea has."

Rolando breaks in, "We need to keep on track, my dear. You were telling them about elemental vampires."

"Yes, thanks for the reminder. Sometimes my head is so filled with the possibilities and theories I get a little lost. Bottom line, I want to show you what happens when a witch is turned. Can you trust me enough to show you all?"

"Just to make sure I'm understanding this right," Jon says. "You intend to project a memory to us from over two thousand years ago? You can remember that far back?"

I know Jon's question is triggered more from what I went through to forget my past. But my choice to forget is obviously not the choice of all vampires.

"The memory is older than I am, it's not mine. You'll understand when you see it. For now—let's consider what I'm offering—a trip to ancient times," she sweeps her arm dramatically, "in the comfort of a living room."

Apprehension fills me. I'm worried this might not be a good idea. Letting anyone in my head is not something I relish. "I've never shared another manipulator's visions, only my own. Can you tell me what to expect?"

"It'll be exactly like the images you've projected to others, except it will be an event in the past and not something a manipulator can change. You will be able to see everything that occurred, as if you were there, living it alongside the occupants in the vision. You'll see it all as the person who lived it, but no one will see you."

"Well of course not. If it's a memory, how could anyone see us?"

"I just wanted to make sure you understood. It's a very disconcerting feeling. Like you've been transported back in time, but invisible."

I open a conjoined mind link between me and the men. *What do you think? Should we go along with it?*

It can't hurt us, right? Rafe asks.

Not that I know—especially if it's a memory. A new illusion crafted to manipulate might contain surprises for whomever it's projected to, but this isn't the same. If she's telling the truth, we won't have any risk—it will be a memory only—and the person who shared it with her survived the experience.

Rafe's assurance sounds in my mind first. *With you by my side, I'm willing to try anything.*

Ditto what the big goon said, Jon adds.

"Okay, we'll do it," I say.

Rolando lets out a sigh. "For a moment there, I feared you'd say no."

"It crossed my mind, trust me. But I want to know what happened."

"You will be happy you got to see the island. It was a magical place."

"How long is the memory?" Rafe asks, always the practical one.

"Hours. It will be an intense sharing." She leans back, getting comfortable. "Take it easy, Dria. This isn't going to hurt." Persephone smiles again in reassurance while I clutch my husband's hand in apprehension.

Never had this happen to you before, huh? He asks through our connection.

We've already covered that it will be a new experience for me.

His mental amusement trickles through our bond. *I meant that you're not in complete and utter control of a situation.*

My mind flashes back to the recent silver torture. *Let's just say when I have lost control, it hasn't been a pleasant experience.*

Suck it up, my lovely husband projects. *Not everything is bad, and not everyone is out to get you.*

More importantly, Jon adds, *we're right here with you. We won't let anything happen to you.*

Yeah, like either of them could stop her from mind-raping me during her projection. I don't like it, but I'm honest enough to admit my apprehensions are probably what Rafe said, the loss of control.

Persephone looks ready to begin, a wrinkle of irritation on her forehead from my lack of trust. "I know it may be hard to grasp after all you've gone through lately, Dria, but I am your friend. Without you knowing it, I've protected your secret over the centuries. I've watched from the sidelines, always ready if you lost control."

"Somehow, knowing you watched and were ready to kill me... well... it's not as reassuring as you might think."

Rolando laughs. "She's got you there."

"How about we start?" And without further discussion, the room around us disappears. A young woman with long dark hair cascading down her back, a coil of tight braids circling the crown, stands in the center of a stone bedchamber. Tapestries hang on the walls and big open windows let in lots of light, their door-like shutters folded back against the wall. There's no glass in the wall openings. By the angle of weak light across the floor, it looks to be the end of the day, the last of the sun's rays before they disappear completely below the horizon.

If she's a vampire, she could be any age over fifty, the point when a vampire can rise slightly before the sun has set.

A man bursts into the room, with no knocking or announcing his presence. "Esmerelda, it's time for the convening. You must come now."

The young woman follows him out of the room. As Persephone said, it's not her in the memory, but someone I don't know. And judging by the appearance of the surroundings, someone I'll never meet. Just how long ago it is, I have no idea, but the ancient did mention millennia earlier.

I can tell by her surroundings, Esmerelda is not in a person of position or power. Her clothes are simple and clean, a loose, shirt-like garment in light purple. The style one might have seen worn by a novitiate in training at a Grecian temple. Our vision follows along with her as she moves, without us having to leave the comfort of the couch. Fascinating. A part of me wonders if my illusions are this complex and complete.

I feel the piece of furniture beneath me and know it's there, but if I allow myself to drift... to disassociate with my physical form, it's as if I'm right in the memory with the young Esmerelda. Truly fascinating.

"You know they hate it when we are late, Esmie. Hurry!"

The young woman rolls her gaze toward the ceiling in

annoyance. "Brutus, you are worrying for nothing. The elders will not even notice if we attend or not."

"It's the most important vote we've ever had. This will be the defining moment of our future. Will manipulators share the governing of Atlantis with elementals, or will our rule stay unchallenged for another quarter century?"

I wish we could hear their thoughts, but we have to assume Persephone brought us to this moment in time for a very good reason. Without any effort, we're pulled along behind the young vampire, getting a bird's eye view of what civilization was like on the ancient, mythical island. I still can't wrap my head around the fact the island actual existed—and then throw in the additional detail that it's the ancestral heart of all vampires? Who wouldn't be in awe?

The two figures wind through narrow passages, wide halls, and enormous empty rooms that look like they were used for specific purposes—like dining, reading, a music hall. I long to stop and stare, to really get an up close look at antiquities that no one has seen for thousands of years... but before my wish can come true, the vampires continue forward, an obvious purpose in their movements.

"Do you really think there's even a chance the elementals will be heard? I predict the presidio will force them to vote how they want."

"Oh no—didn't you hear?" Brutus says. "The witches in the village crafted a huge blocking spell. No one can get into the head of anyone while in the great room and casting their ballot. This vote will be as fair as it can be, if the elementals have anything to say about it."

"But that's just it. They out number us. Of course the vote will go their way. That's the way it's always been. We rule for twenty-five years and then they rule for twenty-five years—each side creating more vampires when they need to swing the vote their way."

"I know my history as well as you do, Esmie. But that doesn't mean it's *always* going to repeat itself. I'm not putting it past the presidio to try anything." He mumbles under his breath. It sounds like "or at least, I hope."

Esmie rushes to follow. "Are you worried for our safety, Brutus? There was only that one time when the elementals regained rule and immediately burned half of the manipulators to death."

The small man shudders. "Don't bring that up. It was once and we all learned from the mistake."

"Did we? Do you recall Neri ordering us to quietly make sure the latest batch of witches born didn't make it to their first year? He was adamant to try and lower the vote any way he could."

"There's still the chance the general population of vampires will vote for the power to remain unchanged."

The two slow their pace, making me think we're getting closer to their destination. When their conversation pauses, I'm able to hear a growing roar up ahead. It sounds huge. Like thousands of voices speaking at once.

"Hah! Do you really believe they will vote to keep *us* in charge? That is, if no one has altered their minds to make them vote for us?" She throws her hands up in frustration. "This whole thing is a farce! Vampires voting to change rule? Why don't we just share the rule? Have it balanced and even?"

"Because then Odelia wouldn't have supreme obedience... and you know how much she craves that."

Their chatter stills when we approach the source of the

noise. We step into a huge coliseum, deep stadium seating lining the walls, all filled with vampires. I've never seen so many undead in one place in my entire life. Easily, the number must be in the tens of thousands.

In the center, on the sandy floor, is a set of curved tables arranged in a circle with eleven chairs around the exterior curve, ten of them occupied. In the center of the tables is a ceremonial fire set in a tall stand, its flame licking high above the seated vampires. Above it hangs a large scale, with huge basins attached to two extended arms. It looks, to me, like a large distorted version of the scales of justice. I wonder what the hell it's for.

"Hurry! The speeches are about to begin."

CHAPTER TWENTY-SIX

RAFE

Watching from the sidelines, literally and figuratively, is quite awe-inspiring. To see a live depiction of an ancient culture no one living has ever laid eyes on—no one besides the undead, that is.

A sound from above pulls my attention skyward. Fabric panels form a ceiling of sorts, the wind billowing across the colorful expanse to make the material float and snap. Everyone appears to be dressed in subtle variations of easy-flowing tunics, of all colors, with very little underneath—due to the tropical climate, I'm sure. I see many people with head coverings, like small squares of finely woven cloth. I can feel the heat of the day seeping through my clothes, even though I'm not really there, so the hats are surprising.

The atmosphere flowing in and around the crowd seems tense but not dangerous. Along with the myriad of food smells and the overwhelming stench of vampires, I'd almost say there's a hint of urgency in the air. This assembly means a lot to the people gathered, of that I have no doubt.

It's like I'm watching a well-done historical drama on a premium cable channel—until I notice the painted masonry work. Even on TV, the creators all forget the statues, columns, and detailed stone reliefs carved into the walls were all painted deep, rich colors, teeming with vibrancy and life. The assault of color on the eye leaves no doubt this is clearly not a film, but a projected memory.

No expense was spared when the artists and craftsmen created the large communal space. A glance at the sand floor in the center, where the tables sit, reminds me starkly that blood sports, as well as peaceful gatherings, were probably commonplace.

Our guide, Esmie, follows her friend deeper into the giant coliseum. "This is the largest vote I've ever seen. Should we be worried?"

"You're damn right we should be," Brutus says, closer to her ear. "I think this is going to be the day things change forever."

We follow the two as they find seats in the stands. Heated conversation, from unknown sources all around them, leaks into my awareness.

"They never should have killed Demetrius."

"Manipulators will pay for his death once and for all."

Confusion blossoms on our two guides' faces, they clearly overheard the statements as well. The news of this death appears to be new to them, too.

Esmie leans closer to Brutus, whispering in his ear, "Did you hear that? When was Demetrius killed? And how?"

The man looks nervously at the center tables on the sandy floor. "I don't know, but there's an empty seat down below.

He's an ancient and should be there by now. They could be telling the truth."

A lone figure dressed in dark purple rises from the semi-circle of seats in the middle, his arms thrust upward to get people's attention. The crowd slowly quiets and he lowers his arms to speak.

"Welcome! You all know why we're here. It's time to vote on upcoming rulership. Today marks the last day of legal rule by manipulator vampires. Each side will voice their concerns and arguments on why they are the better choice to lead us in the coming quarter century. At the end you'll have a chance to cast your voice." He motions to the side, where I can't see. "Official voting stones are ready for you. Place yours in the appropriate slot in the box and it will roll down to the scales over the ceremonial fire. You'll be called by row when the time has come to cast. Until then, I give you Odelia, delegator for the reigning side."

The speeches begin in earnest after that, taking up way more time than I'd have liked. I don't understand why we'd be here to witness the words, promises, and pleas of politicians long dead, until I begin to notice a decided shift in the energy around us from eager and urgent to furious and blood thirsty.

No matter what is being said down on the sand, it seems a large portion of the crowd is collectively making up their minds before the call to vote has even been voiced. I hear murmurings around me—angry, negative voices who have enough combined hatred of the manipulators to make the sun pale in comparison.

"I don't believe Demetrius killed himself."

"I'd like to suck Odelia dry. The lying bitch!"

"I will die before I let another manipulator into my head, dictating to me what is right and wrong."

If my skin is crawling at the words said, then I imagine Dria is squirming in her seat ready to run.

Without warning, the ground rumbles and rain pours on the crowd. I look up, wondering how the rain soaked through the panels so fast, to see droplets issuing from under the canopy of fabric. Tiny storm clouds hover above us, small flashes of lightning sporadically illuminating the roiling clouds.

A tall man, dressed in a gold tunic, stands from the central tables, his voice somehow filling the entire coliseum. "I knew Demetrius well. He would not have killed himself. His death is the work of manipulators!"

The crowd goes wild, screaming and stomping their feet. But his voice carries over them. "It's wrong to force another to your will. It's wrong to get inside the head of your fellow vampire and make them do what you want. There's no trust among us, and it must stop!"

To further punctuate his point, ear-deafening thunder booms and a bolt of unnatural lightning zings down to zap the vampire named Odelia, encasing her in electricity, her clothes catching fire, frying her to a crisp as her death screams rattle across the expanse. The ancients around her flee toward the exits, all except the one who killed her.

For a moment, the arena is shocked into silence, the smell of her charred remains coating the air. Then thousands of voices explode at once, the chatter filled with shouts and angry accusations.

The man in the center speaks again. "No more! We must destroy every manipulator who opposes us. The time has come for equal rule and equality among the most powerful classes of vampires. Unite and throw off our oppressors! We will be told what to do no more!"

Brutus and Esmie cower in the bleachers, shock and fear on their faces.

Magical bolts of power fly through the stands, incinerating vampires on contact. Screams of agony ricochet in the stone-filled space, and people start to push and shove their way to safety.

Brutus grabs Esmie's hand. "Come with me! We must hide until the fighting ends!"

Our view is tugged along with the fleeing pair, no matter how much I might want to watch and see how the battle progresses. Shouts follow us as we scurry down stone steps, making our way to one of the exits.

"They're wearing silver on their heads!" Brutus shouts, pointing to a gleam of polished metal under the fabric squares atop vampires' heads. "There's no way to break their madness!"

Now I understand the hats I saw on a lot of the gatherers. Dria was cowed by a silver hood and a studded mace to the head the night she was taken from me. The combined terror from the panicked crush of people trying to escape seeps through me, as if it were my own. My heart rate increases and the urge to stand and fight sings through my veins.

But I have no choice in what we see, I'm just a free ride on the horrible memory as it unfolds. One thing I notice of the people surrounding us, not all are manipulator vampires, as the color of their robes don't match the ones in the center who've been torched, or the color of the ones in the stands who were cut down as well.

The royal purple Odelia wore isn't very prominent in the

seething mass of individuals, possibly indicating most of the vampires aren't aligned with manipulators. As we flee with the others down the crowded halls, I try and piece together exactly what I saw. The one who called down the first strike was wearing gold, which must be the color of the elemental vampires.

I glance at Brutus and Esmie's robes of pale lavender. Perhaps it indicates they aren't master manipulators yet, I'm not sure. But either way, I'd think any shade of purple would make you a target in this fight.

The building we're in rocks on its foundation, the very earth beneath us rumbling with the power the elementals have called to destroy the ones they seek.

"We've got to get outside before the entire royal compound is destroyed!"

Esmie and Brutus make their way to the far wall, their escape no longer buoyed along by the scared masses running deeper into the warren of rooms and tunneling halls which we first traveled through. Hands held tightly, they slowly make their way to an open colonnade, one with large doors leading onto a darkened patio.

A red glow lights the horizon, but it's not the sun rising hours ahead of schedule, it's the top of a mountain in the distance.

Esmie points and shouts, "They've made the volcano active. It's going to erupt!"

Brutus turns and then tugs Esmie to look in the opposite direction. "There's a glow in the south, as well. That's where Mount Turimy lies. If they've triggered that one, too, they'll destroy the island. Our only hope is the marina. To get on a boat and sail for the mainland. Come on!"

The two run toward a path leading away from the patio, while a crowd of people spill out of the doors the pair exited a moment ago. The golden hue of an elemental robe catches my eye, and a split second later Brutus screams by Esmie's side, falling to the ground and writhing in pain, covered in flames.

The young manipulator doesn't pause, but runs faster and darts behind a tree to put it between herself and the elemental. A second bolt rips through the air, engulfing the tree. Her lavender tunic mark her as a target. Unless she figures it out and takes it off, she's going to be running for her life every step of the way.

A burning desire to help, to do something, builds inside me. I hate the helplessness I'm feeling, the sense of injustice at the complete and total slaughter of people deemed a threat, when no initiating attack came from them. Maybe that's the point, this uprising was long overdue. Maybe the manipulators deserved it, maybe they abused their power for too long.

"Wipe them out! Kill them all! We will never suffer a manipulator to rule ever again!"

"Get her—the one in purple!"

Our flight with Esmie leads us to a cluster of shops and other buildings outside the royal compound. There's no wall or set delineation to mark the end of the grounds, except perhaps for the slight incline we've raced down. The urge to shake the young woman and tear her robe from her, leaves me panting for breath, despite knowing this tragedy has already unfolded thousands of years ago.

I want her to live, I want her to make it, even knowing her predecessors probably deserve everything they've got coming to them. My heart calms when I see her dash into a building, reaching for the hem of her tunic. She peels it off as she runs toward the back of the shop, passing ceramic bowls and jugs on shelves, displayed for purchase.

In the back, she grabs a smock, or covering of some kind, dirty with red clay splotches, and pulls it over her head. In a further attempt to hide her identity, she loosens the complicated braids woven around her head, allowing them to cascade down like snakes, as she strides quickly through a back door.

Intent on her destination, she runs toward the docks, destruction and dying occurring around her. The elementals stream through the city, from all directions, wearing their golden robes and silver-lined cloth hats, killing everyone wearing any shade of purple.

Storm clouds, bigger and darker than the ones from the coliseum, fill the night sky, obscuring the stars and moon. Driving rain pummels Esmie's slight form, slicking the streets, making it harder for her to run. An earthquake rips through the ground, parting the street like a lone crack in the ice of a winter lake. The gap expands while roofing and debris spill from above, clothing and other household goods tumble out of windows as the rumble pitches and heaves the earth in an angry twist.

Trying to avoid the widening fissure in the road, Esmie sidles closer to the dwellings lining it. Water from the rain runs down from the royal grounds, racing toward the new split in the earth, as the smell of charred human flesh fills our noses. Esmie slips in the torrential rainwater racing by, crashing down in a heap with a sharp shout of pain. A family of humans runs past, small children held in the arms of parents while they flee.

The young woman struggles to stand, one hand against a

brick and mud house, leaning to her left as she positions her awkwardly bent right foot to the side. She's broken it in her fall. She looks up and down the street, the chaos increasing with every moment that passes. Dead ahead lies the marina, still about a half mile away.

Dismay fills me as I watch her forlorn form. She must get there! Keep going!

Esmie bends down, places both hands on either side of the break, and forces her ankle and foot into proper alignment, screaming out at the pain. She rests for a few minutes there in the darkness while the city goes to hell around her, so her ankle can heal and she can continue her escape.

We all watch in silence as she scans the burning remains of the city, knowing her only hope lies in getting to a boat in time. If not, I'm assuming the remaining people will have to swim to the mainland, however far away that is. Would a vampire drown when it became too tired to swim? Would sharks feast on anything swimming a long distance?

I shake off the macabre thoughts as she starts to move. Soon, she's ready to continue, stepping hesitantly at first to ensure her ankle won't give out on her. This time, she's even slower than before, picking her way with caution through the crumbling island. Once she reaches the docks, I'm ready for this memory to end. She obviously makes it onboard and to safety or we'd never have seen what she went through up to this point.

I don't want to see any more images of the once beautiful city being destroyed by hatred. I don't want the smell of burning flesh to coat my nasal passages any longer. I grip my wife's hand to ground me in what's real. I want out of this horrible vision, and I want out now.

CHAPTER TWENTY-SEVEN

JON

Voices surround us as we huddle in Esmie's memory, her misery and desperation a living thing. She's made it to a good sized fishing boat with other fleeing Atlantians. They cast off from the docks a little while ago, the boat's occupants staring at their once grand city going up in flames, watching the red glow of lava from the volcano inch down its steep sides.

"This never would have happened if the manipulators hadn't killed Demetrius," one man says, his eyes filled with tears.

Another man shares his opinion. "Place your blame and anger where it should be—we'd still have our city if the damn elementals hadn't destroyed it."

A wizened old woman speaks up, "Never turn a witch, and you'll never have elemental vampires to contend with."

"She speaks the truth," says another refugee.

"Kill manipulators when discovered," adds a woman clutching her tattered clothes to her frail shoulders. "No vampire should have the power to mind control another."

"Agreed!" shout others.

Fear courses through Esmie, palpable through the memory as if it were our own.

"When we get to the mainland we must unite the other survivors. Take back the Seat of Darkness and make it equal for all vampires."

"Look!" someone shouts. "The island is collapsing into the ocean!"

We all look on in horror as the ending of Atlantis becomes clear to those watching the memory unfold. The tropical paradise survived for millennia until vampires discovered it and made it their own.

As the vision fades, Esmie's predicament and eternity of hiding fills me with sadness and dread. It's no wonder Vivian is so paranoid about protecting what she is. There's no way the rest of the vampire race would ever tolerate a manipulator or elemental after this fiasco. And who could blame them?

Slowly, I become aware of the couch beneath me. I'm left feeling drained of energy, bereft and torn. So much destruction, so much death. The end of all that beauty and splendor in the heat of the moment.

I glance at the watch on Dria's wrist, noting it's well after three a.m. We were lost in the illusion far longer than I would have thought—and yet time seemed to fly by.

"From what I was told, after the survivors made it to land," Persephone says, "the remaining vampires huddled together to build a town while the other surviving supernatural species drifted, seemingly happy to get away from the rest of us. And for good reason. Elementals destroyed the most advanced civilization for vampires on the planet, all in the name of power.

"Elemental vampires used their destructive magic to tear apart our home. Their desire to play god ruined centuries of prosperity."

Did we watch the same memory? It looked to me like both sides were guilty of abusing their powers. But I wisely keep my mouth shut, afraid she'll turn that crazy-eyed stare on me.

Rolando clears his throat. "Now you fully understand where the rule to never turn a witch originated. They are where elemental vampires came from."

My mouth opens before I have a chance to think through if I should say anything or not. "Then how are you able to do magic?"

Persephone answers, "The same way Justin can—with spells, incantations, rituals, and with the help of my very powerful vampire blood."

"You became a wizard?" Rafe asks, his tone thoughtful.

My next thought is they have learned nothing from the past and have essentially combined the two deadly classes into one, by making a manipulator vampire who is a wizard, too. What the hell is wrong with these idiots? Don't they recognize they're playing with fire?

Vivian finally speaks, her voice sounding detached and pitched low. "Atlantis was beautiful. The tragedy of its destruction an unacceptable outcome for those of us with the power to change the future."

Persephone's face lights up. "Exactly! I'm so glad to hear you understand. All the killing, the unimportant events that led us here, they matter not in the ultimate goal—to take back vampire rule for those of us who are the strongest."

Every fiber of my being longs to argue, to speak out against this madness. Surely, Viv is just in shock over the events she saw in the memory and isn't thinking clearly. She's hidden her power and used it remotely all these decades for a reason, right? What has happened to her personal mantra of "absolute power corrupts absolutely"?

I look to Rafe and see the same confusion in his eyes I'm sure is in mine. I reach out with my mind, hoping to connect with the two of them again, only to find a block of some sort. It feels the same as when Vivian expanded her awareness earlier to protect me from the ancient's casual reading of my mind—perhaps those shields are still in place.

Squeezing Viv's hand, I try to draw her gaze to mine, to plead with her silently to not agree to their course of action.

"Our new Atlantis will be here, in Buenos Aires," Persephone says. "We will call the manipulator vampires of the world home to roost, and the city will be ours. Our rule will be complete. With no fear of elemental vampires to destroy what we build."

Rolando continues with the crazy talk. "The Tribunal will remain intact, but with manipulators serving as ancients, and within the inner circle as well. With your help, we will rule without opposition."

Vivian nods in agreement, and it takes every scrap of awareness in me to not let my jaw drop open in astonishment. "A noble cause. I can see why you've worked hard to pursue it. I will have a place among the ancients?"

Persephone smiles again, the stretch of her red lips over white teeth disconcerting instead of welcoming. "Of course. I can think of no other we'd want by our side. We need to add your offspring to our numbers, to gain the foothold we need."

"I'm afraid I won't be of much help there. I haven't turned any vampires who showed signs of becoming manipulators.

There were a few, but they couldn't handle the power and had to be destroyed."

"I find that hard to believe," the ancient says, her face no longer looking happy with her crazy glow, more perplexed now.

Rolando rises from the couch and strides to the dining room. "We have a list here." He returns in a moment with a file in one hand. "It contains all the names of the vampires you've turned over the centuries." He opens it and pulls out a sheet. I see a single column filled with names, but it's too far away for me to read. "It's rather light, considering your age."

Vivian's gaze drops to the list and away, returning her attention to the man holding it. "Yes, it is. Due to incurable bloodlust, I didn't allow many to live past a year—the age we're required to report new turnings to the Tribunal."

My mind immediately races to Paul, one of the inn's chefs, who was turned by Vivian a little over seven months ago. If she's keeping to the rules, then Paul hasn't been announced to them yet. Which is good, considering he showed signs of something out of the ordinary when he was able to catch Emiko by surprise and stab her during an organized hunt this past winter.

Persephone leans forward, excitement on her face. "We want you to tell us who on this list could be a manipulator, too. Together we can take back what is rightfully ours."

Vivian takes the list and scans it. Her face remains expressionless, no sign of recognition when she reads. I glance over, as unobtrusive as possible, surprised to see both women and men's names on the list. For some odd reason, I thought Vivian would have only turned men. Wrong again. Go figure.

"Which ones, Dria?" Rolando presses.

"I can't be sure. Very few exhibited signs of being able to manipulate anything but humans."

Persephone looks confused. "Are you telling me you don't know how many could have the power?"

Vivian nods, her face clear of emotion. "Exactly. It's been so long I can't remember."

Rolando says, "Are you sure that's correct?"

I feel a pressure against my mind, similar to when a telepathic conversation is initiated, but not the same. This push means business. Like whoever is doing it wants into my head.

Vivian's grip loosens on mine until she drops my hand and rests hers in her lap. I notice she's dropped Rafe's, too. The pressure on my mind eases a bit, indicating she's the target of the mental press, not me. "Yes, I'm sure."

Persephone smiles, the small grin not reaching her eyes. "Forgive us if we don't believe you." And with that, she links hands with Rolando and Vivian tenses on the couch, her whole body stiffening with a sharp spasm.

"What the hell are you doing to my wife?" Rafe barks. He attempts to rise, but with a motion from Rolando he's pinned to the couch.

"Stay out of it, Raphael, or your wife will regret it," Rolando says.

Adrenaline rushes through me, priming my muscles to fight or flight. What the hell is going on? What am I not seeing?

Vivian screams, grasping her skull, blood dripping from her nose, writhing on the couch in pain. I lunge forward, hands extended, intent on leaping across the coffee table and wrapping my hands around the ancient's throat. But I can't.

Rolando's attention flicks to me and I'm forced back to the couch, staked in place like a bug on a pin.

"Don't fight us, Dria," Persephone says in a strained tone, the effort to break Vivian's mind taking its toll on her. "It will go much easier if you don't."

But the redhead doesn't listen, refuses to relent. The screams and jerks of her body intensify as the two of them plow into her mind for information she may be hiding.

Persephone whispers, "I need more, Rolando, she's very strong."

Their linked hands must mean something. Perhaps he's adding his strength to hers?

Fear lances my heart, forcing more adrenaline into my body. I have to help her! Maybe get them to drop hands. Panic grips me as I watch the horror unfolding, unable to move, unable to do a goddamn thing.

Rage like I've never seen crosses Rafe's face, the intensity of it darkening his skin, forcing multiple veins to stand out on his forehead and neck. He's fighting the binding just as I am, and having no better luck.

The urgent cries ripping from her throat continue, twisting deep into my gut with a pain I've never experienced before. I became hers years ago, a servant to protect and keep her safe—and yet I'm helpless, watching her raped from within.

She is my responsibility! I've sworn to protect her! I must do something!

I force the weakening thoughts from my mind. There has to be a course of action that can throw off their mental attack.

I gather my anger to me, press it into a tight ball of power, and thrust my arms forward in an effort to break the spell holding me. Pressing toward Rolando with everything I've got, claws start to emerge from my finger tips, fur begins to coat their backs as my hands grow larger. The magic from a transformation tickles across my skin, aching to break the hold on my mind and body. Determination swells within me. I will reach that undead bastard if it's the last thing I do.

Abruptly, the screams cut off and Vivian falls limp on the cushions.

"I've got what we need," Persephone says. "Give me a few minutes to clean up the mess and she'll be right as rain in no time."

Spittle flies from my lips as I gnash my teeth and reach with all my might. Rafe yells, the rage and ferocity in his shout a match for what I'm feeling, too.

"Hold them steady, Rolando. I need concentration for this."

His voice sounds strained when he answers, "They're stronger than they look."

"Then knock their asses out, we don't have time for this."

And with that, my world goes black.

I awake first, in the backseat of the car, unsure how the hell I got there. My first thought is of Vivian, and I sit up too fast, nausea twisting my gut and threatening to spew its contents. She's slumped in the front seat of the car, a coat over her face, perhaps to protect her from the sun that's cresting the horizon.

Reaching a trembling hand between the seats, I grasp Rafe's shoulder and shake him awake. He comes to with a jolt, eyes immediately flashing open and looking for his wife. He softens only when he lifts the coat and presses a hand to her cheek.

"She's okay," he says. "It's a restorative sleep."

Tension I was unaware of leaks out of me, leaving me more drained and spent then I ever thought possible. "Are you sure?"

He nods. "I'm linked with her, as are you. You just haven't learned to use it yet." Rafe looks up at the rising sun, the rays blinding us from their position over the large buildings. "A little sun won't hurt her, but I don't want to risk it. We've got to get her inside."

He fumbles for the keys in the ignition and starts the car. His head swivels back and forth, then ducks under the powerful rays to get a feel for where we are. "Holy shit. They drove us a block from the apartment. They knew where we were staying."

"Must have traced us while we were busy tracking the killers. Where to now? The third place you bought?"

He shakes his head and performs a u-turn. "Nope. Back to the first house. We've no threat from the Weres to contend with now, and it has provisions and a better escape route. I doubt they had the address as we'd only been there a few hours."

We travel the distance in silence, residual shock making it difficult to sort through all that's happened. Once we arrive, Rafe gently lifts his wife from the car as I see to the door. He carries her down to the basement and returns to the main floor, meeting me in the kitchen.

"Is she okay?" I ask.

"I can't be sure. Nothing like this has ever happened to her while we've been together. But I think she will be, with time."

"Why?" I ask. "Why the hell did they do that to her? She said she agreed with them, sounded like she was on their side."

"Because they don't trust her. And rightfully so. They want who she's turned, those who may have her power, but they may not want her if she's on the fence about their objective. They may have an easier time persuading younger masters to their way of thinking. By violating her mental barriers, they could see her intent, read all her secrets, and make sure she was worth keeping around."

"And what if she's not? What then?"

"I can only assume they would have disposed of her. We sure as hell couldn't have stopped them."

The feeling of helplessness slinks through me again, and I shake it off, hating the sensation. "We were useless against them. Now I understand why Vivian has always hidden herself, using her gift on the sly rather than exposing herself to the hatred of her kind. That much power is wrong. There was nothing we could do to stop them."

"She believes the power is corrupting. That the darkness inside her is a manifestation of that power—which is why she so tightly holds onto her self-control, never allowing the monster within to have free rein."

"What do we do now?"

"We wait until she wakes. Talk through what happened. See what she thinks. And she'll need your blood when she comes to. It will help her regain strength. A mental attack like she went through will leave her severely drained. This sleep is a way for her body to repair the damage."

I nod, understanding the words even if my brain can't formulate an intelligent response. The spent adrenaline has left me shaky and unsure of myself. I need some of that control he spoke of. I need to feel like I'm not a complete and utter failure. In her darkest hour, I failed her. Unable to stop the two vampires from violating what everyone should be able to protect—the privacy of their own mind.

I stagger toward the front door. Determined not to face another day helpless.

"Where are you going?" Rafe calls.

"To learn a new skill. I'll be back before sundown. I will not fail her again."

B efore I have a chance to reason out where I'm going, my subconscious has already led me in the right direction. I'm a block from Magda's house, no longer hesitant about what I need to do.

I knock on her door, a surreal peace filling me. She opens the door, looking like she's risen from bed, a surprised look on her face. "Jon! I wondered where you wandered off to yesterday. Where have you been?"

"It's been a hellishly long day. Can I crash with you?"

A smile stretches across her face as she pushes the door open. "I'd like nothing better."

I stumble in and she closes the door behind me.

"Jon, are you okay?"

I glance at the tidy, small apartment and determine the open door down the short hall is her bedroom. "No, no I'm not." I shuffle forward and trip on my own feet.

In a split second she's at my side, an arm around my waist as she leads me forward. "Let's get you laid down."

My eyes close before I hit the bed, and I'm out. The exhaustion and shock finally catching up to me.

When I next open my eyes, it's past noon, and the smell of frying bacon wafts through the air around me. Resolve fills my heart, reminding me of what is the most important thing in my life, my sole purpose for living—protecting those I love. And while my heart is no longer filled with misdirected passion toward her, there is no doubt I love Vivian deep into my soul.

Without her, I'd have died years ago. And more importantly, so would an entire pack of Weres. She saved them and me, and refused payment in the end. My dedication to her may have started as a blood debt, but over the years it has transformed into a steel-hard loyalty forged in the hottest flame. I will help her battle what awaits. And I will do it with any means possible.

"Jon?" Magda calls. "Are you up? I hear rustling around in there. I've made breakfast."

"I'll be right in," I answer while rising from the bed. I venture to the bathroom first and then join her in the small living area.

Thankfully she leaves me be for the moment, allowing me to eat without asking the questions I sense shimmering below the surface. Once the first plate is gone, and I've had a chance to eat half of the second helping, she clears her throat.

"What happened to you?"

I grab the mug of untouched coffee and down it, grateful it's had a chance to cool. My voice hitches as I start speaking, the pain too fresh. "I watched my vampire master—the woman I've sworn to protect, bound my life to—get mind-raped by an ancient and a member of the inner circle." Before I have a chance to contemplate telling her the truth, it spills out of me, eager to be told, to share the horror of my failure with someone else.

As the tale unfolds, my soul feels lighter, free of the deceptions I've held between us this whole week. I tell her everything that's happened. I don't reveal why Rolando and Persephone wanted Vivian in the first place, as that's not my secret to tell, but I do tell her what they plan. It's her city and she needs to know what's in store for her and her pack. If the vampires have their way, Buenos Aires will soon become a hot bed of violence and change.

After a few questions to clarify what their plan could mean for the city, she settles on the part that affects her the soonest. "So all along, you've hoped to discover my skill and use it to unite packs? Why?"

"Yesterday, when we fought your packmates, the situation reminded me why it's so important to have a strong leader." I reach across the table and take her hand in mine. "Your pack was subjected to a man who abused those under him. He wasn't a true alpha."

"What do you mean by 'true alpha'? He fought for the position and earned it under pack law."

I shake my head, and grip her hand tighter. "No. Fighting to be top dog doesn't make you a leader. It means you're a good fighter. Ruling those under your care with an eye for their future, their well-being, their happiness... that's what makes you a leader. Hector was a horrible alpha, and so were those who led before him. If they were any good, the pack never would have allowed the subsequent challenges to take place.

"In a war, there are many, many good fighters. But there need be only one general—the right one—to lead those entrusted to him through hell and back."

"We're not in a war. What do your pretty words mean in today's life?"

"Aren't we? Have you looked at your city lately? You've got witches and wizards setting up shop alongside the largest grouping of vampires in the entire world. Your pack of—how many werewolves do you have?"

"After booting out the four yesterday? Thirty-three."

"Your pack of thirty-three needs to survive and thrive among all the other supernatural groups here—and I only mentioned the ones you're currently aware of." Thinking back to what Vivian said the other day, I add, "Did you even know there were fae and demons, too?"

The alpha's olive skin tone pales. "I didn't know about demons."

"My point wasn't to scare you into thinking there was an immediate attack about to happen, but to get you to *see*, really see, that your pack isn't in a good position." I let out a deep sigh, not thrilled with what I have to say next. "You're not the best alpha to lead this pack." Anger crosses her face as I rush to continue, "I'm not saying you haven't tried, but there's too much hatred and dissension among your packmates for you to effectively rule. They need someone else, Magda. You must see it too, no?"

The anger drains out of her as quickly as it came. Tears spring to her eyes and I feel like a shit heel.

"It's not easy, you know. I never intended to rule when I defended myself against Hector. I thought I could choose another mate to rule by my side." A tear trickles down her cheek. "But they didn't want me that way. They were so filled with anger and hurt over what they endured under Hector, they wanted to battle me for the position. I became this hardened bitch to stay alive."

"I understand, Magda. I truly do. That's why I think you

need to share your gift. Let them all know how to change into the hybrid form like you do."

"But they'll kill me!"

"Not if you pick one who can rule first. Take the time to get to know your pack, seek out those with strong opinions and see if they have what it takes to think of others and be a good ruler. Help decide their fate by choosing the one to share your skill with first, explain what you intend to do, and step down as alpha without a fight."

"You really think it's as easy as that? What if they don't listen and kill me anyway?"

"You can do anything you put your mind to. Don't let your fears rule you. Join with me in this idea to unite the packs around the world." I reach my other hand across the table to grab her free one, now clasping both of hers on the smooth wood while I stare intently into her pretty brown eyes. "Your skill could be what makes werewolves finally come together as a cohesive group, able to stand against any supernatural race that threatens us."

Her eyes close for a moment and I hear her heart racing in her chest. "I'm not sure I want to be part of something so large," she says with a quiet voice. Her eyes open and she stares at me. "But I will try and help you learn the skill. You can do what you want with the knowledge. And I..." she lets out a long sigh. "I will do what you suggest and try to select a better alpha. Perhaps one who will show kindness for me and not hate me for the things I've done."

My heart soars, even as I hear hers thumping out a nervous beat. This is what I've been hoping for, and I won't have to manipulate her to get what I want. Life couldn't be any better.

Then I think of Vivian writhing on the couch while Persephone cracked her mind wide open.

Okay, life could be better: None of this shit could be happening. I'd wake up in Candy's arms tomorrow, and my biggest worry—whether Pat and Eric unknowingly locked themselves in a cabin again as wolves and had to break out.

But in the darkness that has been this week, this moment is a bright slice of sunshine. I lean forward and wrap Magda in hug, hoping to convey my gratitude in her trust with the embrace.

"Thank you, Magda. This means a lot to me."

She pulls back and smiles, her hands lingering on my biceps. "Don't thank me just yet, I may not be able to teach you. Have you ever done any meditating?"

"As a matter of fact, I have. I started recently in the hopes of strengthening my mental barriers."

She gives me a sly look under her full lashes. "Ahh... is not everything perfect in paradise? You're trying to hold some of yourself private from your vampire, no?"

She's too sharp for her own good. "Maybe. Maybe not. She's not the only vampire who lives on the resort."

"Fair enough," she says with a nod. "Let's get started. I changed halfway the first time under duress. My wolf was trying to claw to the surface to defend me, and I was holding it back so Hector wouldn't get worse."

Her words trigger a reminder of my actions last night when they attacked Vivian. I too was resisting the change and my magic started to flow out and through my hands. I saw my hands partially shift, but it wasn't a conscious effort on my part.

"But later," she continues, "when I attempted it again, I

couldn't call the change forth. No matter what I tried, it wouldn't come. I'd switch into a full wolf and have to change back. After a few times of trying I was too exhausted by the shifts to keep going."

"So how did you do it?" I ask.

"Eventually, I gave up. I admit, I didn't try more than a few days in a row. But about a week after the initial incident with Hector, I was lying down, tired after a long shift. I began to dream about the night he beat me, but it was different, I was aware it was a dream. My mind was relaxed enough to enter into the space 'between' the change, if that makes sense."

She rushes on, seemingly happy with the analogy and eager to expand on it. "The magic that spills over us during the shift—it's painful in the early years, remember?"

I nod, on the edge of my seat while she explains.

"Before the shift to wolf, the transformational magic seeps through our cells, inciting the change. This 'between' state allows a conscious choice, one I never recognized before because of the pain. Maybe we've all prepared ourselves for the pain for so long, that we're unable to see beyond it, to a state normally hidden by the act of transforming."

She sighs and slumps to the chair back. "I don't think I'm explaining it well."

"No, you're doing fine," I say. "Please, go on."

"While in this half-dream state, I was able to 'see' the change in slow motion, see at the cellular level that I had three choices: human, wolf, and wolf woman—what I later considered the best of both worlds in one form. Previously, I had skipped right to wolf and never knew there was an alternative.

"As I laid on the couch, I felt myself slowly shift. One body part at a time. It wasn't painful, like the shifts were for years, it was... God, how can I explain it? It was like... like water, flowing out of me, rather than the tidal wave of transformation that normally hits when you shift fully to a wolf. Does that make sense?"

Recalling that I had no pain when my hand partially turned last night, I nod again. "Yes, yes it does. But I'm still not sure I'll be able to do it. My shift is very fast."

"I've noticed that. That's why I asked about meditation. I eventually learned how to master the skill through meditating. I had to reach that dream-like state again, but be conscious of my actions, all of them. It took me weeks to perfect it. And by then, Hector hated me so much for fighting back, that he came after me in wolf form when I was alone."

She gets a faraway look in her eyes while recalling the details to me. "It was the first time I'd consciously shifted to a half form without an hour of meditation to assist. It was a calling of sorts, like when you call your wolf to you and the transformation occurs. But different. I felt... still me... but powerful, and more alive. It was exhilarating, even if the sensation was fleeting because I had to fight for my life.

"That was the night I killed Hector. It was self-defense. But if I'm honest with myself, I must admit I did not know the depth of my strength or have much control that night. I killed him easily." She swallows and gazes down at the table. "And perhaps I should have stopped before it was too late."

I scoot my chair closer and tuck a short dark lock behind her ear, then run a hand across her back in a soothing motion. "I'm not going to spout platitudes that you did what you had to do, or that the world is a better place without him in it, but I will say you can't change the past. You need to accept what you did and move forward."

"Thanks. I'll try." She smiles at me, a genuine show of happiness and not a calculated grin meant to entice, like most of her looks since I met her. "Has anything I've shared helped? If you've never encountered a half-shift before, I doubt mediating to achieve it will do any good."

"It has helped, trust me. I have had a partial shift of my hands happen—and it too occurred when I was under extreme duress. I know the feelings you're speaking of."

"But how will your experiences help to recreate the trait in others? How can you teach something that seems more primal?"

I shrug. "I'm not sure. Maybe I'd have to push them into a fight or flight response, and tell them not to shift into a wolf, to go against their instincts." I trail off and remove my hand from her back. "It might work."

"How about we get started on you mastering the skill before we worry about teaching anyone else?"

The corners of my mouth tilt up in a grin. "Sounds like a plan."

For the next several hours, Magda coaches me through meditation and slowing my transformation. The task is extremely challenging for me as I normally shift in the blink of an eye. She patiently guides me through breathing techniques and perceiving the power between the shift, to call upon the third form at will.

We stop when it nears sunset, aware I must return to the safe house to see to Vivian's needs, whatever they may be. I haven't mastered the change yet, still having not been able to call so much as a single sharp claw forth, but I have no doubt I'll get there with time.

"Thank you, Magda," I say at the door. "You've given me a gift I will never forget."

She leans in and kisses me, her soft, full lips resting briefly against my own in a chaste exchange, a shyness in her that was never there before. "And thank you, for giving me back my life. I will do as you suggest and step down as alpha." Her tiny hands snake around my waist and pull me close in a hug. "And maybe then I will find true happiness."

I leave, the door closing quietly behind me, and journey back to the small house in San Telmo. Rafe paces in the living room, glancing up sharply when I open the door.

"It's about damn time. She hasn't woken up. I'm worried something's wrong."

CHAPTER TWENTY-EIGHT

VIVIAN

Music seeps into my dreams, calling me back to the land of the living, despite my enjoyment of the calm, dark silence that filled me while I slept. I open my eyes to see Rafe and Jon sitting on either side of me, worry clear on the faces.

I stretch, raising my arms toward the headboard as a kitten-like mewl of sounds escapes me. "Carry on Wayward Son" by Kansas blasts from the wireless speaker set up on the narrow nightstand. I've always loved this song. So much depth and hope woven through the lyrics. With a shaky touch to his phone screen, Rafe turns the music off.

I sit up and scoot back to lean against the squashed pillows and headboard, pulling the fabric of my nightgown, one I don't remember putting on, over my knees. "What's wrong? Why are you both hovering over me?"

Rafe drops his phone to the covers and forces my legs down, pulling me to his chest in a side-splitting hug. My arms automatically go around him, returning the embrace, his shoulders shake slightly once.

Much to my surprise, Jon wraps his arms around us both, a loud sniff of moisture coming from his nose.

"Uh... okay, guys," I say, my voice even and low. "Not that I'm not enjoying the loving wake up call, but you have to admit this behavior is unprecedented. What's going on?"

Jon lets go first, and then Rafe pulls back, not releasing my shoulders, but staring straight into my eyes. "It's after midnight, liebling. We were—"

He trails off and hugs me again while Jon says, "Fucking scared, that's what."

Alarm seeps through me. "But that can't be right. Why would I sleep so far past sunset? That's never happened to me before. Ever." My stomach tightens, hunger seeping into my awareness. Whatever happened to me, it's made me ravenous.

Rafe runs his hand over my hair, his fear an almost tangible smell in the room. "Do you remember what happened to you?"

I think back to the memory we shared with Rolando and Persephone. The fiery end of Atlantis, the race to freedom and the long, depressing boat ride. No matter how hard I try, I can't recall what occurred after or how we got home.

My brow wrinkles in frustration. "All I remember is the dream Persephone showed us."

Jon grabs my shoulder and squeezes, an uncharacteristic show of affection from him. "Do you remember talking to them afterward?"

I shake my head, concerned by the missing time. "I must not have blown it too badly or we wouldn't be alive."

"Blown what?" Rafe asks.

"Going along with those two crazy bastards."

Jon lets out a deep sigh, tension easing from his frame. "I knew it. I knew you never would have agreed to their idiotic plan."

A rumble sounds in my gut and devastating hunger, bright and pure, lances through me. "I must not have been paying too close attention after the memory, because for the life of me, I don't know what their ultimate plan was."

Rafe cups my cheeks, forcing me to stare into his worried gaze. "Darling, they went into your mind. They took what they wanted to know about who you've turned over the centuries. They want to use your descendants—your blood legacy—to start a new Atlantis, right here in Buenos Aires, and rule everyone within."

"But... but..." I stop speaking as the truth of his words hits me like a blow to the solar plexus. The fear I've always been aware of in the back of my mind, the worst possible scenario I imagined centuries ago, has come to life. That someday, someone would be stronger than me and break my mental shields, that all I hold dear would be subjected to their whims.

"I must see what happened after the shared memory," I say, reaching for both of them, pushing down my need for blood a little longer. "Show me. Let me in to your minds."

Knowing their responses without having to wait, I slide into their awareness, joining us all in a three way mental connection. I shift back through their recollections of the last day, not needing to go too deep, noting their worry, fear, and arguing over what to do when I didn't wake as expected. My heart aches at the pain and frustration I unwittingly caused them.

In a flash, I witness Jon's interaction with Magda, and his attempts to master his transformation. Next, we move backward further still, until I see all that happened after the shared memory of Atlantis ended. Shaken, I drop the mental connection, drawing my knees to my chest again and wrapping my arms around them, a subtle rocking motion seeping through my awareness.

The rocking is me, as I try to hold onto the emotions raging through me. Fury and pulse-pounding rage surge to the forefront, incited by the violation I suffered at Persephone's hands. In the next breath, intense and deep-seated fear cripples me. Could I again be subjected to a similar experience in the future—at any time they're near me? And lastly sorrow—my worries have finally come to fruition. I'm grateful I planned for it, but desperation that I may not have taken enough precaution weighs heavily on my soul.

"Dria?" Rafe prompts, once again prying my arms from my legs and forcing me into his embrace. He's a stubborn son of a bitch when he feels like it, pushing his way into my agony. "Talk to us. What did they learn? Who is in danger of discovery?"

"We can't let them succeed," I say, my voice sounding hollow and distant to my own ears. "Absolute power... corrupts absolutely." A dim part of my brain wonders if I'm in shock. The rocking begins again and I welcome the soothing motion, feeling safe in the comfort of my husband's arms. "We have to stop them."

"Tell us," Jon urges, sliding closer, slipping his arms around my waist and pressing his chest to my back. "Tell us how."

"Never fear. I have prepared myself for this eventuality," I whisper, the edge of my hunger slipping from my grasp, swelling to fill my mind with the only thing that matters —blood.

"What does that mean?" Jon's breath tickles my ear as his delightful werewolf pheromones leak out, not sexual this time, but still tempting me to linger and breathe in his scent, to wrap myself in it and cuddle closer. The hunger surges to the surface with a vengeance, perhaps buoyed by the emotional needs churning within me.

My fangs lengthen and descend, driving home my need for sustenance more than anything else. Without looking in a mirror, I know my eyes have turned black, the heightened state in which a vampire fights, fucks, and feeds.

"I—" Before I can voice my need, Jon lifts his wrist to my mouth, unself-conscious that his arm lies pressed between me and Rafe.

"Take what you need," he whispers in my ear. "We're here for you, Dria."

I stare into my husband's loving gaze as I sink my teeth into Jon's supple flesh. Rich, powerful werewolf blood fills my mouth, a hint of chocolate undertones to tantalize me further. I swallow and moan against his skin, drawing in another deep pull.

I continue for several minutes, taking far more from him than I normally do. But he never flinches. Never voices a single complaint as I draw his life force into my body.

Rafe runs a palm over my cheek, his thumb caressing tiny circles over my jaw. "That's enough, Dria. You don't want to leave him weak. If you need more, I'm here."

I draw away, every corner of my dark soul aching to take more, to drink until he's writhing behind me in ecstasy, reaching his ultimate release as I feed to my heart's content. But I resist. He's not a pawn to use that way. He's my friend and I love him. One light lick seals the small wounds I made, and a shudder races through Jon.

His vibrant blood courses through my veins, filling my limbs with strength and my mind with power. But the craving in me is not satiated. My fangs do not retract.

I look to my husband and smile, a devious sexy grin. His breath hitches in his throat. "More," I say, running a hand down his chest, tweaking one hardened nipple through his shirt. "I need more."

Rafe holds me at arm's length, looking over my shoulder at the man plastered to my back. "Uh... Jon?" he says. A low growl issues from my throat as I stare intently at the thick artery under the skin on my husband's neck. "This may get... intense." My hands become curled, grasping fingers, reaching for him, but he still manages to choke out a last warning. "And uh, naked."

"Oh!" Jon pulls back, taking his warmth with him and leaving my back cold. "Yeah, right. How about I go cook dinner?"

He beats a hasty retreat from the basement, his ears reddening in his flight as he ascends the stairs, shutting the hidden door behind him.

In a flash, I pin my husband to the bed, tearing his shirt down the middle. I latch onto his nipple, sucking it into my mouth, scraping the tip with one fang. My hands don't waste time either, pulling open his pants and thrusting his zipper down.

"Slow down, honey," Rafe says, a glint of humor in his voice. "There's no rush. I'm here for you."

"Lift your hips," I command, not caring about slowing down.

He complies and I yank off his pants, revealing his muscled thighs and growing arousal. I jerk the short nightgown over my head, glad he didn't dress me in panties when he put me to bed.

"I need—" I straddle him, unable to finish my sentence, my desperation making me shake. I aim his arousal at my opening and jam down with my hips, seating him fully in one forceful plunge.

Rafe grunts, his hands clasping my hips in a death grip. "Jesus!" He thrusts upward, lowering to the bed to drive up again, somehow knowing exactly how I need him at the moment.

The werewolf blood heats me throughout, flushing my skin, and driving me crazy with sexual desire. I toss my long hair over one shoulder and lean down, using one hand to tilt his neck to the side. Without warning, I bite into his throat, drawing a yell of pain and pleasure from him.

To his credit, he doesn't miss a stroke, slamming inside me as I drink greedily from his flesh, eager for every drop. "More, Dria! More!" he shouts thrusting wildly and without rhythm.

I oblige, drawing deeply as my climax sneaks up on me. Shudders and spasms of pleasure wrack my body as I ride him like the hounds of hell were chasing me, and he was the steed to deliver me from their clutches. My body slows as my orgasm recedes, my hips moving slower and with more finesse.

Much to my delight, Rafe hasn't peaked yet, he's still ramrod stiff inside me.

I seal his wounds with my tongue, and rise up to meet his eyes.

"We're not through yet, darling." He sits up, with himself still seated inside me, and shifts his legs, turning us so I'm lying under him, my back on the mattress. "And I know you can take more."

Unsure if he means sex or blood, I smile, drawing my knees up and opening my thighs.

"Oh, that's it," he groans with delight, pushing forward.

His eyes find mine, a wildness in his I don't normally see. "Goddamn it, Dria. You scared me." He pants over me, his voice ragged and filled with emotion. "I thought," he thrusts deep, "for a minute there," he draws back out, his arms shaking with the effort to keep going, "that you were hurt." He plunges forward, tears in his eyes. "I can't lose you."

I reach for his face, pressing my mouth over his, showing him what he means to me with my body and soul.

You won't, my love, I say in his mind, my own tears sliding down my cheeks. *Not if I have anything to say about it.*

"More," he whispers against my lips, emotion clouding his voice. "Take more." He lays his chest against mine, angling his neck toward my mouth.

I sink my teeth into his neck as my second orgasm races upon me. His blood fills my mouth and swirls down my throat as I pull with all my might. Warmth fills me as his hips slowly twitch, his body shuddering with the force of his release.

I draw one last pull from his throat, hearing him gasp and feeling him thrust, squeezing out the last bit of enjoyment as he twitches once more within me.

We lie there for a long while, content in the position. When our breathing returns to normal, we slide from our embrace to lie side by side on the bed.

I run a palm up and down his forearm. "I'm sorry. Sorry you were scared. Sorry I did that to you."

He rolls onto his side, drawing his arm over me to pull me

closer. "It wasn't your fault. I'm fine now that I have you in my arms."

In a few more minutes, reality seeps into my awareness. I hear Jon above us, in the kitchen, cooking like he said he would. Life is normal. Or as normal as it can be for us.

I pat my husband's arm and pull away, the loss of his warmth like a smack on the ass—startling and invigorating, convincing me of the need to dress quickly. "We have a lot to discuss. We need to get upstairs to Jon."

He sighs, drawing me back down, forcing me to his chest. "I know. I just want to pretend for a little while longer that everything is okay. That we're home, in our own bed, and none of this week has happened."

I wrap my arms around him, eager to give him the momentary peace he seeks.

W̶e venture upstairs, my lover's hand on the small of my back, Rafe refusing to let go of me for even a second.

Jon looks up from a book as we enter, relief on his face when he sees me. "It's about damn time. I was worried she might have drained you, old man."

Rafe attempts a smile, the expression not quite reaching his tortured eyes. "Never you fear. The day I need another man's assistance—"

Jon waves him away from finishing his thought. "Yeah, yeah. I get it. That's the day you're dead."

"Although," I cheerily add, "With the amount of times we've gone through the mate bond ritual, I doubt even then you'd truly die. More like you'd turn."

"Really?" Jon asks, curiosity lighting his voice. "Why would you go through the ritual more than once?"

Rafe's amusement is genuine this time, laugh lines crinkle around his gorgeous bright blue eyes. "Because sometimes you want to." He reaches toward me, drawing me close for another rib-splitting hug. "Especially when you've got the right partner."

Jon clears his throat. "Speaking of partners—we need to discuss the two creepy ones that messed with Viv's head. What do they know—and cue the horror movie music—how are we going to stop their evil plan?"

Rafe releases me and leads me to a seat, then scoots another chair closer to mine before sitting. His hand rests absently on my thigh as he scans the counter top. "Do you want a coffee, hon? Can I get you a bag of blood? We've got several pouches in the fridge."

I rub my hand over his reassuringly. "I'm fine, darling. Relax. The two of you met all my needs, and then some."

My husband nods and stands, preparing a steaming mug of coffee for himself before returning to his seat, and once again slipping his free hand into my lap.

"How about," I say, looking from one incredible man to the other, "I start at the beginning—my beginning that is. I don't mean all the way back to the nitty-gritty of my turning, mind you, that's too long of a tale, and one I gladly don't recall all of, but back to when I realized I'd turned my first manipulator vampire.

"I knew then I had sentenced the man to death. If he had turned out like the others—without the trait—he would have been safe. Free to live amongst our kind with no fear of retribution. But that wasn't to be the case.

"I'd already been in hiding for over thirty years, and since I staged my death with the rest of my seethe, the Tribunal had no idea I even existed. I realized I'd have to set him up like I did when I disappeared—with a whole new identity, and a story of who changed him and when. The lie would have to be linked to his true age, just in case a sensitive, like Joanna, stumbled upon him and could ferret out an elaborate ruse by sensing his true age."

"What was his name?" Jon asks.

"You see, that's the beauty of my plan. I don't remember."

"What? You can recall the basics, but not the details?"

I nod, eager to finally share what I'd done with both of them. "When I discovered I could choose to forget some of the horrible things done to me when I was captured as a human, I realized I could choose to forget other important things, too. Like whom I turned. And when."

Jon says, "I'm not so sure I understand. How is this supposed to help us find your turns? If you can't remember them then we're shit out of luck."

Rafe squeezes my thigh in understanding. "Well done, liebling. You may have saved all their lives. I don't think I've ever been prouder."

"Jon," I say, focusing all my attention on the confused young man. "Think. You know what I did. You saw proof of it yourself. Even read one on your own."

He gasps, sitting straighter in his chair. "The journals! You wrote everything down before you willed yourself to remember the past differently." He bolts up, pushing back from the table to pace. "Holy fucking hell. Those slim leather books. They hold the key to everything." He makes it to the living room and turns back, his pace clipped. "You knew. You knew that someday, someone would come looking for your turns, to use them against you—or to control someone else."

He jumps, pumping his fist to the ceiling in a celebratory punch of righteousness. "This is huge! If we can get to them before anyone else, we can stop Rolando and Persephone."

The recent goodwill slides from my face, leaving me empty inside. "Yes, we can. Assuming I don't have to kill them myself."

Jon freezes, horror coloring his expression. "What are you talking about?"

"I know deep down, I would never have let them live if I doubted their path, if I ever thought they'd abuse their powers." Tension has my shoulders creeping up to my ears. "But it's been a long time. People change. Power changes them more."

"Nonsense!" Jon shouts, racing for the stairs. "I refuse to believe the worst. Let's get packed and get home. Hot damn!" His voice drifting away as he journeys to his room. "We have a chance and that's more than we had a few hours ago."

Rafe takes another swig of his coffee, lowering it to the table with a smile. "You constantly surprise me, Dria. Such foresight. Outstanding." A thought occurs to him and his brow furrows. "But if you remembered this much, enough to recall the journals, and what you did, how can we be sure Persephone didn't find what you're hiding?"

"Because she never would have known to look for my deception. Depending on the time spent in my head, she would have been looking very quickly, skimming hundreds of years of details to find the relevant information.

"How long did she possess my mind?"

"Minutes, truth be told, though it felt like hours watching

you scream in pain." He's silent for a moment, perhaps reliving the recent event whether he wants to or not. "What about that list they had? Could any of your manipulator turns be on it?"

"I don't remember seeing a list. I can't be sure. Did you get a look at it?"

He shakes his head. "No, sorry."

"My journals should reveal who I reported to the Tribunal and who I didn't. It's a start. At least we can be sure they don't have all the names or even the right ones. Tracking the viable turns we do know of will be our only option in hoping to stop their plan."

"But won't those people be safe already? We can leave them alone."

"I don't want to risk it—and like I feared, they might be corrupted by the power. Persephone can easily track through Tribunal records where I lived and when. Large gaps of residing somewhere without reporting any turns could be a red flag for them, and prompt them to investigate any and all seethes reporting from the area."

"That should slow them down a bit."

"Exactly what I was thinking."

I hold his hand on my leg and think of my past. All I've lost and gained with living in the present. Sadness trickles through me, I'm not sure from where. "I won't read them," I say, my voice so quiet it's a mere brush of air in the room. "I cannot live through the pain again." I glance up at the man I love more than life itself. "Will you do it for me?"

My husband pulls me close again, like he can't get enough of me, the fear still gripping him from my sleep that went on too long. "Anything. I will do anything for you."

"Are you sure?"

319

His lips settle against mine. *Yes. I'm sure.*

A fter we're packed and waiting for the plane and pilots to get ready, I receive a text from Justin asking if we found Rolando and reminding me I owe him payment for his services.

The jet won't be able to take off for a few hours, so we drive to Justin's to tie up loose ends. It takes some time, but we explain the events as best we can, letting him know his magic is still valid, and it was a spell that turned his blood to dust and called forth the invunche and hombre gato—leaving out the parts about my being a manipulator and the deadly duo mind-raping me.

"Are you sure?" he asks, apprehension in his voice. "I haven't tried a damn thing since the tracking spell." The young man shakes his head. "Didn't want to risk it."

I lift a shoulder. "As sure as we can be. We'll know for certain when you attempt a spell with your blood."

"Okay, okay." He runs a hand through his longish black hair—at least today it looks clean. "I'll try something after I master the meditating and aura cleansing Bart told me about. I'm not taking any more risks with being sloppy." His eyes dart nervously toward the sink. "I've done that for way too long. This was the wake-up call I needed."

Justin stands and goes to the counter near the sink. He hands me a glass flat-bottomed vial—similar to what we store the shots of my blood in at the resort—a much better selection for storing a valuable liquid than the porous clay pot the witch used.

With an eye on the clock, I reach for the knife on the table.

In one smooth slice I open my wrist, angling the wound over the vial. Once it's filled, I stopper the top and watch the cut heal.

"Thank you for helping us, Justin. I'm well aware you didn't have to." I slide the payment across the table to him. "You surprised me with your fortitude and dedication. Can I call upon you in the future if I have need of your services?"

Justin blinks, taken off guard with my pretty words and request. "Do I have a choice?"

I smile while rising from the table, thrilled he understands. "Not really."

"Are you done?" Jon calls from the front room. "I'm so ready to blow this popsicle stand."

Rafe strides into the kitchen and glances at Justin, then me. "I'd like a word with the wizard, if you and Jon don't mind."

Intrigued, but willing to wait and see what he's planning, I nod. "We'll see you in the car."

"Sure," Justin says, stretching out his long legs and lacing his arms behind his head, "don't bother to ask the wizard. I'll just sit here and mind my own business."

I smile as I pass my husband. "He's all yours."

CHAPTER TWENTY-NINE

RAFE

I pull back a kitchen chair and slide into the seat. Justin cocks an eyebrow, an insolent expression on his face.

"What's up, Rafe? You've got me all to yourself."

Unwilling to waste time, I jump right to the chase. "How much money do you make as a wizard?"

He unlaces his hands and sits up straighter. "Uh—and why does that matter?"

"Just answer the question. I want to make you a job offer, and wanted to know where to start." At his look of surprise, I continue. "The exchange rate for the US dollar is really strong right now compared to the Argentine peso."

"The cost of living is different here, you know. It's hard to compare what I earn to the US job market."

I smile, noting that he's still not answering my question.

"I do all right, man." He looks around his small home, perhaps realizing the tiny dwelling doesn't jive with his claims. "I put a lot into savings."

I dip my chin in acknowledgment. "Smart man. Saving is always a good thing."

The wizard fidgets in his seat. "Spell ingredients cost a lot, too."

"I bet." I wait him out a bit longer, sure I've intrigued him now.

"How much money are we talking—and what's the job?"

Bingo. I knew I wouldn't have to wait too long. Know what inspires a man and you know how to entice him.

"Five hundred thousand dollars. A one year contract. You'll be required to move frequently."

Justin starts to cough before I can relay the rest of the information. "Holy shit," he croaks, his voice rough and broken. "Think I just choked on my own spit." He pounds his chest, then clears his throat. "Just what the hell do you expect me to do for that kind of money—kill someone?" His eyes bug out in worry. "Several someones?"

"No." I smooth my hand over the table, enjoying the texture of the polished wood. "You'll be teaching me magic. Every day. Until you've taught me everything you know."

"Just you, no one else?" he asks.

I nod.

A lazy grin crosses Justin's face. "Now that's a deal I can handle." He thrusts out his hand. "You've got yourself a magic teacher."

We shake on it and a huge smile splits my face. I can't wait to see what Dria says to this idea. "Good. Go pack. We leave for Alaska in an hour."

Justin looks put out, but I know it's an act. His excitement fills the air between us, more than likely he's never had an opportunity like this offered to him before. This job will change his life, and he knows it.

"Jesus, talk about short notice. All right then, looks like I better get packing." He stands and heads upstairs, calling behind as he goes. "Grab a box from out back and pack my spell books, would ya? Wouldn't want to make us late for the flight."

I snort at his audacity, and open the back door for a box. He'll certainly be surprised when he discovers we own the plane. There's no chance we'll miss the flight.

As the pilots finish their pre-flight check, I power up my laptop in the hangar's back lounge, ignoring the tension coming off my wife. She wasn't thrilled with me hiring Justin, but Jon's enthusiastic acceptance of the plan softened her ire.

I understand her fears and worries, probably better than she does. But I will not allow either of us to face an enemy so grossly unprepared. My solution makes sense, and it will give me peace of mind in case we run into anymore vampire wizards in our quest to find Dria's turns. At least one of us will have the mojo to stop them before we walk into another mess unprepared.

When Jon and Justin leave to load the bags onto the plane, she stirs from her position across the room, where she's been sulking for the past twenty minutes or so, and walks toward me at the table where I'm working on the wizard's employment contract. Silly man refused to get on the plane until everything is signed. I shake my head in disbelief. Like I'm not a man of my word and can't be trusted or something.

"I still don't like it," she says, a touch of a petulant whine in her tone.

"I know."

"But do you truly understand *why*?" This time she sounds annoyed. I look up, eyebrows creeping up my forehead. "I don't like the position you've put me in. It goes against promises I've made to you. I never want to violate your trust."

"I need to do this, Dria. It is for us, for our safety, that I want to learn what he has to teach."

"But you know—you agree—we cannot allow a vampire wizard to knowingly come into existence. The power is too great. And yet here you sit, blatantly flaunting that fear." She runs both hands through her hair, uneasiness making her hands jerky, while staring toward the door where the two left a few minutes ago. Her voice sounds quieter now, filled with dread and angst. "I'll be the one who will have to wipe the knowledge from your mind if you die and turn."

I stand and move closer to her, cupping her cheeks in my palms and tilting her beautiful face up to mine. "*If*, darling? There is no *if*, only *when*." I lean down and kiss her gently. "And we will survive where other couples have not. I swear it to you."

"All right," she relents, tension spilling out of her, but not the sadness. "We'll try it your way. But you can't practice mind manipulation like you have been." A shudder runs through her, despite the warmth in the lounge. "It's too dangerous. The darkness will have too many opportunities."

"Opportunities to do what?"

"To drag you under." Tears fill her eyes. "To own your soul."

I lean my forehead against hers, breathing deeply before replying. "I know you'll never let that happen to me."

"No. No, I won't." The look in her eyes reveals a steely determination to face a task she loathes, and to do it to her own husband.

I have no fear in me like she does. I trust her with my heart and my soul, what more is it to add my mind to the list?

The door opens and we break apart, both of us unwilling to share what we've exchanged with the other two.

Justin strides in, oblivious to the energy between us. "How's that contract coming, Boss Man?"

"Good. I just need your full name so I can print it out. Once we both sign it, and the flight attendant notarizes it, you'll be a legal employee of the V V Inn." I wink at him. "Complete with that fifty-thousand dollar advance to your bank account I mentioned in the car."

"Sa-weet! Monson is my last name. Spelled M-O-N-S-O-N, not with a U like most people think. Justin A. Monson."

Dria and I both freeze, the name an all too familiar one. I cut my gaze to my wife, who stands with her mouth open in shock.

Could it be the same family? I ask her telepathically. *What the hell are the chances of that?*

She closes her mouth and stares at the wizard. *Fate works in mysterious ways. And it's never good to question her, she can be a fickle bitch.*

"What's wrong?" Justin asks. "Did I miss something?"

I enter his name into my laptop at the appropriate spot on the contract and hit print. "No, nothing at all. In fact, more things may be right than you think."

He looks at me with a confused what-the-hell-does-that-mean expression on his face, while Dria hands him a pen.

"Your life will never be the same when you arrive in Alaska," she says with genuine happiness for him. "Of that, I guarantee."

~~*~~

A personal note from C.J.: If you enjoyed this book, please consider leaving a review on the product page where you purchased it. Reviews help readers discover new series and perhaps try an author they never heard of. Thank you.

To receive notice of my next release, please join my newsletter! Copy and paste this link into your browser window: smarturl.it/cjenews

Other Titles by C.J. Ellisson

The *V V Inn* Series:
Death's Servant (prequel story)
Vampire Vacation
The Hunt
Big Game
Death Times Two
Blood Legacy
Sharpen the Blade
Blood Reckoning (coming soon!)

Romance Titles:

Vanilla on Top
Vanilla Spice
Avoiding Mr. Right
Loving Ms. Wrong
Johnny Living Dangerously (erotica)

ABOUT THE AUTHOR

C.J. Ellisson is a *New York Times* & *USA Today* bestselling author, who writes supernatural suspense, mystery, and romance. She lives in northern Virginia with her husband, two teenagers, three dogs, and two cats—reporting to love the energetic zoo that's become their home.

When forced to give up a career due to her decreasing health, C.J. turned to writing in 2009 and claims the escape helped save her sanity. She battled severe chronic illness for years and has finally reached the end of her long-term treatment.

Instead of dozens of pills, IVs, exhaustion, and pain, C.J.'s life is now filled with writing, exercising, eating healthy, and running a novel-writing club at her daughter's school. It all leads to a fun-filled, busy day, and she's incredibly grateful to be so involved in life again.

C.J. loves to hear from readers! Connect with her at:
www.cjellisson.com
cj@cjellisson.com

ACKNOWLEDGMENTS

I began writing *Blood Legacy* alongside four eighth-graders in an after school NaNoWriMo club devoted to writing a novel in thirty days. It was a momentous occasion for me, as I hadn't created anything new in over eight months. The students were incredibly enthusiastic and their energy was contagious, reminding me of why I love to write in the first place.

All four reached their 30k-word goal by the last day of November 2014, while I still had plenty to write on my much larger manuscript. **Addison Conner** (my daughter), **Shay Dylan**, **Dana Trace**, and **Dalia Medina** will hopefully have their stories published by this summer, and I will gladly support them when they do. I couldn't be prouder of these young ladies. They've accomplished something many adults will never be able to do in their lifetimes. Thank you, ladies, for all the write-ins and inspiration. You helped me find my writing mojo again.

In addition to my students, I'd like to thank my alpha

readers. These ladies read the chapters one at a time in a private Facebook group, offering feedback before the work went to my editor. They were invaluable with their observations, suggestions, and overall support. Big thank you to **Michelle Chauvin-Archut**, **Lisa Errion**, **Sandy Schairer**, **Katrina Hough**, **Gwenda Bourgeois**, **Laura Ward**, **Lisa Moss**, **Kay Ramsey**, **Kim Engstrom**, **Carol-Jean Fierro**, and **Chelly Pazdan**. You ladies rock!!

I had two editors on this book who deserve a shout out: **Tina Winograd**, thanks for always being a voice of reason I can count on, and **Taylor Law**, who worked all hours of the night to help me reach my deadline. Thank you both for the hard work and time you put in.

Thank you to the fabulous **Readers** who reach out online and via email. Your support and interest in my work is what keeps me writing on a day to day basis. Due to my health issues, I've been more of a homebody for the past six years than any other time in my life. Your kindness is both humbling and awe-inspiring. Thank you for being a part of this fantastic journey with me.

And last, but never least, thank you to my supporting family. You've been incredible during the years of intense medical treatments with IVs that left me tired and sick, by helping to cook meals I was too tired to prepare, and reminding me time and time again to slow down and focus on my health. I know, as do the doctors, if it wasn't for all of you I wouldn't be here. Thank you, **Pete**, **Addison**, and **Jack**—from the depths of my soul.

CONTRIBUTORS

The following individuals inspired names for characters appearing in this book. They either thought the name up, volunteered the use of their name, I stole their name because I liked it, or they supported me so much I wanted to thank them:

Andy Lipshultz: It started as an April fool's joke, but then I twisted things and named a character after him (and basically stole his name, too).

Asa Monson: My nephew, whom I based a character on and stole his name.

Ashley Gonzalez: She suggested the old wizard's name, Bartholomew, in a Facebook post on my author Page.

Cy Whitfield, aka Michael Stern: My brother, whom I based a character on his Second Life persona, and named the character after him.

Diane O'Neill-Mason: She volunteered to have her name used.

Eric Monson: My nephew, whom I based a character on and stole his name.

Elsa Cisneros: I named a character after her.

George "GJ" Marko: I named a character after him.

Jessie Patterson: She suggested the name Magdelena for the female alpha werewolf in this book.

Justin Monson: The oldest nephew of the three. I based a character on him and stole his name.

Patrick Larson: I gladly wrote him into the story, with his permission, so he and Eric could continue to have adventures together forever.

Paul R. Ocker: I named a character after him.

Michelle Pazdan: I named a character after her.

Rolando Ray: He thought of the name Ivan (the villain from book one), which won in an online vote—and I stole his name.

Romeo LoGiurato: I stole his name.

GLOSSARY

Asa - fledgling vampire and the security and munitions expert at the V V Inn.

Bartholomew - aka Bart. Old wizard in Buenos Aires who uses animal blood to work his spells.

Blood Coffee - a mixture of half-blood and half-coffee, favored by undead everywhere.

Blood Bond - a term used to describe the exchange of blood between either a human and a vampire, both ways, or a master vampire and a member of their seethe. It enables telepathic communication between them through the bond, if desired.

Bonded Mate - a deeper connection than a servant, this bond allows the non-vampire to stop aging and share a significant amount of power associated with the bonded vampire. A complex ritual and exchange of large amounts of blood must take place for this bond to occur. The only way to break the bond is through death or a rare deep mind manipulation severing the link.

Chelly - See Michelle.

Companion - a human who has donated blood to a vampire and been accepted into the vampire's care for future feedings.

Coraline - a member of the Inner Circle who cares for and guards the Tribunal of Ancients.

Cy - Vivian's contact in New York, whom she turned when she discovered him close to death in an alley outside his bar over forty-five years ago.

Diane - An employee on the resort. Dr. Cook's adult daughter and a witch.

Donor - a human who donates blood to a vampire, willingly, with no connections.

Drew - a one-hundred-and-fifty year old vampire, and newer member of Vivian's seethe.

Dria - the master vampire narrating part of the story, aka Vivian and Alexandria.

Enforcer - a highly skilled vampire assassin, used as an instrument of justice by the tribunal.

Emmanuel - bartender at Lupine Luna in Buenos Aires, aka Manny.

Elsa - Romeo's werewolf mate.

Emiko - the rogue designated by the Tribunal to be hunted at the resort (book two).

Eric - a new werewolf from Romeo's pack.

Fledgling - term used for a vampire under the age of five years.

George - Security at the Tribunal of Ancients.

Gwendolyn - a witch in Buenos Aires the trio turns to for answers.

Hombre Gato - or Cat-man, is a legendary creature that possesses both feline and human features. This South American folk tale is particularly popular in Argentina, especially in rural and less populated areas.

Invunche - In the Chilote folklore and Chilote mythology of the Chiloé Island in southern Chile, the **imbunche** or **invunche** (mapudungun *ifünche*: "deformed person", also "short person") is a legendary monster that protects the entrance to a warlock's cave.

Joanna - a young vampire vacationing at the inn, and a member of Liam's seethe.

Jonathan - Vivian's werewolf servant and the head groundskeeper on the property.

Liebling - German endearment, meaning darling.

Lucas - a vampire in Argentina who hates Vivian for killing his old lover.

Magdelena - the female alpha who runs the Buenos Aires werewolf pack.

Manipulator - a rare breed of vampire able to mind control other vampires. Usually hunted down and killed by their own kind to ensure they do not gain power over their fellow vampires.

Master Vampire - a vampire who heads their own seethe, or is independent of a seethe. One not requiring the blood of a master to gain in power, but has accumulated enough strength to hold their own in a battle where an older vampire may try to drain a younger one for their blood.

Mate - see **Bonded Mate.**

Michelle - aka "Chelly", an employee at the inn, who also doubles as a blood donor. Recently bound to Drew as a vampire servant.

Old Blood - a term used to describe the blood a seethe member gets from a master to increase their own power. Contains the added benefit of increasing a vampire's perceived undead age if the blood is strong enough and consumed regularly.

Pat - a new werewolf at the resort, originally from Romeo's pack.

Paul - a gourmet chef imported from the lower forty-eight, married to Bunny.

Rafe - Vivian's bonded mate for sixty-five years, and co-owner to the inn.

Rolando - a member of the inner circle, part of the Tribunal of Ancients located in Argentina.

Romeo - Jonathan's old Alpha, but not the Were who changed him.

Seethe - A vampire family, or group of vampires, with a master vampire at its head.

Servant - see **Vampire Servant**

Tribunal of Ancients - the governing body of ruling ancient vampires, entrusted with maintaining the secrecy of the existence of vampires from the human race.

Turning - term used for when a human has been changed into a vampire.

Turns - term for those changed into a vampire.

Vivian - the nickname for Dria, a play on words from *The V V Inn*.

Were - shorthand for werewolf.

Vampire Servant - a human or Were who has donated blood to a vampire and ingested the blood from the same vampire. A mind connection can be established (and broken), allowing telepathic communication. The servant feels a desire to protect and serve the vampire above his or her own needs.